THE PER MIRROR

THE PAPER MIRROR

a Dick Hardesty Mystery by

DORIEN GREY

GLB PUBLISHERS®   San Francisco

Published in the United States by
GLB Publishers
P.O. Box 78212, San Francisco, CA 94107 USA

Cover by Mark Shepard
and GLB Publishers

Library of Congress Control Number:

2005930126

ISBN

1-879194-57-0

978-1-879194-57-1

First Published Oct. 2005
10 9 8 7 6 5 4 3 2 1

WITH THANKS

No book writes itself, and with this, the tenth book in the Dick Hardesty Mystery series, it is well past time for a special dedication to those people without whose help and support you would not be reading these words. You may not recognize some of the names here, but they are very important to me, Dick, Jonathan, and the entire gang.

First I'd like to express my profound gratitude to Bill Warner, publisher of GLB Publishers, who was willing to give me, as an unknown writer, a chance when the bigger boys wouldn't give me the time of day.

Secondly, thanks to my dear friend and webmaster, Gary Brown, who has been there for me every step of the way despite the geographical distance between us. His humor, intelligence, and willingness to put up with my endless bitching, moaning, and plunges into the pool of self pity and frustration have guided me through many a dark tunnel.

Thirdly, to those special friends I either had coming in or who have climbed on my rickety bandwagon along the route, to whom I have been able to turn for information while researching the books, and whose input has immeasurably helped give the books whatever verisimilitude they may have. In no particular order, they are: Nowell Briscoe, Tom Fearn, Jay Hartman, Karl Overholt and everyone else to whom I've ever asked a question concerning how things work.

Fourth, to those reviewers, fellow writers, and friends I've made through the books: Beth Anderson, Jay Hartman (again), Bil Buralli, Ralph Higgins, Molly Martin, Denise Pickles, Cindy Penn, Liz Burton, Richard Labonte, and those wonderful people who have been so kind as to feature me and/or my books in one way or another on their internet sites.

To those of you whom I should have mentioned and did not, please excuse me—you know who you are, and that you have my sincere thanks.

And a very, very special thanks to you, who by reading my words bring the characters and stories to life. Words on a page are nothing until they are filtered through your eyes and into your brain and, I would be delighted to think, your heart.

You are all my family, and I treasure you.

Dorien

DEDICATION

TO THOSE WHO
NEVER PRESUME
TO SPEAK FOR GOD

CHAPTER 1

Words are humanity's most versatile tool, and our civilization could not exist without them. Strung together, they can be stronger than steel or as light as dreams. We use them to teach, and to learn, and to record our past. Libraries are the repositories of words, and I think it's because I've always been aware of the power of words that I find libraries so fascinating.

But just like the books they house, libraries sometimes have secrets within, and secrets are not always good things. While we use words to record facts, we also use them, consciously or unconsciously, to record ourselves. Writers of fiction, particularly, reflect their innermost selves and their innermost secrets through their words. Perhaps that's why they polish them so. For them, words are paper mirrors.

* * *

The phone rang just as I was finishing the crossword puzzle and thinking about having another cup of coffee.

"Hardesty Investigations," I said, picking up the phone, as always, on the second ring.

The voice on the other end was taut as a violin string: "We have another one," it said.

Shit!

Well, before I get into details, a little background might be in order. It had started about two months earlier....

* * *

"We're no fun anymore," Jonathan said one evening as we lay in bed.

"What do you mean?" I asked. "I think we're a barrel of laughs. You had Joshua in hysterics with your impression of Cookie Monster."

"Uh-huh," he said, unconvinced. "He's four years old. He thinks everything is funny." He rolled over in bed, toward me. "You know what I mean...ever since Joshua arrived, we've turned straight."

I rolled over and faced him. "What the *hell* are you talking about?" I asked.

He sighed. "Well, we've got a kid now—and I wouldn't change that for the world—but we're turning into the Cleavers. We hardly ever see our friends anymore. We don't go out to gay places hardly at all. I miss it...don't you?"

As a matter of fact, I did. And ever since Joshua, Jonathan's four-year-old nephew, had become a permanent fixture in our lives, we really hadn't had much time for a "just us grown-ups" social life. We were able to get together with our old gang from time to time, but usually just for dinner and a drink after. My own party days of endless cruising, tricking, bar-hopping, and out-all-nights had ended when I met Jonathan, but at least we'd still had a lot more freedom than we'd had lately. Not that we minded, really (I kept telling myself): we just lived in a different world now. There are tradeoffs, but maybe we had traded a little bit too much.

That's one reason we were happy to accept when Glen O'Banyon, the city's top gay attorney with whom I'd worked frequently, invited us to a party for the opening of the new Burrows Library—by far the biggest predominantly gay social event of the year.

Chester Burrows was a local eccentric, very rich (which is society's dividing line between "eccentric" and "crazy"), and a world-class collector of books and manuscripts, many of them very rare and worth a fortune. Though no particular fuss was made about it, the collection included what was thought to be the largest private hoard in existence of books on the subject of homosexuality. If a book, from Gutenberg on down, even mentioned the subject, it was said to be in Burrows' collection. He guarded his collection with a tenacity well beyond the border of paranoia, and while everyone knew it existed, he allowed very few people access to it, even for purposes of research.

As a result, when upon his death at the age of 89 his will set up The Burrows Foundation and donated the gay portion of the collection to the very small local Gay Archives, scholars and researchers were chomping at the bit to get at it. In addition to the collection, the will bequeathed the Foundation $1,000,000 for a new facility to house both the archives, which were at the time crammed into a small store-front building on a side street in The Central, and the Burrows collection.

By extreme good fortune, the Foundation, upon whose board Glen O'Banyon sat, was able to obtain the elegant old

T. R. Roosevelt Elementary School building on Ash St. just two blocks south of Beech, the heart of The Central. The building had been vacant for years and only a constant series of legal battles by historical preservationist groups had prevented it from being demolished some time ago. Its purchase as home for the Burrows Library was welcomed by everyone, the only stipulation imposed by the preservationists was that the exterior of the building—a Victorian gem—be unchanged.

A mysterious fire at Burrows' estate shortly before the collection was moved to the new facility had threatened the collection, but was discovered and extinguished in time—none of the original manuscripts were lost, and only a few of the more modern works were damaged, most of them replaceable from other sources. Still, it gave impetus to getting the collection to the new facility which had an elaborate fire protection system.

* * *

I'm really not all that big on fancy social occasions, but it was a nice opportunity to get out, and Jonathan, of course, was excited at the prospect of mingling with the rich and famous of the gay community. He was particularly looking forward to the opportunity of possibly meeting one of his favorite writers, Evan Knight, whose gay novels, set in the 1930s and 1940s, were extremely popular—he even had a large following among open-minded heterosexuals. Knight had been something of a protégé of Burrows'—rumor of course had it that he was something more than that—and would, with Burrows' nephew, officiate at the Library's opening.

As soon as we received the invitation, Jonathan called Craig Richman, the 16 year old son of Police Lieutenant Mark Richman with whom I'd also worked frequently, to book his babysitting services for the night of the opening. Craig was a really nice kid who'd recently come out to his folks, and his dad was all in favor of his having some adult gay role models. Mark Richman was definitely a man ahead of his time—especially for a high-ranking member of the police department. Relations between the police and the gay community had improved tremendously in the past few years, and the waters between the department and the community were for the most part calm. But while there was increasing tolerance among the department's hierarchy, there is a considerable difference between tolerance and acceptance. We'd not yet reached the point of all standing around in a big circle holding hands and singing "Kumbaya."

Anyway, Craig Richman was a great kid who also had a tremendous crush on Jonathan. It was really fun to watch because he tried so hard not to let it show. And Jonathan, of course, pretended not to notice. Best of all, Craig and Joshua had become fast friends since the first time he'd baby-sat for us, so Joshua put up relatively little fuss whenever Jonathan and I did make the time to get out by ourselves. Because the Burrows opening was a very special event and we'd probably be out later than usual, Jonathan arranged with Craig's mom to have him spend the night. Our couch was pretty comfortable for sleeping, and while I'm sure Craig would have preferred it if *I* slept on the couch, he was all for staying over, and his folks okayed it.

By luck, all our core-group of friends would be at the by-invitation-only opening, too: Bob Allen and his partner Mario, as part of the contingent of bar owners and managers, Tim and Phil—Tim as an assistant medical examiner in the coroner's office and Phil as a well-known model for Spartan Briefs—and Jared and Jake: Jared (a former beer truck driver) as a professor of Russian literature at nearby Mountjoy College, and Jake as owner of a large construction firm. I think Jonathan and I got invited just because Glen O'Banyon was a nice guy and had the clout to do it.

Jonathan suggested we run out and rent tuxedos for the event, but I assured hm that while it would indeed be a fancy affair, I was sure it wouldn't be quite *that* fancy, and that I doubted that any of our friends had even considered it.

"Well, maybe you should call Mr. O'Banyon just to be sure," he said. "I wouldn't want our group to be the only ones there not wearing a tuxedo."

"I'm sure there will be a lot of women there," I said, "and I can almost guarantee you they won't be wearing tuxedos."

"You know perfectly well what I mean," he said in exasperation. "And you keep being a wiseguy and we'll be playing a little game of 'The Put-Upon Lover and the Guy Who Ain't Gettin' Any'."

I threw my hands in the air in surrender. "Okay, okay, I'll call."

* * *

The above took place on a Thursday, with the opening set for a week from the coming Saturday, so on Friday morning I called Glen O'Banyon's office and, assuming correctly that he might not be there, asked to speak to Donna, his secretary. Donna was, I'd long ago determined, the quintessential executive secretary and well worth every penny O'Banyon paid her. She was the perfect combination of business and personality, and always made everyone with whom she talked feel like his or her business was at the head of O'Banyon's list of importance.

She told me that O'Banyon was at home working on an upcoming trial, but that he'd be calling in and she would have him call me as soon as he could.

* * *

I'd been lucky enough to have been keeping fairly busy the last several weeks, which helped refill the coffers after yet another lengthy involvement in a case for which I wasn't being paid, and was devoting the day to preparing my final reports...and billings...on two of them. As usual, I got so wrapped up in what I was doing that I wasn't really aware of the passage of time, until the growling of my stomach told me it needed attention.

I was just about to pick up the phone to call the diner downstairs and order something to bring back to the office when it rang, startling me.

"Hardesty Investigations," I said, waiting for the second ring before picking it up.

"Dick, hi. It's Glen. Donna tells me you called."

"Yeah, I did. I hate to bother you at the office about personal things, but Jonathan made me promise I'd check with you to see about the dress code for the Burrows opening. He seems to think it's a black tie and tails event."

O'Banyon laughed. "I'm sure there'll be a couple tux queens there, but I sure won't be one of them," he said. "Tell Jonathan anything other than bib overalls will fit right in."

I was relieved to hear it. "Thanks, Glen. Again, sorry to bother you about something so trivial, but..."

"Not at all," he said. "As a matter of fact, how would you like to join me for a beer at Hughie's at about 3:30? I've been working my tail off on this upcoming trial, and I could use a break. And for some reason, I'm in a Hughie's mood."

"Sure," I said. "I'll see you there." I heard the click of the receiver hanging up.

* * *

Hughie's. Well, that brought back memories...lots of memories. Hughie's is a hustler bar about two blocks from my office, and it's where I met Phil (back when he was hustling under the name "Tex"), and it's where I met Jonathan. I used to go there pretty frequently after work in my single days, not for the hustlers but because Hughie's is one of the few places that serves dark beer on draft, in old-fashioned frosted mugs. Nothing better on a hot day.

I'd met Glen O'Banyon there a couple of times, too, always related to business, and seeing one of the best, most successful, and richest lawyers in the city dressed in torn Levis, baseball cap, and a football-logo sweatshirt never ceased to amaze me. He'd told me he didn't get out much, and when he did, he wanted to go someplace people wouldn't be buttonholing him for legal advice. Hughie's was the place.

I ordered a BLT and potato salad from the diner, refilled the office coffee pot, and went downstairs to pick up my order.

* * *

I'm not sure how many times I've said it before, but there's really only one way to say it: Hughie's was...well, Hughie's: a big, dimly lit space off the hallway of time, totally unaffected by the passing years. It never changed. Dark, mildly clammy from the air cooler, always smelling of spilled booze and cigarette smoke, same 3:30 hustlers (well, different guys, but interchangeable) waiting for the offices to close and the johns to come in for a little pre-heading-off-to-the-suburbs action.

And Bud, of course, behind the bar. I could count on the fingers of one hand the number of times I'd been in Hughie's and Bud had not been there. And though I couldn't honestly remember the last time I was there, the minute Bud saw me walk in the door he reached into the cooler for a mug and poured me a dark draft, having it ready for me when I reached the bar.

"How's it goin', Dick?" he asked with the same detached tone he'd used from the first day I entered the place. Hearing it, I was sure I'd been in the day before.

"Pretty good, Bud. You?" The usual expressionless shrug in response as I opened my billfold and handed him a bill. No Glen. A really hot hustler in a tight short rolled-sleeve shirt which made him look—not coincidentally, I'm sure—like James Dean in *Rebel Without a Cause*, gave me a sexy smile, which I returned with a nod.

Ooops! Wrong move, Hardesty, one of my mind voices cautioned as the guy picked up his beer and headed in my direction. *Butt out!* my crotch responded sharply, and I was once again aware why I didn't come into Hughie's much since I'd gotten together with Jonathan. *"Here there be tygers,"* another mind voice cautioned, piously.

Luckily or unluckily, depending on whether you were my conscience or my crotch, Glen O'Banyon appeared at my elbow, and the approaching guy stopped short and took a seat at the bar about ten feet away.

"Interrupting something?" Glen asked with a smile.

"Fortunately, yes," I said, turning to shake his hand, noting he was in his baseball-cap-sweatshirt-jeans uniform. In the artificial dim light of the bar, it looked as though his hair was becoming greyer than last time I'd seen him.

"Glad you called," he said. "I needed an excuse to get out of the house for a while."

I smiled as he motioned to Bud for a beer. "I do what I can," I said.

"So Jonathan's looking forward to the opening?" he said more than asked.

"Like a racehorse at the starting gate," I said. "It was really nice of you to invite us."

He shook his head. "No problem," he said. "How's it going with a kid in the family?" he asked, handing Bud a bill and taking a swig of his beer.

"I assume you mean Joshua," I said with a grin. "Surprisingly well, actually. He's a great kid."

"So, you got any pictures?"

I shrugged, feeling a little sheepish. "Well, we're not *that* far into the 'perfect family' mode yet. But Jonathan did mention having some taken. He would."

We idle-chatted for several minutes, and then the talk got around to the Burrows and the generous donation to the community.

"Pocket change," Glen said. "Though to hear Zach Clanton

tell it, it's taking food out of his kids' mouths."

"Zach Clanton?" I asked. "Who's he?"

"Zach...Zachary Clanton is the oldest of Chester Burrows' two nephews."

"Ah, I said. "I thought Burrows only had one."

"One gay one," Glen amended. "One straight. Zach's the straight one, and if it were up to him, there wouldn't be a new library."

"I thought the bequest was in Chester Burrows' will," I said.

Glen nodded, then took several long swallows of his beer, nearly emptying it. I motioned to Bud for two more.

"It is," Glen said. "And Zach is none too happy about it, you can be sure. Luckily, he had no say in the matter. As the two heirs to Burrows' fortune, both he and Marv Westeen, Zach's cousin and Chester's other nephew, are on the Foundation's board of directors, and it hasn't been easy. The will actually states the bequest to the Foundation is to be *'up to'* $1,000,000—rather odd wording, but that was Chester Burrows for you—and Zach sees that as meaning that every dollar not spent by the foundation is fifty cents in his pocket. He couldn't see spending good money for establishing a separate library when any number of established institutions would be happy to take the entire collection. I suspect Marv is the one who talked Chester into making the bequest in the first place. Marv convinced the old man it would mean a lot to the gay community, and it will. I'm sure there's an incredible amount of historical material buried in there, things no one is even fully aware of yet. If the entire collection had gone to a larger institution, chances are it would have been given a lot less attention than it will have now."

"I gather you knew the Burrows family before all this came about?" I asked, taking a bill out of my wallet and laying it on the bar. O'Banyon nodded.

"Not all that well, really, but I've handled some things for them from time to time. I actually only met Chester Burrows once in person. Most of my dealings with him were by phone. He was *really* a recluse. Zach and Marv's mothers were his sisters, and when they died I got to know 'the boys' in the course of handling their mothers' estates. Marv I like; Zach, as I may have indicated, is a real pain in the ass."

"He sounds like a real winner," I said. "How does he deal with his cousin and uncle being gay?" I wondered.

O'Banyon grinned, exchanging his empty bottle for the full

one Bud handed him."Well, he doesn't—or at least didn't while Chester was alive—have much choice in the matter if he wanted a share of Chester's fortune. Chester's money had supported both Marv's and Zach's families, and Zach's not stupid. He's a closet homophobe, but always tried to cover it up while Chester was alive. He obviously hates faggots, but certainly wasn't above sucking up to Chester every chance he got—he went so far as to name his first kid after him.

"He and Marv aren't exactly close, as you might imagine, but there apparently wasn't any open hostility between them while Chester was alive. Marv's pretty quiet, like Chester, and while Zach did his best to butter up the old man whenever he got the chance, Chester seemed more partial to Marv, though it was a little hard to tell with somebody as tightly-wrapped as Chester. Marv and Zach shared equally in the will, though."

"How about this Evan Knight?" I asked, reaching for a fresh napkin to wipe off the bottom of my beer mug, from which the thin outer layer of ice was rapidly melting. "Where does he fit into the picture?"

"Kind of a strange duck," O'Banyon replied rubbing the back of an index finger across the corner of his mouth. "But I guess all writers are, in one way or another. From what I understand, he was just about the only human being Chester Burrows might have considered as being a friend. There's about a 45-year age difference between them, so I tend to dismiss the rumors about their being romantically involved...but who knows? I have no idea how they met, but I do know Knight acted as something of a curator for the collection for many years before he published his first book."

"Well, he's Jonathan's favorite writer, I know," I said, "and he's really hoping to meet him."

"I'm sure that can be arranged," O'Banyon said, raising his bottle to his lips.

We talked for another ten minutes or so, then I looked at my watch. "Uh, oh," I said. "I'd better get going."

O'Banyon finished his beer. "Yeah, me too. Glad we had a chance to get together."

"So am I," I said. We left the bar together, stopped outside long enough to shake hands, and went our separate ways. "See you next Saturday," I called over my shoulder in afterthought. I turned, and he waved without looking back.

* * *

The weekend flew by, as weekends tend to do, though with a definite difference between pre-Joshua and post-Joshua weekends. Saturday, in addition to our routine laundry/grocery shopping/housecleaning chores, we had to add a search for some new clothes and shoes for Joshua who, I projected from his current rate of growth, would be somewhere around 11 feet tall by the time he was 18. Raising a kid certainly wasn't going to be cheap. We ended up getting him two pair of shoes—one for "good" and one for school and play—plus two new shirts, and two pairs of pants.

And Sundays had changed, too. While pre-Joshua Sundays involved sleeping in, a quiet morning reading the paper, then brunch either by ourselves or with friends at a gay restaurant/bar, we now were more likely than not awakened shortly after dawn by a hungry Joshua, his ever-present favorite toy, Bunny, under one arm. A great deal more time than used-to-be was devoted to reading the comics aloud and examining all the photographs in the paper. Then Jonathan would get himself and Joshua showered and dressed and go off to the M.C.C.—Metropolitan Community Church—so Joshua could attend Sunday School as he'd always done with his parents. While they were gone, I'd finish reading the paper and take my time getting showered and dressed.

We still went out to brunch nearly every Sunday, sometimes with friends, but very seldom to our pre-Joshua places.

As I say, I was well aware of just how drastically my life had changed since Jonathan—and now Joshua—had come into it. I wouldn't give it up for the world, but there were times I missed my little revolving door of tricks, partying, and general harmless debauchery.

* * *

The week, too, raced by and before I knew it, Saturday had rolled around again and it was the day of the opening. When Joshua heard Jonathan mention the word "Library", he wanted us to be sure we would bring him back some books. ("With big words!" he insisted. He recently had become fascinated with adding multi-syllable words to his vocabulary, and the bigger the better. 'Constantinople' was a favorite, though it was rather hard to fit into a conversation.) Rather than explain that while this library had lots of books with big words, not many of them would be of interest to little boys, we made a conciliatory swing through The Central during our regular Saturday chore routine to buy him a couple new books for his growing collection. His parents had given Joshua a love for books, and we definitely wanted to encourage it.

And Joshua was, of course, even more hyper than usual over the prospect of spending the night with his buddy, Craig—who, we promised him, would read him one of his new books at bedtime.

The party started at eight, so I drove over to the Richmans' to pick up Craig at around five thirty. Jonathan called in a pizza order shortly after I'd left so that we'd be able to eat as soon as I returned with Craig.

I mentioned that Craig was 16, and gay. His parents were amazingly supportive —especially, again, considering his dad was a high-ranking police officer—and I was flattered that they tacitly passed on to me—and trusted me with—the role of surrogate dad when it came to questions involving coping with being gay in an all-too-straight world. So when I'd pick him up for babysitting, we'd spend the ride to the apartment talking about how his life was going, gay-related issues he might be coping with at school, etc. He eventually reached the point where he felt comfortable enough (though I'll admit I was a little edgy about it) to ask some pretty sexually-based questions: what certain expressions meant, what was safe and what wasn't. He wasn't all that sexually active yet, but he was a 16 year old boy with the usual raging hormones, and he was meeting other kids at school who were more than willing to experiment, even though they might not turn out to actually be gay in the long run. (When you're 16, sex is sex.) He didn't see the necessity for using condoms, but I kept hammering away at it every time I could, and I think he finally started coming around.

* * *

The pizza had just arrived when we got to the apartment so we ate right away, then Jonathan and I got ready. Jonathan had already given Joshua his bath and put him in his p.j.s so that Craig could just put him to bed when the time came.

We left the apartment around 7:30 and headed back to The Central. As I suspected, parking was a real problem.

Having been built in the early part of the century as an elementary school not needing student parking, the parking lot beside the old T. R. Roosevelt Elementary building would be ample for day-to-day use, but hardly for a large gathering like this one.

We managed to find a spot a block and a half away and walked back to join the impressive number of people going in. A nice looking guy in his early 30s but walking with a gold-handled walking stick, though with no sign of a limp, was coming toward us, heading in the opposite direction.

"'Evening," Jonathan said pleasantly as we approached him. His head jerked slightly as though he'd just been insulted. His lip curled into a sneer and he passed us without a word.

Jonathan merely shrugged. "Friendly guy," he said, not looking back.

We turned our attention to the building just ahead of us. It did look great. I'd been watching its progress over the past couple of months, and merely sandblasting and tuckpointing the exterior gave it a whole new look of elegance. Some consideration had been given to simply building an entire new facility, but they could not have done nearly as well as they had by going with the renovation. The old "T. R. Roosevelt Elementary" had been removed from above the main door, replaced with a matching stone engraved "The Burrows Library." It really was a feather in the gay community's cap to incorporate its own archives with the prestige of the Burrows Collection.

The bulk of the restoration had, of course, been in the building's interior, which had been largely gutted and redone. The original wide stairway leading up from the entrance to what had been a first floor hallway sided by classrooms now led to a huge open space—a large two-story reading area in the middle, with a circular service desk in the exact center of the room, and a couple of informal smaller areas off to each side with comfortable chairs and sofas beneath open stairways leading to the second floor—flanked by rows of open stacks on either side of the main room. This space was devoted largely to the existing archives brought over from their old home off Beech. It was estimated that only a small portion of the Burrows collection would be readily available to the general public.

The second floor would house the more esoteric and valuable works of the archives and the Burrows collection, and access to it would be limited and supervised to prevent theft or damage. The basement, which was off-limits during the opening because it housed the largely as-yet uncataloged manuscripts and documents, would never be open to the public. From what I'd heard, it roughly duplicated the layout of the main floor, but the large center area was where the cataloging took place. When the Burrows cataloging was completed, part of the room would be set up in individual cubicles for researchers to work privately. There were plans to start a Personal History department, seeking the personal letters of gays and lesbians, so the cataloging would be largely an ongoing project even after all Burrows' material had been cataloged.

Two attractive young women, each in a white blouse and black skirt, stood at either side of the top of the stairs checking the invitations. We showed ours to the one closer to us, who smiled and said, "Welcome to the Burrows." Passing her, we entered the main room. Two small bars had been set up for the opening ceremonies, one at each side of the room, and a long table of hors d'oeuvres was in front of the service desk. All were doing a brisk business, and there must have been well over a hundred people already there when we arrived, with more coming in every minute. Off to one side of and slightly behind the hors d'oeuvre table was a raised platform with a lectern, apparently set up for the official opening speeches.

I recognized probably half of the people there, if not from knowing them personally then from having seen them at various events over the years. There were several, however, that I'd never seen before—further evidence that the community was growing rapidly. Jonathan spotted Jared and Jake—they were pretty hard to miss in any crowd—near the bar to the left, and we went over to join them. I'd never seen either of them in a shirt and tie before, and they looked terrific.

"Hi, Jonathan," Jake said with a grin when he spotted him. He gave me a winking nod, then turned his full concentration back to Jonathan, saying: "You're looking particularly hot tonight! Why don't you ditch the old man, and we can go exploring the stacks together?"

Jake had learned some time ago that Jonathan flustered easily under sex-teasing, especially coming from someone as spectacularly sexy as Jake, so he did it every chance he had.

We exchanged handshakes all around and Jonathan, seeing Jared and Jake had full drinks, stepped to the bar to order a coke for himself and a bourbon-seven for me.

"Quite a crowd," Jared observed with a slight gesture of his glass to indicate the entire room.

I nodded. "Yeah, the cream of the crop. I imagine just about everybody who is anybody in the gay community is here, or will be before the evening's over. Where are the Burrows heirs?"

Jake gave a heads-up nod in the direction of a large cluster of people near the other bar across from us. "They're the two in the tuxes."

Jonathan, who had rejoined us, handed me my drink and said: "See? I told you!"

"You're right," I said, "two hundred people, two tuxes. You wanna go home and change?"

He reached over and grabbed my ass, giving it quick but painful squeeze.

"And look!" he said excitedly, indicating a tall, handsome man about 40 with salt-and pepper hair, standing in another group not far from the Burrows heirs. "There's Evan Knight! I recognize him from his books!" Definitely looked like an author to me. "Can we go meet him?"

"Sure," I said. "But let's wait a bit. He's obviously busy now."

"Well, yeah," Jonathan said a bit impatiently, "but I'll bet he'll be busy all night. He's a famous *author*."

"Okay, okay," I said. "Let me see if I can get Glen to introduce you."

"Us," Jonathan corrected. "*Us*. Don't you want to meet him, too?"

Frankly, my one previous run-in with a famous author had not been a particularly pleasant experience. But that was then and this was now, so... "Sure," I said.

We all made our way over to the buffet table, and were joined on the way by Tim and Phil, both looking as though they'd stepped off a magazine cover. It never ceased to amaze me how much Phil had changed from the day I first met him when he hustled me at Hughie's. He was a diamond in the rough even then, and he'd polished up nicely. And I don't know what there is about a large group of good looking guys dressed to the nines that raised their sex appeal through the roof.

I kept watching for Glen O'Banyon, but only caught fleeting glimpses of him as he moved from group to group. Our own little group, brought to full company strength by the arrival of Mario and Bob, was having a great time talking among ourselves as though we never saw each other—and I realized again that we really hadn't been all together very often since Joshua arrived.

"I suppose we should go mingle," Jake said after another round of drinks. "I for one am not above mixing business with pleasure, and there are a couple people here I really should talk to." We all agreed, and drifted off in different directions.

"There's Mr. O'Banyon," Jonathan said, gesturing toward one of the bars, "and he's with Mr. Knight!" He immediately grabbed my free hand and pulled me toward them. I needed another drink, anyway.

"Hi, Mr. O'Banyon," Jonathan said a little breathlessly as we reached the bar.

O'Banyon grinned. "Hi, Jonathan, hi, Dick."

We shook hands, and he turned to Evan Knight, who was looking at Jonathan with a bemused smile that I thought had just a touch of the predator in it.

"I don't think you know Evan Knight," O'Banyon continued. "Evan, this is Dick Hardesty and his partner, Jonathan..." he hesitated and I realized he might never have heard Jonathan's last name.

"Quinlan," Jonathan added quickly, extending his hand. "I'm a huge fan, Mr. Knight—I've read every one of your books."

"That's very nice of you to say, Jonathan" Knight said, taking Jonathan's hand. "And it's 'Evan,' please." He cocked an eyebrow and studied Jonathan's face. "You look familiar," he said. "Have we met?"

I'd have thought a writer would be able to come up with a little more original line than that one.

Jonathan shook his head. "I don't think so," he said.

After another slow scan of Jonathan's face, he reluctantly released Jonathan's hand and extended his hand to me. "Nice to meet you, Dick."

I started to say something when one of the tuxedo-wearers, looking singularly unhappy, hurried over and whispered something in O'Banyon's ear. O'Banyon's eyebrows raised, then dropped into a frown. The tuxedo moved off quickly, toward the front steps.

"Something wrong?" I asked.

"I'm afraid so," he said.

I didn't know whether I should ask, but I didn't have to.

"It seems we have a body in the basement," he said.

CHAPTER 2

The other tuxedo came over to consult with O'Banyon and Evan Knight. I started to excuse ourselves, assuming they'd want to talk in private, but Glen held up his hand to indicate we should stay.

"What are we going to do?" the tuxedo asked. "The police will be swarming all over the place in a few minutes. Shall we just cancel the whole evening?"

Glen shook his head. "No, I don't think so," he said. "Everyone's here; calling it off would just stir things up more than they need to be. Unless the police have some objections, let's just go on with it as planned." He glanced at his watch. "It's almost time for the dedication to start, anyway. As soon as Zach gets back, we can begin."

O'Banyon's reference to Zach indicated that the other tuxedo—the one standing with us—was Marv Westeen, Chester Burrows' gay nephew. Not a bad-looking guy, somewhere around 40. There was something about his face that I found puzzling until I realized it was devoid of lines or wrinkles...or character. The effect was rather like a nice looking window-display mannequin come to life.

Evan Knight apparently took the announcement of a body being found in the basement as not particularly noteworthy—a form of writer's stoicism, perhaps—and appeared to have other things on his mind: in this case, Jonathan. He'd hardly taken his eyes off Jonathan since we'd been introduced, and under normal circumstances my "Me Tarzan! Boy mine!" reaction would have fully kicked in by this point. But for some reason, I always find myself distracted by having someone turn up dead in my immediate vicinity.

Glen and Marv Westeen excused themselves to get things ready and moved off, but Evan made no attempt to go with them.

"So tell me, Jonathan," he said, with a small smile, "are you a writer?"

Jonathan was obviously pleased that he'd think so, but said: "Oh, no. I'm just a reader."

Knight reached out and touched Jonathan's arm. "*Just a reader*'?" he said. "Please, don't sell yourself short. Where would writers be without readers? We're symbiotes, you and

I."

Gee, Hardesty, one of my mind voices observed sweetly, *don't you wish you'd learned to read? Maybe you could be a symbiote then, too.*

"What do you do, if I might ask?" Knight said, again speaking directly to Jonathan.

"I work at Evergreens Nursery," Jonathan said. "I'm going to school for an associate's degree in horticulture."

"Really?" Knight said. "Good for you! Do you do landscaping?"

Jonathan looked a little perplexed. "Evergreens does," he said. "I'm not in business for myself...yet. I'd like to be someday."

Knight gave him a smile warm enough to toast bread. "I'm sure you will be," he said. "I've just bought a new house in Briarwood, and I'm going to need some landscaping. Do you have a card?"

I had no idea whether his little web-spinning operation was as transparent to Jonathan as it was to me, but probably not. The fly seldom knows what's going on. But the spider does. And so did I.

"No," Jonathan said, apologetically, "I'm afraid I don't."

Knight gave him an a-little-too-warm smile. "No matter," he said. "Evergreens, eh? I'll keep that in mind."

I'm sure you will, I thought. I figured it was about time to break this little courtship dance up.

"If you'll excuse us, Evan," I said, "We should go find our friends before the ceremony starts."

Evan gave me a knowing smile—I thought it had just the slightest hint of a smirk, actually—into which I read volumes. "Of course," he said. "It was nice meeting you...both...and I trust I'll see you later."

We shook hands, and Jonathan, totally oblivious to the fact that he had obviously just been writ large on Knight's menu board as 'Special of the Day,' said: "I'd love to talk to you about your books sometime."

"I'd like that," Evans said. "Very much." He shot me a very quick glance that, like his smile, spoke volumes.

"Gee, what a nice guy," Jonathan said as we walked away.

Since my gut was telling me I couldn't trust the "guy" any further than I could throw him—and I was tempted to try—I reserved comment.

We spotted Tim and Phil just as Bob and Mario came up

behind us.

"What's up with the police?" Mario asked. "I went to the bathroom, and they've got the stairway to the basement sealed off. There are cops everywhere. There are even a couple blocking the main doors. Talk about paranoia: my first thought was 'Great, they've got us where they want us.'"

While I was pretty sure the show of strength wasn't specifically to harass us, it was evidence of the fact that the police were still rather uncomfortable about dealing with situations involving large numbers of homosexuals—as if they never knew what we might do next.

"There was some sort of accident in the basement," I said. "Somebody's dead."

"Any details?" Bob asked as the four of us approached Tim and Phil.

"None so far," I said. "I'll try to find out more later."

By looking back toward the entrance, I could see Zach Clanton moving through the crowd toward the central service desk, where Glen O'Banyon, Marv Westeen, and several other members of the Burrows Foundation board had assembled by the jerry-rigged speaker's platform.

Evan Knight joined the group and he, Westeen, Clanton, and O'Banyon mounted the platform. The crowd closed in around the service desk, and Glen moved to the podium.

"I'd like to welcome you all," he began, "to the new Burrows Library...."

* * *

It took forever to get out of the place. The police were taking the names of everyone in attendance—which, again despite the vastly improved relations between the gay community and the police, was not received well by those who too-clearly remembered the bad old days of bigotry and open harassment on the part of the department.

While we were working our way slowly toward the main entrance, I managed to spot Glen O'Banyon still by the service desk, talking with a policeman, and excused myself from the group to go talk with him. "I'll meet you out front," I told Jonathan, and inched my way upstream through the crowd. O'Banyon didn't seem surprised to see me. He said something to the officer he was talking with and came over to meet me.

"I know it's none of my business," I said, "but I was

wondering if you had any idea what's going on?"

"Not much, I'm afraid," he said. "The police aren't saying much. All I could find out is that one of our catalogers, Taylor Cates, somehow fell down the back stairs leading to the rear exit and apparently broke his neck."

"I thought the basement was closed," I said. "What was he doing there?"

O'Banyon shrugged. "The cataloging areas are off limits to just about everybody," he said. "They usually keep it locked, so Taylor was there in case some board member might want to give someone a guided tour. It was Irving McHam who found him." He motioned with a head nod toward a tall, almost skeletal red-head deep in conversation with two of the Foundation's board members. McHam, I'd read, was the library's new Director and head librarian, who had been brought in from Chicago's Newberry Library.

"Then why would Cates be using the back exit stairs, I wonder?" I said.

"Good question," O'Banyon said. "I have no idea. That stairway leads to a emergency fire exit—no one can use it from the outside, and an alarm would have sounded if someone had tried to open it from the inside. I can't imagine why he'd be back there."

"Maybe somebody was at the back door trying to get in?" I suggested.

"Unlikely," he said. "There's a big sign on the outside of the door telling people to use the front entrance. As I said, they couldn't get in, and Taylor couldn't have let anyone in without sounding the alarm. Apparently the police checked, and the door was locked."

"Can the alarm be turned off?" I asked.

"I imagine so," he said, "though I don't know that Taylor even knew where the switch was, or why he might want to turn it off even if he knew how."

"Well, I gather there are some pretty valuable manuscripts and documents down there," I said. "Maybe Cates found something valuable and was trying to sell it."

O'Banyon looked skeptical. "I really doubt it," he said. "From what little I know, Taylor's character was above reproach. He was totally dedicated to his work, and just didn't strike me as the kind of guy who might do anything illegal." He thought a minute, then said: "Of course there's no doubt there's a lot of valuable material down there, and that's why the cataloging area is treated like it's Fort Knox. But it'll be months before anyone has even an idea of the value of what's there. The fewer people who have access to that area, the less the chance of someone walking off with something."

The room had fairly well emptied out, and I saw Jonathan, who had apparently hung back waiting for me, talking with a policeman with a pad and pencil.

"I guess I'd better get going," I said. "Thanks again for inviting us, and I'm sorry about the accident."

We shook hands, and I moved toward the front entrance as Glen turned to walk over to join Irving McHam and the other board members.

Jonathan stepped away from the cop as I came up.

"Can I have your name, address, and phone number, please?" the cop asked politely. Since there'd been a death at a large gathering, I knew it was just routine, and I gave him the information, which he duly wrote down. The odds were overwhelming that Taylor Cates' death had been an accident, but just in case, it was wise to know who had been in attendance if they had to do further checking.

"I told the others to go ahead and we'd meet them at Ramón's," Jonathan announced as we went down the steps and started toward the car.

* * *

Sunday was kind of fun, actually. Thanks to Craig, who was sleeping on the couch, it was to him Joshua went running the minute he woke up, and Jonathan and I were able to sleep about half an hour later than normal. When we got up, Craig, Joshua, and Bunny were at the kitchen table having a bowl of cereal and a glass of milk.

"Hi, Uncle Jonathan! Hi, Uncle Dick!" Joshua said happily in a stage whisper which made him sound as though he was coming down with some rare children's ailment. But Craig looked up at us and grinned, then said to Joshua: "It's okay, Joshua. We can stop playing now."

"Playing?" Jonathan asked.

"Yes!" Joshua said brightly. "We're playing 'Whisper'. I won, didn't I, Craig?"

"Yep," Craig replied, his face solemn. "Fair and square." Then he reached out and, grinning, tousled Joshua's hair.

"You want to come live with us?" Jonathan asked Craig,

jokingly.

I could hear Craig's mental *"Yes!"* clear across the room; I don't think Jonathan caught it.

After Jonathan and I had our coffee and toast, Jonathan asked Craig if he'd like to go to the M.C.C. with him and Joshua, if his folks wouldn't mind. "Sure!" Craig said. "That's the gay church, isn't it? I've always wanted to go, but didn't have anybody to go with. My folks always go to St. Mark's. Can I go call them and ask?" Without waiting for an answer, he got up and headed for the phone. I gave Jonathan a knowing smile and he looked totally puzzled. "What's that for?" he asked, and I merely rolled my eyes to the ceiling. "Oh," he said, finally making the connection. "Well, it's okay if he comes with us, isn't it?" "Of course it is!" I said. "I'm sure he'll enjoy it."

"Yeah," Jonathan said, glancing from Joshua to me, "I just hope he doesn't enjoy it *too* much, if you know what I mean."

I knew. "Puppy love never killed anyone," I said.

"I love puppies too," Joshua said. "Can I have a puppy?"

* * *

While the three of them were at church, I read the paper. There wasn't anything in there about the death of Taylor Cates, though there was a small piece in the Arts & Leisure section on the opening of the Burrows—obviously written well in advance of the event in order to get it in Sunday's paper. The "G" word wasn't mentioned, but I was nonetheless pleased to see we'd reached the point where large gay events were even mentioned in other than the gay press. It was a very small article but it was a start.

When the Three Musketeers returned from church, we took Craig with us for brunch at the Cove, a nice little family restaurant on the edge of The Central. Naturally, there was a large contingent of gays including one group of four obviously gay teenagers. Craig was immediately smitten by one of the group, and they spent most of brunch cruising one another despite Joshua's persistent attempts to keep Craig's attention focused on him.

Ah, youth!

* * *

I checked Monday morning's paper for any mention of Taylor Cates' death at during the opening of the Burrows, and found nothing at all except for an obituary:

Taylor James Cates, 29, 2424 Beckham Place, died Saturday as a result of a fall. He was preceded in death by his parents, Peter and Yolanda Cates. Services will be at the McGraw Funeral Chapel on Tuesday at 2 p.m.

I really hate obituaries. In Cates' case, 29 years of a human life were reduced to two short sentences. Well, life ain't fair sometimes.

May we quote you on that? a mind voice asked.

I got wrapped up in some paperwork on a just completed case when the phone rang. I glanced at my watch and was surprised, yet again, to see it was 1:15 already. Why hadn't my stomach let me know?

"Hardesty Investigations," I said, picking up on the...yeah, you know by now... second ring.

"Dick," Glen O'Banyon's familiar voice said, "What's your schedule tomorrow morning?"

"Clear at the moment," I said without having to check. "Something I can help you with?"

There was only a slight pause, then: "There just might be," he said. "Can you come by my office at, say, 9:30?"

"Sure," I said. I didn't ask for details, since I'd worked with him long enough and on such a variety of matters to know that it could be any one of a number of things. He'd tell me in good time . "Oh, and thanks again for inviting us to the opening," I said. "We had nice time—that poor guy's accident aside, of course. Have you found out anything else about it?"

"Actually, that's what I want to talk to you about," he said. "I'm waiting for more information and hope to have it by this afternoon."

You're slipping, Hardesty, a mind voice said, disapprovingly, and maybe it was right: my immediate reaction to his asking to see me had not been that might be related to the accident.

"Okay," I said. "I'll see you at 9:30 tomorrow, then."

Well, if I hadn't been curious before, I certainly was now. Being of a somewhat suspicious nature—and given the fact that I am a private investigator, after all—I had to wonder if Glen had reason to suspect Taylor Cates' death just might not have been an accident—and what led Glen to think so. Well, little point in speculating until I knew more of what was going on.

* * *

Joshua greeted me at the door holding a Munchkin-sized loaf of bread in a Munchkin-sized wrapper.

"Look what I got, Uncle Dick," he said happily, holding the bread at arm's length out toward me.

"That's great, Joshua," I said as Jonathan came out of the kitchen for our now-traditional group hug. "Where did you find a loaf of bread like that?"

I should have learned by then that when you ask a four-year-old boy a question, you should, depending on the kid's degree of enthusiasm for the subject, be prepared for a deluge of information, some of which may actually be related to the question. It seemed that the Bronson sisters, who ran the day care center Joshua attended, had arranged with some other day care centers to have the older kids tour a local commercial bakery. I learned this by patching together Joshua's account of his adventure and Jonathan's interspersed interpretations given between living room and kitchen and preparation of my Manhattan. At the end of the tour, all the kids had been given perfectly proportioned miniature loaves of bread.

It was only through Jonathan's diplomacy and art of persuasion that the loaf had lasted this long, Joshua, of course, having wanted to eat it immediately. But Jonathan had promised that we'd make a very special dessert (toasted, buttered, and sprinkled with sugar and cinnamon) of it after dinner, and that seemed to hold Joshua at bay.

After dinner I watched some TV while Joshua played on the floor. Jonathan, I was a little surprised to see, did not haul out his school books as usual, but instead sat reading (or rather 're-reading') *A Game of Quoits*, a mystery novel by... guess who?... Evan Knight. I'd read it at Jonathan's insistence right after he first got it, and had to admit it was pretty darned good. The guy had an uncanny ability to evoke the sense of time of the book, which was set as were all his books in the late 1930s through the late 1940s. Considering he'd probably just been born around that time, I had to hand it to him.

* * *

I got off the elevator on O'Banyon's floor at 9:20. Only 10 minutes early! I was proud of myself. The receptionist sent me back to the small waiting room just off O'Banyon's private office, where his secretary, Donna, offered me a cup of coffee. Since I'd come directly from home without yet stopping at my office, I accepted the offer with thanks. My high opinion of her was reinforced when she remembered I took it black.

I was standing at the window, looking out over the city, when O'Banyon hurried in, briefcase in hand, surrounded by an almost palpable aura of business and efficiency.

"Hi, Dick," he said, without stopping. "I'll be right with you."

He went into his office, followed by Donna with a note pad.

You know that old expression, "How the other half lives"? Well, Glen O'Banyon was pretty much "the other half". He had more power, prestige, and money than I could ever imagine having, but somehow he still kept one foot firmly on the ground, and I admired him for it.

A moment later, Donna came out of Glen's office and said: "You can go in now, Mr. Hardesty," holding the door open for me. She indicated the now-almost-empty coffee cup in my hand. "I can take that for you, if you'd like."

I smiled my thanks as I handed it to her, and she closed the door behind me. O'Banyon gestured me to a chair, and I sat.

"I've got to be in court in 45 minutes," he said, settling back into his own chair behind his large but not ostentatious desk, "but I wanted to talk with you in person about this…matter."

"Taylor Cates' death," I said, and he nodded.

He ran a thumb across the space between his nose and upper lip. "Yes," he said. "And we…several members of the Burrows board and I…would like you to look into it."

I pondered that one for only a moment.

"Aren't the police doing that?" I asked.

He nodded. "Oh, yes, but I doubt they have much to go on. It *looks* like an accident, but…"

"…but you don't think it was," I said, completing his sentence for him.

He gave a slight shrug. "Well, that's just it—we don't know. We're concerned that with the Burrows being so visible a symbol of the community, it might somehow have become a target for some radical group or another; or just a single homophobic nutcase. The police have talked to each of the board members, but frankly, we aren't that directly involved with the operational day-to-day details of running the library. Irving McHam called me after they'd spoken to him and was a little conflicted. He had told the police what he knew, which wasn't much, but nothing more."

"Meaning?" I asked

He gave a cocked-head shrug. "Just that he had a strong feeling that something was not right."

I didn't ask why McHam hadn't said that to the police, but I understood. Just as the police are a still a little leery of us, there was still a distinct…hesitation…in getting them involved in community affairs unless it was absolutely necessary. But obviously he felt strongly enough to mention his feelings to O'Banyon.

"Nothing more specific?" I asked.

O'Banyon—odd, I thought, how I insisted on always thinking of him as O'Banyon, though I called him Glen when we talked—pursed his lips and glanced out the window beside his desk. "He has been bothered about the same questions you brought up right after the accident about the circumstances of Taylor's death…a fall down a set of steps he should never have been on in the first place, and why he was even in that part of the library.

"Pretty obvious questions. The police had asked why Taylor might have been on the stairs: might he have been going out, or coming in, or answering a knock at the door, or…. Irving told them that it was unlikely that Taylor would have been leaving the building for some reason or trying to let someone in, but he was understandably pretty distraught at the time, and didn't go into detail. When the police noticed a pack of cigarettes in Taylor's shirt pocket, they apparently assumed he'd been stepping outside for a cigarette, but they didn't say anything, and Irving didn't think to tell them that Taylor followed the rules too closely to ever leave the catalog area unattended by going outside to smoke. I guess they were satisfied and didn't follow up any further. Apparently, since they talked with Irving the night of the accident, they didn't interview him again. But the more he thought about it, the more strongly he felt that something wasn't right, and he called me. He is convinced that Taylor was on to something prior to his death, though he has no idea what.

"So after talking with Irving I decided to bring his concerns up to the board, and four out of five of us—I don't think I have to mention the dissenter—agreed we should ask you to look into it, just on the outside chance Irving's concerns should have some basis in fact. We want to keep the whole thing as quiet as possible, of course, which is another reason not to involve the police. We'll do everything we can to cooperate with whatever police investigation there may be, but we're not going to start waving flags and pointing off in all directions."

"I'll do my best," I said. "What do you know of Taylor's personal life? Did he have a lover? How did he come to work with the collection?"

O'Banyon gave a quick sigh. "As I told you the night of the opening, I didn't really know him all that well. He had just earned his Masters in Library Science, and Irving was very impressed with him. He came to us, interestingly enough, on Evan Knight's recommendation. I assume he and Taylor had something going there for awhile. But like most of Evan's affairs, I doubt it lasted all that long."

"Yeah," I said, grinning. "I got the impression Knight was sizing Jonathan up like a spider eyes a fly."

"Well," O'Banyon said, returning the grin, "I'd keep an eye on him, if I were you. Evan's as slippery as they come, and a real con man. From what I understand he's not very keen on the idea of monogamy…his or anyone else's. As a matter of fact, I hear he looks on guys in relationships as a special challenge. Jonathan strikes me as just the kind of guy Evan would consider fair game—especially with you around."

"I'll keep that in mind," I said. I suddenly remembered the program we'd been given at the opening—Jonathan never throws anything away. "I was a little surprised to see that Knight's name wasn't on the list of the Foundation's Board of Directors," I said. "I'd have thought, considering his closeness to Chester Burrows, he might have been."

O'Banyon shook his head. "No," he said. "The board was limited to five members to make it easier to operate, and Evan is just a bit too much of a loose cannon. We're having enough trouble with Zach Clanton as our resident nay-sayer. I don't think Evan minds not being saddled with the responsibilities of board membership as long as he feels he still has some influence as Chester Burrows' confidante."

He glanced quickly at his watch. "Anyway, the facts are these: we're sitting on a potential gold mine of material with the Burrows collection, and we don't even have an idea yet of what we've got. There is the outside possibility that Taylor

Cates might have come across something valuable enough to have gotten him killed."

In a warehouse full of old books and manuscripts? I thought. In a detective novel, maybe, but in real life? I couldn't imagine how, but a job's a job, and if O'Banyon wanted me to check it out, I'd be more than happy to oblige.

"So will you look into it?"

"Of course," I said.

"Good! Any questions?" he asked.

"Not at the moment," I said. "I assume I'll have full access to the library and its staff, as well as the board members."

O'Banyon nodded. "Of course," he said. "I've asked Donna to make you a list of the board members' addresses and phone numbers, as well as those of Irving McHam and Evan Knight; I'm sure you'll want to talk to some of them." He looked at his watch again and sighed, then pressed a button on the intercom on his desk.

"Donna, could you bring in those papers on the Feinberg case...and that information for Mr. Hardesty?" Without waiting for a response he turned the intercom off, and his attention back to me. "Sorry to have to cut this short, Dick, but..."

"I understand," I said, getting up from my chair as he rose from his to shake hands.

As I turned toward the door, there was a gentle knock, and Donna entered, a large legal binder and a plain envelope in one hand. She paused to give me the smaller envelope with a smile: "The addresses you wanted," she said, then continued on to O'Banyon's desk as I left the office.

As I listened to the soft whoosh of the elevator's descent, I had some niggling second thoughts about having taken the job just because it was offered to me. I'd feel pretty bad about taking money just to spin my wheels and get nowhere. Did I really think Taylor Cates could have been murdered? He had died in a fall. Accidents happen all the time. So does murder, unfortunately. But usually, in a murder, it's in a setting with a little bit of mystery or intrigue. A corporate headquarters, maybe, or a military base. But, again, what could go on in a library that might lead to murder?

CHAPTER 3

Well, no sense in wasting time. As soon as I got to my office I sat down and opened the envelope—I hadn't even stopped to pick up the morning paper. There were six names on the list, complete with addresses and phone numbers: Irving McHam, Zachary Clanton, Marvin Westeen, Thomas McNabb, William Pearson, and Evan Knight.

Of the six, I'd only officially met Westeen, and, of course, the ever-popular Evan Knight. I knew Thomas McNabb only by reputation—he was a prominent realtor, and had been instrumental in acquiring the old T.R. Roosevelt Elementary property for the library. William Pearson, the only black member of the board, had a variety of high profile business interests and some not so well publicized, such as ownership or part ownership of a number of the larger and more popular gay bars and restaurants. He was well respected for his philanthropies in both the black and gay communities. That there were no women on the board had been a source of minor controversy, but the selection of the board was generally understood to be more a matter of financial and political clout than of gender.

Since McHam, as the library's new director, had been, however briefly, Taylor Cates' defacto boss in the cataloging of the Burrows collection, I thought I'd start with him. Of all the principals in the library, with the possible exception of Evan Knight, McHam was in the best position to know what, if anything, Taylor might have come across that may have resulted in his death—if it had indeed not been an accident.

The Burrows' phone number wasn't in the directory yet, but I assumed the number on the list Donna had given me was for the library and not McHam's home, and I called it right after making a pot of coffee.

"Good morning, the Burrows Library and Archives," a pleasant female voice answered.

"Good morning," I said. "Is Mr. McHam in?"

After the usual game of 'May I tell him who's calling' and polite answer, she told me she would get Mr. McHam for me. A minute or so later there was a click and a definitely male: "Yes, Mr. Hardesty, what can I do for you?"

I was a little surprised by the deepness of his voice, but then I remembered we hadn't officially met at the opening, so I guess I'd never heard him speak.

"As I'm sure you know, I've been hired by the Burrows Foundation board to look over the circumstances surrounding Taylor Cates' death. I was wondering if we might get together to talk about it," I said, "since I gather you knew him as well as if not better than anyone at the library."

"That's probably true, I suppose," McHam said, "though our relationship was strictly work related."

That's interesting, I thought. *I don't recall implying it was anything else. Why would he mention it?*

"Understood," I said, "but I would like to hear whatever you *do* know about him. The more I can find out about him and whether there might be any reason to suspect his fall was not an accident, the better. Perhaps there was something in the work he was doing...."

"We've just begun the work of cataloging, really," McHam said, "and it is a monumental task. Evan Knight had done some preliminary work, but he is only one man, and not really trained in library science and current standard cataloging procedures, so we are in many aspects starting the process from scratch."

I didn't want to get into a long discussion of library science and current standard cataloging procedures just then—or ever, now that I think of it—so I just said: "So when would it be convenient for us to meet?"

"When would you like?" he asked.

"Well, the sooner the better, I think," I said.

He was silent a moment, then said: "I'm interviewing potential catalogers this afternoon," he said, then paused, as though he had said something he shouldn't. "I mean," he continued, "I know it's only been a few days since Taylor's death, but we're now short two catalogers, and we have a tremendous lot of work to do."

Two catalogers? I wondered what became of the other one, but decided to wait until I met with McHam to ask.

"I won't take up much of your time, I promise," I said.

"I should be through by three. Would that be all right?" he asked.

"Three will be fine," I said. "I appreciate your cooperation."

"I'm happy to help," he replied. "Until three, then." And he hung up.

* * *

After we hung up, I thought of calling Evan Knight. He'd apparently known Taylor Cates in a slightly different way, but he might very well have some pertinent insights into Taylor as a person. I knew full well part of my aversion to seeing him again was my Scorpio jealous/possessive nature, which I've tried with only relative degrees of success to keep under control most of my life. I consoled myself with the thought that he would have pissed me off even if he'd been making so obvious a pass at anyone else's lover.

But I thought I'd better see what McHam had to say, first. It might give me some clues on how to handle my meeting with Knight.

Once I'd gotten McHam and Knight out of the way, I'd contact the other Board members, though I suspected that with the possible exceptions of Chester Burrows' nephews, who'd been around it all their lives, none of them were all that familiar with the collection or Taylor Cates' world.

* * *

After lunch, I busied myself with what little outstanding work I had on my desk, to clear my slate for working on the Cates case.

I arrived at the Burrows at ten minutes 'til three, and parked in the almost-full side lot. I walked into the encompassing calm of the library and climbed the steps to the main floor, going directly to the circular desk. There were probably fifteen or so people seated at tables and in the smaller sitting-room areas, and another ten or twelve people visible in the stacks at either side of the room. A very handsome young redhead was pushing a cart with books from the desk toward the stacks, apparently to be put back on the shelves. He gave me a very nice smile, which my crotch and I returned. A middle-aged woman was behind the desk, putting cards into a Rolodex. She looked up and smiled as I approached.

"May I help you?" she asked softly.

"Yes," I said. "I have a three o'clock appointment with Mr. McHam."

"Ah, yes," she said. "Mr. Hardesty. I'll let him know you're here."

She picked up a phone from somewhere beneath the counter and punched one of several colored buttons. She then said something I couldn't hear and hung up.

"Mr. McHam asks that you go right up." She pointed back toward the front entrance. "Take the stairs or the elevator to the second floor, and it's the farthest door on your right."

I thanked her and followed her directions. I noticed the young guy with the book watching me, but he quickly looked away when he saw I was aware of him.

Just as well, a mind voice said, though my crotch thought it would be a very nice idea for me to go over and say hello.

I took the stairs.

The farthest door on the right had a small but dignified sign beside it, saying: "Irving McHam, Director." I knocked and heard a basso-voiced, "Come."

I entered to find McHam just rising from the chair behind his desk. He was a little less gaunt than I remembered him as being, and his long-ish red hair was, I could see at this closer distance, flecked with grey. I walked over and took his extended hand. No smile. No sense of antagonism or displeasure, either. Just…businesslike.

"Please," he said, gesturing me to a chair in front of his desk, the surface of which was almost invisible beneath neat piles of books and papers. "Sit."

I did, as did he, and he got right to business.

"So how can I help you?" he asked. It struck me as unlikely that his name and the word "mischievous" would ever be used in the same sentence.

"I was wondering what you could tell me about Taylor Cates…anything you might know about his personal or professional life. Do you know if he had a lover, or any enemies? Had he been acting strangely lately? Glen O'Banyon gave me the impression that something about him was not quite right, and I hoped you might clarify that for me."

McHam gave a quick head-raised nod after I'd finished. "Yes," he said. "Well, I have only been with the Burrows less than six months. I arrived about two months before the transfer of the collection from the Burrows estate. It has been, as you can imagine, a very hectic time." He pursed his lips slightly, as if in thought. "I admired Taylor's devotion to the task and his sharp mind. He had, as I think you know, just completed his Masters degree in Library Science. He was very ambitious—which almost verged on aggression at times—and would have gone far in the field.

"I try to keep a professional distance from my employees and co-workers," McHam continued, "so as to his personal life,

I knew very little. He had a roommate, I know, and he never indicated they were anything more than that. He was something of a perfectionist, and he worked such long hours here I rather doubt he had much time for a personal life. As for enemies, well, I wouldn't use so strong a word, but there was some bad feeling between Taylor and one of our other catalogers we subsequently had to let go."

I assumed that clarified his earlier remark about being 'two catalogers short.' "Oh? What was that all about?" I asked.

He gave a small sigh and leaned slightly forward in his chair. "Well, as I've said, Taylor was a perfectionist and he was rather intolerant of those around him who were not. Dave...Dave Witherspoon...was the first cataloger we hired, even before the collection was moved from the Burrows estate. I think he rather enjoyed holding that fact over Taylor's head. Both were recent graduates of Mountjoy, but I got the distinct impression they really did not care for one another, though they were both sufficiently professional not to let it interfere with their work."

"Have you any idea what their problem was?" I asked.

He shook his head. "Not really, other than the fact that I think Taylor, however irrationally, somehow resented the fact that Dave had been hired first. They were equally ambitious, so I suppose a certain degree of rivalry was only natural. But Dave was far more...'laid back,' I think they call it...and that bothered Taylor a great deal.

"And when Taylor came to me, telling me that Dave had been taking files home with him, which is strictly prohibited, and which Dave did not deny when questioned, I had no choice but to let him go. Rules are rules for a reason."

"And how did Witherspoon react to being fired?" I could easily see why Witherspoon might be really pissed at Taylor, but I couldn't easily stretch being pissed like that into a motive for murder.

McHam looked at me oddly. "How does anyone react to being fired?" he asked. "He was not happy, I'm sure. Nor was I, frankly. Dave is an excellent cataloger, and any library will be lucky to have him. I wrote him a letter of recommendation, and he was, in fact, at the opening."

"How long before Taylor's death was he fired?" I asked.

"Maybe a week and a half," he replied. "Dave approached me at the opening to ask me to consider rehiring him. I was sorely tempted, given all the work to be done, and I do believe he learned his lesson, but considering the tensions between him and Taylor, putting the two of them back together just would have been too counter-productive. He left and I've heard nothing from him since—though I am giving strong consideration to rehiring him now that Taylor is...gone. And assuming he's not already found another position."

"And Taylor had no little flaws—his perfectionism aside—of his own?" I asked.

McHam paused a moment before saying: "Taylor's only flaw, if it can be called that, is that he had the training and duties of a cataloger but the heart of a researcher. While he never would have admitted it, I noted that he had a tendency to become occasionally distracted from his cataloging by his desire to know more about the work being cataloged. He, of course, didn't see the difference. He was constantly sending me notes on interesting bits of trivia he found in the works he was cataloging. It got to the point I simply didn't have the time to read them all."

"Did you get the impression that he was being...distracted...at the time of his death?"

"As a matter of fact, yes. He was cataloging the work of Jerromy Butler and his son, and seemed to have become fascinated by it."

The name rang a bell. "Jerromy Butler?" I interrupted. "The 'Fires of Hell' Evangelist of the '20s and '30s? What would his works be doing here?"

McHam allowed himself a small smile. "Well, of course his works would be here. Chester Burrows collected anything and everything, positive and negative, on the subject of homosexuality. And since for puritanical religious fundamentalists, the subject of homosexuality is high on the list of things to rail against.... If, to Oscar Wilde's generation, homosexuality was 'the love that dare not speak its name', to Jerromy Butler and his ilk, homosexuality was a sin so heinous the word itself was almost never directly used.

"Interestingly, it was the Butler papers that Taylor had wanted to work on from the moment he learned we had them. But I'd already assigned them to Dave Witherspoon. After Dave left I turned the Butlers over to him."

"Any idea why his particular interest in Butler?" I asked.

He shook his head. "Not really, other, perhaps, than that Butler was a well known public figure. Taylor seemed particularly fascinated by the fact that in addition to Butler's vitriolic public writings—books, sermons, and religious tracts in which the subject of homosexuality comes up frequently if obliquely—there are apparently a rather large number of more personal papers...particularly letters to his son, Morgan, his only child and the apple of his eye. There are also a sizeable number of Morgan's own papers included with those of his father, and it was Morgan who donated the papers to Chester Burrows shortly before his own death.

"In this case, Taylor's distraction produced something of a coup which will have to be left to researchers to explore further...Morgan Butler married and had a son, but was apparently gay. He killed himself in 1953 at the age of 31."

I just shook my head. "Interesting," I said, and meant it.

McHam gave me another small smile. "I'm glad you think so. Contrary to popular belief, librarians do not lead lives of unremitting dullness."

"Wasn't Butler from here, originally?" I asked, mentally rummaging through the stacks of trivia scattered around the shadowy alcoves of my mind.

McHam nodded. "He was, yes. Morgan died here, and Morgan's son still lives here, I understand. He has been threatening suit to have Butler's papers removed from the collection. He has a snowball's chance in hell of doing so, of course, but he can try."

"Well, I can understand his not wanting it made general knowledge that his father was gay..."

"If he even knew," McHam interjected. "He was very young when Morgan killed himself. It well may not have been the kind of thing that would even have been mentioned to him."

I had to admit there was a lot more to his business than meets the eye. But interesting as it was to learn that the notorious preacher had skeletons in his closet, I couldn't see much of anything in it that could possibly get Taylor Cates killed.

"How did you happen to find Taylor's body?" I asked.

"I was just making a routine check of the building, making sure that everything that should be locked up was...with crowds of people around, I wanted to make doubly sure. And the door to the catalog room was unlocked. It shouldn't have been. Taylor had been working at a desk near the door. There was an opened box of material on the desk—again, there shouldn't have been. The door was to be kept locked to prevent just anyone from walking in, and while I knew he would be working to pass the time, he had instructions not to leave materials loose on the desk if he let someone in."

He looked down at his desk as if in thought before continuing. "Those two facts alone set me immediately on edge. I called to him and there was no answer. I began looking for him and that's when I found his body."

"Is there any other reason to think it might not have been an accident?"

McHam leaned forward in his chair, his elbows on the desk. "I'm not really sure," he said, "but Taylor had no reason to be in that part of the stacks, let alone on a set of steps that led to an unused door. The police apparently assumed that Taylor was going outside for a cigarette, or that someone had knocked on the door and he had gone to answer it. I told them that either assumption was highly unlikely, however logical."

"How is that?" I asked.

"Because knowing Taylor, even as little as I did, I know that Taylor would never have just left his post, cigarette or no, and that everyone knew that door was to be used as an emergency exit only. Even if someone had knocked—and again there is a sign on the outside of the door directing people to the front entrance—he would not have broken the rules by opening it."

"Taylor never broke the rules?"

"Actually, no," he replied. "And he was intolerant of anyone who did. That's why he reported Dave Witherspoon for taking materials home with him. Some people may see it as being petty, but Taylor did not."

"What were the papers he was working on at the time of the...accident, if I may ask?" I...uh...asked.

"Morgan Butler's, I believe. I didn't have time to look at them more closely than to make sure they were in chronological order and put them back in the box and return the box to the shelf. Looking back on it, I realize that was a rather strange thing for me to do under the circumstances, but I really wasn't thinking clearly at the time."

"Were any of the papers missing, could you tell? Is it possible someone might have been trying to steal them?"

He knit his brows and looked at me. "I really don't know," he said. "But I'd think it highly unlikely. Morgan Butler had no particular distinction of his own; I'd imagine if anyone were out to steal papers, it would be Jerromy Butler's they'd be after.

"Jerromy Butler's papers had already been cataloged, however, and we were just finishing up with Morgan's. I'll have both sets gone over again to be sure nothing's missing. But as for anything of Morgan's that had not yet been cataloged, I'm afraid we would have no way of knowing if anything were missing or not. Though again, I really can't imagine that there would be."

We talked for a while longer, but I felt I had gotten what I needed to know for the moment.

"Oh," I said in afterthought, "Would you happen to have both Taylor's and Dave Witherspoon's phone numbers? I think I'd like to talk with Taylor's roommate, and definitely with Witherspoon."

"They should be right here," he said, opening a side drawer in his desk and bringing out a small metal box filled with 3x5 cards. Flipping through them expertly, he paused at two cards long enough to write something on the notepad in front of him, then tore off the top sheet of the pad, tapped the tops of the 3x5 cards to get them all even, closed the lid of the box, and slid the torn-off piece of paper across the desk to me. "Here you are," he said.

I folded the paper and put it in my shirt pocket. "Well, thank you again for your time and your help," I said. "I'll let you get back to work now."

He gave me a small smile. "Yes," he said, "there is a lot to do."

We shook hands, and I left.

*　*　*

When I got home from work, Jonathan seemed to be in a particularly happy mood. He and Joshua were just finishing up their feeding-of-the-fish ritual. I hadn't really expected Joshua's two little fish to have survived as long as they had, due to Joshua's firm belief that if a little food was good for them, a lot was better. But Jonathan had gotten him slowly used to the idea that goldfish do not require quite the same amount of food as a great white shark.

After our group hug, Joshua went running off in pursuit of whatever it is four-year-old boys always seem to find to pursue, and I followed Jonathan into the kitchen for my evening Manhattan.

"So what's up?" I asked him as I took a glass from the

cupboard and he opened the refrigerator for his Coke and some ice cubes.

"Guess what happened today?" he asked, answering a question with a question.

"Something good, obviously," I said, and he grinned broadly.

"Yeah! I was out on a job, and when I got back, my boss told me he'd gotten a call from Evan Knight, who wants his whole yard landscaped, and he mentioned that I had referred him to Evergreens! The boss was really impressed."

I doubted the boss had any idea who Evan Knight was, but the prospect of a full yard landscaping project in the Briarwood area would undoubtedly be profitable.

I was happy for Jonathan's boss. I was happy for Jonathan's getting the credit for bringing in new business. I was not, however, particularly happy with the possibility of Jonathan's being drawn any closer to Evan Knight's little web.

"That's great, Babe," I said. "Will you be working on the job?"

I realized that last question was my Scorpio side raising its ugly head.

"I hope so," Jonathan said. "I'd really like to see where Mr. Knight lives. My boss is going over there tomorrow morning to talk to him about what he'll want done, and to give him an estimate. I hope we get the job."

Oh, I'm pretty sure you will, my Scorpio said. Damn it, why the hell was I being jealous? I had no reason to be. Except that I'd met people like Evan Knight before, and I know the games they like to play with people like Jonathan who tend to take everyone at face value and are sometimes way too trusting. But I realized at the same time that I had too strong a tendency, sometimes, to treat Jonathan too much like a kid who needed constant protection. He was an adult, and he didn't need me hovering over him all the time.

Yeah, a mind voice reluctantly agreed. *Still....*

* * *

I was a few minutes late getting to work the next morning, thanks to Joshua's somehow managing to slosh an entire bowl of cereal and milk over himself at breakfast. So while Jonathan cleaned up Joshua and changed his clothes, I cleaned up the kitchen. Kids can be a real joy sometimes. This was not one of them. Once at work, I waited until I'd gone through my morning newspaper/coffee/ crossword puzzle ritual before calling Dave Witherspoon. I hoped to get a little better idea of what kind of guy Taylor Cates really was, even though I was quite sure that under the circumstances what he had to say would probably be less than flattering. And while I sincerely doubted that Taylor's having gotten Dave fired would be enough reason to kill, stranger things have happened, and it was always wise to check out every possibility.

And speaking of possibilities, it was still a very real possibility that Taylor Cates had, for whatever reason, simply fallen down the steps.

Uh huh, a mind voice said. I determined to give our friend Tim Jackson a call. Since he worked at the coroner's office, he may be able to tell me a little more about the actual cause of Taylor's death. But that would have to wait until I got home.

I dialed Dave Witherspoon's number and, considering that it was by now nearly 9:30, was not overly surprised to get an answering machine. Witherspoon may have already found another job and was at work—though there aren't that many libraries in the area, and even fewer research libraries—or he was out looking for work. I left my name and work number; if I didn't hear from him by the time I was ready to go home, I'd call again and leave my home number, too.

Part of me wanted to talk to Evan Knight next, but the rest of me suggested that it might be best to hold him until last. On the one hand, I didn't want to be influenced by these little games I suspected he might be playing with Jonathan and needed some time to regain my objectivity. On the other hand, of course, waiting would allow me to see how this landscaping gambit—if it was indeed a gambit, as I suspected it was—played out.

And okay, I admit it: if Jonathan was going to be working in close proximity to Knight, I wanted to keep Knight reminded that I was in the picture.

You're really weird, Hardesty, an unidentified mind voice observed.

Guilty as charged.

I decided to go with the least-most-likely-involved board members first, to see if they might by chance have any idea at all of what was going on. It was really unlikely, I knew, but I couldn't afford to overlook anyone or anything. I decided to start with Thomas McNabb, the realtor.

When I did call, I was informed that he was out of the office showing a property, but would return my call as soon as possible. I left my name and number, and hung up. I thought it interesting that someone who headed one of the city's larger real estate organizations would still be going out and showing properties himself. But then I realized that may be one of the reasons his company got so big in the first place.

Rather than wait for him to return my call, I next tried William Pearson's number. I was a bit surprised when he answered the phone himself.

"William Pearson," the voice said.

"Mr. Pearson," I said, "this is Dick Hardesty, of Hardesty Investigations. Glen O'Banyon gave me your number."

"Ah, yes, Mr. Hardesty," he said. "I was rather expecting your call. I gather you've agreed to look into this...unfortunate incident at the Burrows?"

"Yes," I replied, "and I was wondering if there might be anything you could tell me about Taylor Cates or the collection that might have some bearing on my investigation."

There was a slight pause, then: "I'm afraid I really can't be of much help as far as the collection is concerned," he said. "I don't have very much direct contact with the day-to-day operations of the library. I did know Taylor Cates, though not all that well. He was a weekend bartender at Steamroller Junction from the time it opened until about three months ago."

Steamroller Junction was one of the biggest and most popular of the gay dance bars, though the last time I'd been there was, in fact, on its opening night, not too long after Jonathan and I got together. I'm not big on huge crowds or noise, and Steamroller Junction had both.

"Did you happen to know anything at all about his personal life?"

Another brief pause. "No, I'm afraid not. He was personally recommended to me by someone whose opinion I respect. Usually, I'm not all that directly involved with the staff of my various businesses—unfortunately, there just isn't time to know everyone. I do know the manager subsequently thought very highly of him, too, and that he apparently never missed a shift. I wish I had more employees like that. Teddy had told me Taylor was a college student at the time, but had no idea he was working for the Burrows until the night of the...accident."

"Teddy?" I asked, the name striking a bell.

"Teddy Wilson, one of the performers who's worked in several of my clubs over the years. He goes by the name of Tondelaya O'Tool. Maybe you've seen one of his shows."

Teddy! T/T! One of the best drag queens in the business! Well, well, what a small world!

"Of course I know Teddy," I said. "He's fantastic. I last saw him at the opening of Steamroller Junction, as a matter of fact."

"He'll be back in town in two weeks for a benefit for the Hospice Project. He's performing in Atlanta now, but when he heard of the benefit he wanted to be part of it. There aren't many people like Teddy around these days."

"Indeed there aren't," I said. "I'll definitely be there."

"Well, I'd advise you to get your tickets in advance," he said. "It's going to be a sold-out event. We'll have a full-page ad for it in this week's *Rainbow Flag*, and the box office will be open every day starting Monday."

"I wouldn't miss it for the world," I said. "Thanks for the heads-up."

Okay, Hardesty…first things first, my mind voice said. *Taylor Cates, remember?*

It was right, of course, so I pulled myself back to the moment. "Do you happen to know how Teddy and Taylor Cates knew one another?"

Pearson paused a moment, then: "I don't know how well you might know Teddy," he said, "but as I say, he's truly one of a kind…he's got a heart as big as all outdoors. As I recall, Teddy told me that Taylor had lived next door to him as a kid, and really looked up to him. In those days, Teddy didn't have many people looking up to him. He never forgot it. And apparently they stayed close over the years. When Teddy called a day or so after the accident to discuss some details of the benefit, I mentioned to him that Taylor was dead. He hadn't heard, and it seemed to really hit him hard."

"Do you have any reason to think Taylor's death might not have been accidental?" I asked, getting to the core of my call.

I could almost see him shaking his head. "None at all. But Irving McHam and Glen O'Banyon apparently had sufficient concerns to convince me to agree to have it looked into. We certainly can't afford even the hint of a scandal."

I didn't see any particular point to setting up a face to face meeting, based on our phone conversation, but I gave him my phone number and asked him to please call me if he remembered or thought of anything that might be pertinent. He agreed, I thanked him for his time, we exchanged good-byes and hung up.

The fact that he had some dealings with Taylor Cates, however peripheral, might warrant a follow up later, depending on what more I might find out about Cates' life. And that Teddy Wilson...T/T as I always called him...had known Taylor definitely warranted a follow up. Besides, it would be great to see T/T again.

I got out the piece of paper on which I'd written down Cates' phone number, picked up the phone, and dialed.

It rang four times, then: "Hi. I'm not in right now, but please leave a message and I'll get back to you."

Never having heard Taylor Cates' voice, I didn't know if the voice was his or his roommate's.

"Hi," I said. "My name is Dick Hardesty, and I was hoping to speak to someone about Taylor Cates. I'd appreciate it if you could give me a call sometime either today or tomorrow—Thursday—at my office." I left my number, and hung up.

Within ten minutes, the phone rang.

Busy day, I thought as I picked up the phone.

"Hardesty Investigations," I said.

"Dick! This is Tom McNabb, returning your call. Sorry I wasn't in when you called earlier." The voice was warm, friendly, and reminded me of the phrase 'hale-fellows-well-met'.

Considering that we had never met, the first-name familiarity threw me off for a second. I suppose he probably tailored his personality to fit his perception of the people he was dealing with—which again may be one of the reasons he'd become so successful. "I appreciate your calling," I said, avoiding using either "Tom"...with which I'd feel a little uncomfortable since I didn't know him (call me old-fashioned)...or "Mr. McNabb" which might seem a little awkward since he'd called me "Dick."

Get on with it, Hardesty, one of my mind voices said impatiently.

"I was wondering," I continued, "if you might have any information about the incident at the Burrows' opening involving Taylor Cates' death."

There was only the slightest of pauses, then: "I'm afraid

not. Evan Knight introduced us, once, and I had seen Taylor a couple of times shortly before the opening when I had occasion to be at the library, but that was it. His death was a real shame, though, and especially so that it had to happen at the Burrows."

Well, I hadn't really expected that he'd be able to shed much light on the matter, but I found the fact that Evan Knight had introduced him to be most interesting. "You say Evan Knight introduced you to Taylor...at the library, I assume?"

"No," McNabb replied, "I was out to dinner one evening about three months ago and ran into Evan at the restaurant. Taylor was with him."

"Interesting," I said. "Did you get the impression they were dating?"

McNabb laughed. "I know Evan too well," he said. "I have no doubt Taylor was his date that evening, but that it might have been anything more than that is highly unlikely. I found it interesting, though, that Taylor seemed like such a serious fellow... not the kind of personality Evan usually finds attractive."

"So you and Evan are friends?" I asked.

"I don't know that I'd go so far as to say 'friends,'" he said. "But we've known one another for a long time, and I must say he's come a long way."

"I'm sorry?" I said. "How do you mean?"

"Evan worked for me for a short time when he first got out of college," he explained. "He has a real way with people when he wants to apply himself. His problem was that he couldn't be bothered most of the time. I liked him, but he was just too unpredictable when it came to his work, and I had to let him go. He went through a series of jobs and never stayed with any of them very long. Then he met Chester Burrows and went to work for him as his personal assistant. Chester was more than a little reclusive, as you know, and Evan was his bridge to the 'outside' world for the last years of Burrows' life. And then, four or five years ago, Evan's first book was published. Frankly, I was impressed. I never knew he had it in him. But I'm glad he's finally pulled himself together on at least one level."

I took a moment to mull that over before asking: "Do you recall anything unusual the night of the opening, before Taylor's body was discovered?"

"Not a thing," McNabb said. "I didn't even know Taylor

was in the building until I heard that he'd died."

I couldn't think of anything further for McNabb at the moment, so I thanked him for his time, and we said goodbye and hung up.

The phone had no sooner hit the cradle than it rang again.

"Hardesty Investigations."

"Dick, it's Jonathan." *Of* course *it's Jonathan*, I thought with mild frustration over why he always found it necessary to identify himself. "I was wondering if you could pick Joshua up from day care and then maybe stop at the store and get some milk. I'm with my boss and we're on our way over to Evan Knight's place to give him a quote on his landscaping."

"How come you're going?" I asked, immediately regretting letting my Scorpio petty jealousy spring to the fore. I usually kept it under pretty strict control. But for some reason, with Evan Knight....

Luckily, Jonathan didn't seem to pick up on it. "My boss was supposed to go over by himself, but he and I had to go pick up some mulch and he was running late, and..."

"That's okay, Babe," I said. "I'll go get Joshua. No problem. We'll see you when you get home."

Damn, I hate being a Scorpio at times. I'll bet my bottom dollar that Othello was a Scorpio, and we all know what happened to him.

Time to go home.

* * *

Joshua was his usual effervescent self, giving me a detailed account of his day at 'school,' as he always called it, which as usual seamlessly blended reality and imagination as only a four-year-old boy can blend them. And stopping at the store for milk was, as usual, an adventure in itself. I deliberately only took a basket rather than a cart in hopes it might dissuade Joshua from trying to put everything within reach into it. Of course, I wasn't much better. I can never go to the store and just buy what I went there for—a fact of which the store owners and designers are very well aware. We ended up with the milk, a large box of a new cereal being advertised on all the kids' shows on TV, which Joshua spotted half an aisle away, a dozen chocolate covered donuts, a package of knockwurst, and a can of sauerkraut. (No, I have no idea why, either. It just seemed like a good idea at the time.)

Jonathan arrived home shortly after Joshua and I had declared a truce in a battle over his insistence that he eat the entire box of cereal the minute we got home, despite the proximity of dinner. He settled, after rather heated negotiations, on a small glass of milk and a plum.

Between the battle and Jonathan's arrival, I managed to put in a call to Tim and Phil. I knew they wouldn't be home yet, and that Tim probably wouldn't have the information I needed at his fingertips anyway, but I left a message telling him what I needed and asking if he could give me a call when he found out.

After our group hug and settling down in the living room with my Manhattan and Jonathan's Coke—Joshua was playing in his room—I had a chance to ask Jonathan how it had gone at Evan Knight's place.

"Fine," he said. I noticed a certain…hesitation…in the way he said it. "We got the job, and we start tomorrow. It'll be a pretty big project, and he wants it done by this Saturday. He's having a big party."

I looked at him closely. "Anything wrong?" I asked.

He didn't look directly at me when he said: "No. Nothing."

"You're sure?"

"I'm sure," he said. "He asked us to the party."

???, I thought. "He asked you and your boss to a party?" I said, confused, at the same time sensing my Scorpio rising.

Jonathan shook his head and took a long swig of his Coke. "No. You and me. My boss had to run out to the truck for his calculator, and Evan asked me while he was gone."

"What did you tell him?" I asked.

"I said I'd ask you."

"You don't sound too enthusiastic about it," I said.

He looked at me. "Oh, I am!" he said. "There's going to be a couple other writers there and some other important people. I'd really like to meet them."

I could still sense something in there he wasn't saying. "So you want to go?" I asked.

"Yeah," he said, though with just a hint of hesitation, "if you do."

Well, let's see here. Something was going on that Jonathan wasn't telling me. I didn't trust Evan Knight for one second when it came to his motives, and I felt like saying 'No, I don't want to go,' but realized if I did, I'd be giving in to those Scorpio traits I've worked so hard to overcome. Besides, I'd like to get a little closer look at the situation, to see how Jonathan and Evan Knight interacted. I trusted Jonathan completely, but...

"Sure," I said. "It might be fun."

Liar! my Scorpio said.

CHAPTER 4

"I'd better call to see if Craig can come over to watch Joshua," Jonathan said, setting his Coke down on the coffee table and getting up from the couch. "Saturday's kind of short notice, but we'll see. And if he can't make it, we don't really have to go."

What is going on, here? more than one of my mind voices wanted to know. To say I was more than a little confused and more than mildly uncomfortable for no specific reason is an understatement. I knew Jonathan was easily impressed, and that to actually know someone as "famous" as Evan Knight meant a lot to him, and the idea that there might be other well-known writers at the party was probably an irresistible draw. So why the perceived hesitance?

"That's great, Craig!" I heard Jonathan say. "Around 6:30 or 7, then? Thank your mom for us."

He hung up the phone and came over to take his seat next to me. "We're all set. His mom will drop him off here," he said, as Joshua suddenly appeared in front of us, holding Bunny.

"We're hungry," he announced.

* * *

After dinner and dishes, I remembered about William Pearson's saying that T/T would be back in town in two weeks for an appearance at Steamroller Junction.

"As long as we're on a roll with our social life," I said, "I was thinking maybe we could get the gang together to go see him," I said. "But we'll have to act fast so we can get tickets before they're sold out."

"Sure!" Jonathan said enthusiastically. "I really like him."

So did I, and the fact that he had known Taylor Cates and might be able to tell me something about him made the prospect of seeing and talking with him even more appealing.

While Jonathan was giving Joshua his ready-for-bed bath, I called Jake to ask if he and Jared would like to go to the benefit.

I wasn't sure that he'd be home, but dialed his number anyway, and was glad to hear him answer on the first ring.

"Jake, hi...it's Dick. How's it going?"

"Hi, Dick," he said, sounding glad to hear from me (okay,

so I still harbored my little fantasies). "Everything's fine. Been busy as hell, but that's okay. How about you?"

"We're doing fine, too," I said. "We haven't talked to you since the Burrows opening, and thought we should give you a call."

"Glad you did," he said. "It was a nice event, except for that accident. I even managed to make a contact and land a job."

"Oh?" I said, curious. "Who with?"

"Evan Knight, the author. He came over to us after the ceremony, and when I told him I was a contractor, he told me he was considering converting his basement into a 'playroom' and wondered if I might be interested in doing it for him." He paused for just a moment. "Well, that wasn't *all* he wanted...he made that pretty clear from the get-go...and he's a pretty hot guy, so I took him up on the contracting offer, and Jared and I took him up on the other." Another pause, then: "Hey, like I said at the opening , I'm not above mixing a little business and pleasure. He's invited us to a party he's having this Saturday."

Small world! I thought. And I also began to wonder just what kind of party Evan Knight was planning.

"Yeah," I said. "We've been invited, too. Jonathan's boss is doing some landscaping for him."

"That's great!" Jared said. "It'll be good to get together again."

"Ah, and speaking of which...," I began, and told him about T/T's upcoming appearance at Steamroller Junction.

"Sounds like fun," he replied. "I'll ask Jared when I talk to him."

"I'll be talking with Tim tomorrow, I hope," I said, "and I'll check with Bob and Mario, too. I can pick up the tickets for everybody, as soon as I know for sure if we all can make it."

"I'll get back to you as soon as I can," he said.

Joshua, scrubbed, hair slicked back, skin polished to a high shine, and wearing his Dr. Dentons, came running from the bathroom to tug impatiently at my pants leg. "Story time!" he said.

I heard Jake laugh. "Ah, the joys of unclehood," he said. "I'd better let you go. Give Joshua—and Jonathan—a big hug for me."

"Okay," I said, bending down to pick Joshua up with my

free arm. "We'll see you Saturday."

"Story time! Story time! Story time!" Joshua sing-songed as I carried him to his bedroom.

* * *

I was standing by the coffee maker, cup in hand, staring at it intently in hopes my concentration might speed up the burp-and-hiss process, when the phone rang. Breaking off my battle of wills with the machine, I stepped to my desk and, reaching across it, picked up the phone just before the answering machine could click on.

"Hardesty Investigations," I said, coffee cup still in hand.

"Hi," the male voice said. "I got a message to call you."

Great. I'd left messages for several people the day before, but I thought I recognized it as the voice on Taylor Cates' machine and took a chance.

"Thanks for returning the call," I said. "You were Taylor Cates'…roommate…I assume?"

"Roommate, yes," the voice said. "Why are you calling me?" He had a slight…what? Not an accent, but…I pegged him as being Afro-American. Interesting in that I realized I had no idea whether Taylor Cates himself was black or white, and why that might surprise me slightly I had no idea. Why had I assumed he was white? What the hell difference did it make?

On with it, Hardesty, a mind voice prodded impatiently.

"I was hoping you might be able to tell me a bit about him," I said.

"Like what?"

Obviously he wasn't going to make this easy.

"Like how long you were roommates, how you met him, what kind of guy he was, whether he had a lover or was seeing anyone, if he'd been acting any differently in the weeks leading up to his death. That sort of thing."

"What business is it of yours?" he asked.

This is definitely not Mr. Warmth, here, I thought.

"It's my business because I've been hired to look into anything that might have contributed to his death. His employers want to be certain there is no possibility that it was anything but an accident. I'm sure you can understand."

There was a very slight pause, then: "Yeah, I suppose so. But there's not much I can tell you. I answered a classified in *The Rainbow Flag* about a year ago. Taylor and I didn't have all that much in common. He was way too quiet; never let himself just relax and have a good time. Always working, or running up to Carrington for classes. We didn't really see that much of one another—I work the night shift, for one thing—but it all worked out and we got along okay when we did see each other."

"So he didn't have a lover, or wasn't seeing anyone?" I asked.

"Nobody special, that I know of. The only guy I ever knew about was some writer, but that was only for a couple weeks, but that's about it. An occasional date now and then."

That 'some writer' was, I assumed, Evan Knight.

"Did you ever meet the writer?" I asked.

"Yeah, one time. I wasn't impressed. The guy was a real arrogant asshole—the kind of guy who thinks his shit don't stink."

"Any idea why they stopped seeing each other, do you know?"

"Nope. I guess Taylor just got wise to him. I don't know...he never said."

"And did you notice anything different about Taylor in the couple of weeks before he died?" I asked.

A longer pause. "Not really. After he got that new job, I saw even less of him than I had before. But that last week or so, he *was* a little...I don't know how to describe it...wound up, maybe? Like he'd been drinking too much coffee, ya' know?"

"But he never gave you a clue as to what about?"

"Nope. Like I said, we shared the apartment but not much else."

I decided I'd kept him about as long as I needed to. "Well, I appreciate your talking to me," I said. "I'd like it if you'd keep my number, and if you think of anything, please give me a call."

"Okay," he said. "That's it?"

"Uh, yeah, I think so," I said, and I heard the click of the receiver as he hung up.

* * *

Well, that was helpful, I thought as I replaced the phone on its cradle,...*but not very.* Other than coming to the conclusion that Taylor Cates was black—which had absolutely no bearing on anything except my tendency to too often assume things that turn out to be incorrect—and reinforcing my opinion of Evan Knight—there really hadn't been much there. Another teasing tap dance around the strong probability that *something* was going on in Taylor Cates' life toward its end but without getting one inch closer to what that something might be.

Logic said it had to be something with his work, and with his cataloging. But I had a hard time imagining how the papers of a notorious fundamentalist preacher of the 1920s and 1930s and his son could possibly get him killed. Whatever it was Taylor had found, if he'd found anything at all, I doubted it could hardly be considered 'stop the presses!' news after all this time. Still, I'd check it out.

But first I wanted to give Dave Witherspoon another call. I remembered I hadn't left my home number, and he may have gotten home after I'd left work. I called him again.

Same machine, same message. I once again asked him to call me and left my home number this time.

Not two minutes after I put down the receiver, the phone rang again, and I was surprised to hear Tim Jackson's voice:

"You called, Master?" he asked, giving me a quick mental flashback to the time before Tim met Phil or I met Jonathan, when Tim and I used to get together for a little horizontal recreation. My crotch gave a small nostalgic sigh, but didn't say anything.

"You're in early," I said.

"Yeah, Phil had an early morning photo shoot so I got up when he did," he said. "You wanted to know about Taylor Cates?"

"Yeah," I said. "Anything peculiar in the autopsy? Exactly what was the cause of death? Somebody suggested a broken neck?"

"No," he said. "Severe head trauma consistent with a fall down a set of metal stairs. A really nasty indent to the skull just behind the right ear, where apparently he hit a sharp corner on the way down. That was probably the one that did it."

"Any signs of a struggle?" I asked, grabbing for straws.

"None," he said. "Were you expecting there might be?"

"Other than the fact that one doesn't normally just fall backwards down a flight of steps, not really," I admitted. "Just checking."

"Ah, okay," he said. "Anyway, the M.E. listed it as an accidental death, which will probably mean the police will close the case."

My pause to think his information over was interrupted by Tim's saying: "Well, I hate to cut this short, but I've got a probable drug overdose waiting for me and I'd best get to it."

"Thanks, Tim," I said, then quickly remembered the benefit. I filled him in quickly and he said he'd check with Phil and call us back that night.

I next put in a call to the Burrows and asked to speak to Irving McHam.

"Yes, Mr. Hardesty," McHam's deep voice said. "What can I do for you?"

"I was wondering if I might come over and take a look at the Butler papers."

There was a significant pause before he spoke. "I…uh, I suppose. May I ask the reason? Are you looking for something in particular? And there are at least a dozen boxes of the Butlers' papers."

"I believe I'd be most interested in Morgan Butler," I said, "since you said they were the ones Taylor was working on when he died. If I could just come have a look at them I might know what I'm looking for if I find it."

You want to try that one again? several mind voices asked in unison. But before I could rephrase it, McHam spoke.

"Well, I'm of course happy to give you my full cooperation," he said, his reluctance coming through loud and clear. "But I'm sure you understand you won't be able to take anything out of the cataloging area. We are not only understaffed at the moment, but very busy, and…"

"I understand completely," I said, "and I'll try not to either get in the way or keep anyone from their work any longer than necessary. So would it be possible for me to come by today?"

Still another pause just long enough to clearly indicate he's just as soon I didn't, before he said: "Of course. I'll be expecting you."

"Thank you for your cooperation," I said. "I appreciate it. I'll see you in about an hour."

We exchanged good-byes and hung up.

I poured myself a cup of coffee and sat down at my desk to read the paper.

* * *

I'd never been in the cataloging room before and I was reminded of a gigantic rummage sale, except instead of lamps and end tables and macrame plant holders, there were boxes—boxes of all sizes and shapes filled most of the center of the large space, stacked on the floor in no discernable order that I could see. McHam, who had escorted me in, noticed my reaction.

"I know," he said with a sigh. "After the fire at the estate, we were desperate to get the collection out. We had to resort to putting things in whatever containers we could get. Normally, we would never use anything but archival boxes, which are made of acid-free material to slow down the deterioration process of the papers." He gestured to one side of the room, where there was a huge stack of new, identical black boxes measuring about a foot tall by a foot wide by two feet deep. Most of the boxes scattered around the room were similar but older and looking a bit battered. "Most people would be amazed at how truly fragile paper can be," he continued, "and how fast it can deteriorate, depending on its composition, the ink used, etc. So it's important that we get everything into the archival boxes as soon as possible."

As on the main floor, the center of the room was flanked by row upon row of floor-to-ceiling shelf units, most of them empty. A few were beginning to be filled with neat rows of the new archival boxes, neatly labeled, as order was made out of the chaos in the rest of the room.

Three college-age women and a man in his fifties—the on-duty catalogers, I assumed—were seated at long tables piled with open boxes and stacks of papers, letters, and what looked to be manuscripts. McHam escorted me in and led me to one of the young women, seated at the table closest to the door.

"Janice, this is Mr. Hardesty," he said as the woman looked up at our approach. "He would like to look through Morgan Butler's papers, and perhaps you could help him find what he's looking for."

Yeah, like I knew, I thought.

He turned to me. "Janice has been doing a thorough review of all the Butler papers to see if anything might be missing," he said, indicating a stack of about twelve older-looking archival boxes on the floor flanking her chair, and two open on the table in front of her. I remembered that McHam told me Evan Knight had done some cataloging at the Burrows estate—I wondered if the Butler papers might have been among them. "Everything seems to be in order thus far," he continued. "Still, we want to be thorough."

He glanced around the room, then at his watch. "If you'll excuse me," he said, "I have some matters which must be attended to. I hope you find what you're looking for. Let me know if there are any problems."

"I will," I said. "Thank you again."

He nodded, turned, and left, closing the door behind him.

I looked at the stacks of paper Janice was apparently working on.

"These are the last of Jerromy Butler's private correspondence," she said. "I've not yet started on his son's, which aren't completely cataloged yet."

She nodded, and indicated the boxes on the floor beside her. "Box #12-A," she said, "are Morgan's personal correspondence. 12B is nearly empty; just a few articles he'd written for some educational journals, and a couple of apparently unpublished book manuscripts."

"Manuscripts?" I asked. "Fact or fiction?"

"I'm not sure," she said. "As I say, Taylor hadn't yet gotten all the way through everything when he…fell. His list should be in there."

"Do you mind if I take a look?" I asked.

"Of course," she said, and indicated a chair at the other end of the desk. "There's some clear space down there. Please try not to get them out of order, though."

"I won't," I promised. As I bent over to pick up the two boxes, I noted that they were apparently older versions of the new archival boxes stacked against the wall. A large white stick-on label on one end identified its contents. One said, in large, neat handwriting: "Butler, Jerromy: Son Morgan, Correspondence 1938-1953," the other "Butler, Jerromy: Son Morgan Misc. Writings 1948-1953." Apparently once cataloged, the material would be put in the newer boxes for storage on the shelves.

Setting them on the floor by the chair at the far end of the table, I opened the "Correspondence" box first. Heavy, tabbed cardboard dividers separated the material by year. On top of them was a lined yellow notepad that appeared to be a list of the contents of the box. I sat down and carefully pulled out those behind the divider marked 1953.

I idly leafed through the letters I'd pulled out and was surprised to realize they were all apparently carbon copies—and almost all handwritten! Who makes carbon copies of handwritten letters? However, when I started reading quickly through the neat script, I could immediately see how Taylor could have gotten so distracted from simply cataloging letters and papers. These were bits and pieces of a human being's life. The paper had once been blank, and the words that filled it now had been placed there, albeit through a sheet of carbon paper, one after the other, by a living entity, inhaling and exhaling as he wrote, transferring parts of himself through his fingertips to the paper, to be carried across the years.

I had to force myself not to be drawn into the vortex of actually reading each letter, and tried to just skim them, like a stone skipping across the pond of time. I found it interesting that the few typed letters—also carbon copies, of course—were to his wife (I assumed) and to his father. Now that was pretty interesting, I thought. He handwrites letters to his friends and types them to the two people who one might suppose were closest to him? I also noted that the majority of the letters to his wife and father tended to be short and from what little I saw, quite dry, while those to various friends and colleagues—I gathered he was a high school English teacher—were quite lengthy and showed both intelligence and wit. Apparently he had been in the navy in WWII, and of the last 20 letters or so, most were to someone then still in the service named Scot—one "t". I skimmed them, and they seemed pretty innocuous from a quick-scan point of view. Probably an old service buddy. There were no letters from Scot to Morgan.

Making sure the letters I'd read were all neatly back in the order I'd gone through them, I replaced the lid and exchanged the box for the one on the floor. Opening it I noted it contained some manila file envelopes and a stack of dozen or so thick spiral notebooks like high school and college kids use for classes. I went quickly through the manila folders first, which contained a number of relatively short typewritten manuscripts of articles he'd apparently done for educational publications and a few short stories. From my cursory scan, they all appeared to be well written and seemingly very authoritative. Whether they'd been published or not, I couldn't tell. Returning them to the box, I pulled out the stack of spiral notebooks, which I gathered were the book manuscripts. They were numbered, "1-9" and "1-4" Neither book was titled, though the last page of notebook 9 had the word "Trash!" scrawled across it. I had no idea if this was to be the title or whether it was Morgan's assessment of his own work. I started with notebook 1 and skimmed through it. The plot, from what I could tell, seemed to be along the lines of a 20th Century *The Scarlet Letter*...there was a conflicted preacher and a young woman and the overall impression I got was that while the writing was good, the plot and the characterization were...well, perhaps summed up by Morgan's own note. But he had finished it nonetheless (the words "The End" on the last page sort of clued me). If he'd ever attempted to have it published I had no idea, though I strongly doubted it. There was no clue as to when it had been written.

The second, interestingly, appeared to be the narrative of a sailor returning from WWII to confront his domineering father's plans for his future. Obviously it had been written sometime between 1945 and Morgan's death in 1953. It was told in the third person and I assumed was fiction. From what little I read, it seemed to be really well done, in that I had to consciously pull myself away from it. Flipping through the last notebook, number 4, I saw the writing ended abruptly about two pages into Chapter 9. I kept thumbing through the blank pages, hoping there might be something else written there, but there was not. I did note that a couple of pages apparently had been torn out at the very end.

On a whim, I took another look at the last twenty or so letters in the first box, dated from May 12th to August 11th of 1953—a few days before he died. The last letter to his wife was dated the 10th. She and their son were apparently on an extended visit to his wife's parents, and gave absolutely no clue that he was about to kill himself. The only possible sign was in the last line of the letter, in which he said: "Tell Collin I love him very much." Other than that, it, like every letter to his wife, was pretty bland; almost impersonal. Aside from that note to Collin, I didn't get much of a sense of...well, warmth. There were hints of something beneath the surface, and I wondered if perhaps they were having marital problems. (Well, if Morgan was indeed gay, that there might have been marital problems wouldn't have been surprising.)

But it was the letters to Scot that I read more closely, and while they appeared to be nothing more than just friendly letters to an old buddy, I could definitely sense something a little less casual between the lines. There were some sidelong references to Morgan's military days and frequent, obviously fond, reminiscences on things the two had done together—a trip to Rome, for example, was written of with much warmth. And, in the last few letters particularly, there was somehow an almost tangible feeling of...again, what? Tension: of desperation and sadness. Probably just my own Scorpio-romantic nature, seeing these things which were not specifically stated, but I could sense the words were some sort of carefully constructed dam behind which huge volumes of confined feelings were pressing. The last letter to Scot was dated August 11, 1953. It was also apparently the last letter he ever wrote.

I really wanted to know more about Morgan Butler.

You've got a lover, one of my mind voices reminded me gently. *You don't need another one. And especially a long-dead one. You're supposed to be working on a case here, not running off on some sort of romantic tangent.*

It was right, of course: my mind voices usually are. But I somehow felt that in this case, the two were not mutually exclusive...that in some way, Morgan Butler was linked to Taylor Cates' death across all those years.

* * *

I spent far more time at the Burrows than I had intended to. I found it interesting that there were no references in any of his letters to any novels, including the ones in front of me. And while I couldn't find exact dates for either book manuscript, I had the strong feeling that it was his death that interrupted completion of the second one.

I came away from the library with a determination to find out whatever I could about Morgan Butler.

* * *

I arrived home before Jonathan and Joshua, who were stopping for a haircut, and had fixed myself a Manhattan and just sat down to turn on the TV when I happened to glance at the bookcase by the door. I noticed several books were missing and, puzzled, I got up and went to see if I could figure out which ones they were. Well, actually, I pretty much knew before I got there. The four missing books were those by Evan Knight. Jonathan must have taken them with him to work and brought them to Knight's house for signing.

So? a mind voice asked.

So why hadn't he mentioned it? I wondered.

What? the mind voice asked, much more sharply. *Since when does he have to report to you on everything? Jeezus, Hardesty, what's going on with you?*

I was afraid I knew, and I wasn't the least bit happy about it. This whole thing with Evan Knight and Jonathan had been poking at the worst part of my Scorpio nature. That I knew Knight was a predator was one thing, but combining that with my sense that Jonathan had been acting a little strange lately...no, I didn't like it at all.

Luckily, my little toe-dip into the Depression Pool was interrupted by the phone.

"Hello?" I said, picking it up. I'd at long last broken myself of answering with my name.

"Is this Dick Hardesty?" the male voice asked.

"Yes..." I said, not quite sure who was on the other end of the line.

"This is Dave Witherspoon," the voice said. "Sorry I didn't reply sooner, but we just got back into town."

"I'm glad you called, Mr. Witherspoon," I said. "I'd very much like to talk with you about Taylor Cates. I am trying to find out whatever I can about him, and since you two worked together..."

"Yes," he said. "Taylor. I assumed that's what you wanted when I heard the 'Dick Hardesty Investigations' part of your message. Unfortunately, I don't really know what I can tell you. I'm sorry he's dead, of course...as I'm sorry for anyone's death, but we weren't exactly close."

"Well, would it be possible for us to get together for an hour or so? I do have some questions I think you could help me answer."

He sighed. "I suppose. But it can't be until next Monday, I'm afraid. My lover and I are leaving town again for a few days."

"That'll be fine," I said. "What time Monday would be convenient for you?"

There was a slight pause, then: "Well, we're flying back Sunday evening. Let me call you at your office Monday morning and we'll see what my schedule is."

"That'll be fine," I said. "Thanks. I'll look forward to seeing you then."

"Thank you," he said. "Monday, then." And we hung up.

* * *

I'd returned to the couch and was staring at the TV when Jonathan and Joshua came in. I got up and went over for our group hug, noting how hot Jonathan looked with his new haircut—he'd gotten it cut really short, which was sexy as all hell. Joshua seemed a bit subdued, and I noticed his hair looked the same as it had when he'd left for day care. I asked Jonathan about it, and he gave Joshua a rather stern stare.

"Joshua decided he didn't want his hair cut. He decided it loudly and at great length, and since there were a lot of other people in the shop waiting, I figured 'the heck with it.' But we had a long talk about it in the car, and I don't think we'll be going through that same little number again. Right, Joshua?"

Joshua looked mildly crestfallen, stared at the floor, and nodded.

I noticed, too, that Jonathan had been carrying his bookbag, which he set on the floor next to the bookcase.

After the hug, Jonathan and Joshua headed to the kitchen and I returned to the couch and my Manhattan.

"I was going to put dinner on," I called into the kitchen, "but I wasn't sure what you're planning on having. I don't think the meatloaf is thoroughly thawed yet."

"That's okay," Jonathan called back. "I figured we'd have macaroni and cheese."

"And *hot dogs!*" Joshua added enthusiastically, pulling himself out of his sulk and contemplating his favorite meal.

When they came back into the living room, Jonathan went over to his book bag and opened it, replacing four books on the shelf.

"Evan Knight's?" I asked, knowing fully well they were. God, I can be an asshole!

"Yeah," Jonathan said. "He told me yesterday that if I wanted him to autograph them for me, he would. That was really nice of him."

Wasn't it, though? a mind voice asked sweetly.

Knock it off! a chorus of others demanded.

"Did he say anything else about the party?" I asked.

Jonathan finished putting the books away and got up to carry his book bag into the bedroom. He paused in front of the bedroom door and turned toward me. "Just that he's really glad we're coming," he said. "He said he'd been telling a couple of his writer friends about us, and that they're looking forward to meeting us."

Uh, Jonathan. a mind voice said,...*excuse me, but...?*

When he returned to the living room, stopping to pick G.I. Joe up from where Joshua had dropped him, he said: "It really sounds like it's going to be a nice party. He said he'd hired some really popular bartender."

A little bell went off in my head. *Oh-oh!* I thought.

"Did he mention the guy's name?" I asked.

"Yeah, but I'd never heard of him before. A Kirk-something? You know him?"

Oh, yes! Just about every gay guy in town knew Kirk Sims. Kirk was indeed a great bartender, and specialized in private parties. Kirk was also known to have one of the largest schlongs in captivity, and for a sizeable gratuity, he'd be happy to take it out and stir your drink for you.

So it was going to be one of those parties, eh? I used to love them when I was single, but with a partner....

"So are you just about through with the landscaping?" I asked.

"We finish up tomorrow," he said, scooping Joshua up from the floor and sitting down beside me. "I guess he wanted it done for the party, so we had a lot of guys working on it."

Joshua, who had been helping Cowboy defend an empty-cereal-box fort, immediately tried to scramble down from Jonathan's lap, but Jonathan held him tight.

"I've got to go back over there tomorrow afternoon to deliver some plants for the party," he said offhandedly, staring intently at Joshua with a mock scowl and rocking him back and forth.

"Let me *down!*" Joshua demanded.

"*No!*" Jonathan replied, freeing one hand to tickle Joshua's belly, which of course sent the kid into spasms of laughter and flailing legs.

I recognized this for what it was—a distraction from the announcement that Jonathan would be going back to Evan Knight's house the next day. I really had to bite my tongue from asking: "Alone?"

* * *

After giving Joshua his bath, getting him into his pajamas and into bed, and reading him a story, Jonathan and I watched some TV before going to bed ourselves. As we got into bed, I was aware Jonathan was staring at me.

"What?" I asked.

He looked quickly away and climbed under the covers. "Nothing," he said.

"Oh, no you don't," I said, joining him and pulling him toward me. "What's going on?"

He locked his eyes on mine for a moment, then said: "Are you jealous?"

That one caught me by surprise. "*Me?*" I asked, hoping I sounded incredulous.

"You," Jonathan replied.

"Do I have reason to be?" I heard myself asking and immediately wished I hadn't.

He gave me a small smile, and moved closer. "Of course not," he said. "It's just…"

"Just what?" I asked.

He sighed. "It's just that…well…Evan is a really nice looking guy and he's famous, and he really seems to like me…"

"And I don't?" I asked.

He gave me a nudge. "Well, of course you do! That's not the point!"

"What *is* the point?"

"The point is that I'm human, and so are you, and that just because we're together doesn't mean we're never going to look at another man again." He looked at me intently before continuing. "That also doesn't mean we're going to *do* anything about it, but a little fantasy every now and then never hurt anybody. And don't tell me you've never had any! I've seen you look at other guys."

He had me there, of course.

"And if I thought you ever really meant to do anything about it," he said, "I'd be worried. But I know you wouldn't. And I won't either. If we can't trust one another to know where the lines are, we're in deep trouble."

That was the first time since we'd been together that the subject had ever seriously come up, and he was completely right.

"Jeezus, I love you," I said, grabbing him to me.

He pulled his head back far enough to give me a big grin. "Show me," he said.

And I did.

CHAPTER 5

Defenestration: the act of throwing something or someone out a window. It was a word in my Friday morning crossword puzzle and, I found later that day by spending a couple of hours in the city's main library, the cause of death for one Morgan Butler, age 31. The window in question was on the 17th floor of the Montero Hotel. What he was doing there was not explained. He was, the obituary dated August 14, 1953 noted, survived by his wife, Emily, his four year old son, Collin, and his mother, Gretchen. He was preceded in death by his father, the Reverend Jerromy Butler. He had been an English teacher at Catherby Academy, a prestigious private school on the east side. Burial was at Rosevine Cemetery.

I was struck by the thought, immaterial though it may be, that Collin Butler had been Joshua's age when his father died. It must have been tough on the kid, growing up without a father—if, indeed that's what he did. I wondered if his mother might have remarried.

Well, at least I'd confirmed that Morgan Butler had been living here at the time of his death—that would make it easier to find out other things about him.

Out of curiosity, before I'd left the office I had checked the phone book under "Butler" just to see if Collin Butler might be listed. Sure enough, there he was (I didn't think the chances were great that there would be more than one Collin Butler in town).

I was tempted to call him, but then remembered what Irving McHam had said—that Jerromy's grandson had tried, or was trying, to have the Butler papers removed from the collection. I wondered if it was because he might be a zealot like his grandfather and didn't want Jerromy Butler's name to be in any way associated with a bunch of fags. I also didn't know if Collin was aware that some of his father's papers were also included in the collection. It was highly unlikely that Collin might know that his father was possibly gay: Collin was only four when his father died and it's also very unlikely his mother would have brought the subject up even if she knew. And there was in fact no definite proof—at least not in the materials I'd seen at the Burrows—that he really was gay.

I would like to talk to Collin Butler, but didn't want to get the Burrows in any trouble until I knew more about who he was and exactly on what grounds he wanted his grandfather's papers removed. I made a note to check back with Irving McHam and perhaps with Glen O'Banyon to see what I could find out.

And just what did all this have to do with Taylor Cates' death? Who knows? Maybe nothing, maybe something, maybe everything. Part of the fun of being a private investigator is sorting through piles of jigsaw puzzle pieces, trying to see what pieces might fit together.

I checked my watch just as I was getting ready to leave the library and saw that I might just have time to get in touch with McHam and see what he knew about Collin Butler's efforts to remove his grandfather's papers from the Burrows collection. I decided to return to the office and call him from there. I knew if I went to the Burrows, I'd be tempted to take another look at Morgan Butler's papers, and that could wait until another time.

Even so, it was close to 3:30 by the time I dialed the Burrows and asked to speak to Irving McHam.

"Yes, Mr. Hardesty," McHam's deep voice said. "What can I do for you?"

"I was wondering," I began, "if you could tell me a little bit about Collin Butler and on what grounds he's trying to remove his grandfather's papers."

"I think you'd be better off talking with Glen O'Banyon," McHam said. "I really don't know all that much about it, other than that he's claiming ownership of all the Butler materials."

"I thought you'd told me Morgan Butler had donated them to Chester Burrows." I said.

"I did. They were specifically bequeathed to Mr. Burrows in Morgan Butler's will, which fairly well knocks the legal legs out from under Collin Butler's claim," he said.

Interesting, I thought. And it certainly lent weight to the possibility/probability that Morgan Butler was gay.

"Morgan Butler knew Chester Burrows, then?" I asked

"I really don't know the circumstances of the bequest," he replied. "Perhaps Glen O'Banyon could help you there."

"Do you know anything more about the possibility of Morgan Butler's being gay?"

There was a slight pause, then: "Other than what Taylor mentioned shortly before he died, no. It seems he'd found some evidence of it in Morgan's papers, but I really didn't have the time to follow up on it. There is just so very much else to be done."

"How big a loss would it be to the collection if Butler were to be able to withdraw his grandfather's material?" I asked.

"The Butler papers are a very important part of the collection, of course," he said, "but they represent only a very small portion of the total collection. Their loss would be a great shame, but it certainly wouldn't cripple the library in any significant way, if that's what you're wondering."

"Well, yes, I guess I was," I said.

"So you will refer your other questions to Mr. O'Banyon, then?" he asked, obviously ready to end the conversation.

"Yes, I'll do that," I said. "Thank you for your help."

"You're quite welcome. Good afternoon, then."

"And to you," I said, and we hung up.

I looked at my watch and decided that 3:45 on a Friday afternoon was not exactly a good time to try to call one of the city's busiest lawyers, so I put it on my mental agenda for first thing Monday morning, did a few minutes' puttering around the office, and left.

* * *

It being Friday, we'd promised Joshua we'd take him to Cap'n Rooney's Fish Shack for dinner. Cap'n Rooney's was right up there with macaroni and cheese and hot dogs on Joshua's list of fine dining, and I had to admit I kind of liked it, too: especially the malt vinegar for the thickly-sliced "chips."

Jonathan did not say a word about his trip to Evan Knight's, and I didn't ask him. Before we left for dinner, Tim had called to verify that he and Phil would be glad to join us at Steamroller Junction the following Saturday to see T/T's show. I hadn't had a chance to call Bob and Mario, who were also big T/T fans, but Tim said he and Phil were going to stop by Ramón's later that night and would ask. Our social life was definitely picking up.

* * *

Saturday passed as Saturdays do with by-the-numbers chores, highlighted only by Joshua's knocking over a small plant stand while engaged in a chair-cushion battle with Jonathan. Only one African violet was seriously wounded in the melee, and Jonathan had Joshua help him carefully dip the stems of the broken leaves into some rooting stimulant and place them in a styrofoam cup filled with vermiculite to root so there could be even more African violets than we already had.

I was mildly trepidatious about Evan Knight's party—in large part, to be honest, because we'd not been to a large private party consisting largely of guys we didn't know for I don't know how long, and my crotch, stubbornly refusing to accept the concept of monogamy, invariably tried to get me in trouble. That, and because of my double-standard concerns over the Evan-Jonathan dynamics. Well, we'd just have to wait and see.

Craig Richman's mother, who had agreed to let him spend the night again, dropped him off at around six-thirty so we wouldn't have to go over and get him, and we once again ordered in pizza. Craig had brought along a small duffle bag with a change of clothes in anticipation of accompanying Jonathan and Joshua to the M.C.C. in the morning. It appeared we were establishing a nice sort of routine, and I was grateful once again to the Richmans for their confidence in us.

Since it was still fairly early, we decided to take full advantage of our evening out and stop by Ramón's our-selves...Tim had said he and Phil would be going out there Friday night...for a quick drink and to say hello to Bob Allen. It was early enough that we were able to actually talk for a bit while I had an Old Fashioned and Jonathan had a tonic and lime and fended off the sexual teasing of Jimmy, the bartender. Bob said Tim and Phil had mentioned T/T's show, and that he was sure he and Mario could juggle their work schedules so they could go. I told him, as I'd told the rest of the gang, that I'd pick up the tickets Monday after work.

We arrived at Evan Knight's at around nine and found a place to park about three houses down. This was indeed the Briarwood area, but the homes on this particular street were somewhat smaller than the ostentatious behemoths that made up most of the area. Still, it was a pretty impressive place, and I made a point to compliment Jonathan on the really good job he and Evergreens had done on the yard.

We passed Jake's pick-up, directly in front of the house, and went up the lighted walkway to the massive double front door. We could hear the sound of music and laughter coming from somewhere at the back of the house.

We rang the bell, and the door was opened by a spectacular

number in break-away black pants, a cummerbund, no shirt—one look at him made it clear why—and a white bow tie.

Ah, that Evan Knight, a mind voice—my crotch, I suspected—said admiringly: *Class all the way!*

"Good evening, gentlemen," the hunk said with a smile that made me weak in the knees. "Please come in."

He showed us through the small foyer into the large living room. There were probably a dozen guys scattered in small groups around the room, and another shirtless Chippendale should'a-been with a tray of hors d'oeuvres was approaching three guys near the window. I was rather surprised to realize I didn't know a single one of the people in the room.

You've been out of circulation far too long, a mind voice observed wistfully.

"Mr. Knight is out by the pool," our shirtless wonder said, gesturing with one beautifully-biceped arm toward open sliding glass doors at one end of the room. "The bar is just to your left as you step onto the patio."

The doorbell rang, and our hunk smiled and said "Excuse me," and turned to answer it.

We made our way through the living room, exchanging nods of greeting with a few of the other guests, and stepped out onto the large patio, where another dozen or so guys stood in small clusters or milled about. Five more were in the pool. Obviously, none had remembered to bring their bathing suits. I noted that one of the five was Jake, and from what I could see, even through the water...oh, lordy!

We turned to the left and approached the bar, which was set into a small alcove and had another gaggle of guys standing around it, admiring the bartender in a red jacket, white shirt with a red tie. I recognized him immediately as Kirk Sims, whom I'd seen bartending at several parties in my single days. As we got closer to the bar I could also see he was not wearing pants.

Jared stood just a little way to one side of the group, a fresh drink in his hand, and a bemused smile on his face. He saw us and gave a grin and a heads-up nod of greeting as we walked over to him.

"Hi, guys," he said, putting one large arm around Jonathan's shoulders. "Glad you could make it."

"Us too," Jonathan said, grinning. "We just saw Jake in the pool and were wondering where you were."

Jared took a long sip of his drink. "I'll be going in in a few minutes," he said. "Just wanted to have another drink first."

"Shy?" I asked, teasing.

"Oh, *sure,* Dick, sure," he said. "You going to come join us?"

Got 'cha there! A mind voice observed. "Uh, I don't know yet," I said. "We just got here and hadn't thought about it."

"Well," Jared said, "why don't you go get you and Jonathan a drink, and think about it?"

"Tonic and lime?" Jonathan said, and I nodded and walked to the bar.

"Yes, sir?" Kirk asked, the perfect bartender.

"A beer and a tonic and lime, please," I said.

He reached beneath the bar's counter and pulled out a beer, then scooped some ice into a tub glass, smoothly opened a bottle of tonic water, filled it and garnished it with a large slice of lime. "Would you like that stirred?" he asked politely, lifting up the front of his shirt to reveal a "stirrer" of truly monumental proportions. The other guys around the bar all laughed.

"Not just now, thanks," I said, and he just gave me a raised-eyebrow grin.

"Chicken!" one of the other guys said good-naturedly.

I just returned his smile, took a few loose bills out of my pocket to drop in the tip jar, then took our drinks and returned to Jared and Jonathan.

"Why didn't you let him stir it?" Jonathan asked with a grin.

"Hey, you can always go back," I said.

The three of us talked for a few minutes, moving a bit further from the bar, which was becoming quite active.

"He's straight, you know," Jared said, nodding toward Kirk.

"*Straight?*" Jonathan asked, incredulous, having watched as Kirk expertly stirred a couple of drinks.

"Wife and two kids," I said, having heard his story before.

"But then how can he...?"

"Have you seen that tip jar?" I asked. "He never does anything with anyone, but he sure knows a good thing when he's got it."

Jared had just verified that he and Jake would be joining us for T/T's show when Evan Knight came over to greet us."Jonathan!...Dick!" he said, apparently already having greeted Jared and Jake earlier. "Glad you're here. Got everything you need? There's a buffet table in the dining room if you'd like something to eat."

"Thanks, Evan," I said. "We're fine for now."

Someone just entering the patio called his name and he excused himself and moved off. Jared finished his drink and looked toward the pool, where Jake was in intense conversation with a crew-cut hunk, either currently or recently in the Marines, if one could believe the large 'USMC' tattoo on his shoulder.

"I think I'll go join Jake," he said. "You coming?"

"Maybe in a bit," I said, then turned to Jonathan. "You want to go in?"

He looked slightly conflicted. "Well, yeah, I'd like to, but we don't have our bathing suits, and…"

"…and we'd stand out like sore thumbs if we did," I noted.

"Yeah, that's true," he said.

Just then Evan Knight appeared again.

"Dick," he said, taking me by the arm. "There's someone here really anxious to meet you. I told him you're a p.i. and he might have some business for you."

"Well, sure," I said. "I…"

"And Jonathan, while Dick is talking shop, why don't you come with me and meet a couple of my writer friends."

Ah-Hah! I thought. *Divide and conquer! This guy's good. A weasel, but good.* And I couldn't protest if I wanted to without looking like a possessive ass.

"Sure!" Jonathan said.

Knight led us into the living room and over to the fireplace, where a nice looking guy in his early 50s was standing alone, looking at some photos on the mantle.

"Dick," Knight said, "this is Drew Rothworth. We'll leave you two to talk while Jonathan and I go say hello to some people."

And like that he led Jonathan away. *Damn!* I had the distinct impression I'd somehow just been had.

I was aware that Rothworth was extending his hand, and I turned my attention to him. "Nice to meet you," I said.

* * *

It turned out, not surprisingly, that Rothworth, who told me he'd seen me several times in the bars over the years but had never come up and introduced himself, was less interested in my professional services than in a discreet testing-of-the-waters cruise. Had I been single, I might well have taken him up on it, but under the circumstances I as discreetly as possible brought up Jonathan and Joshua and our monogamous relationship. He was a nice guy, though, and we ended up talking about a number of general topics. Typical cocktail-party conversation.

I could see Jonathan across the room with Knight and two other people. About ten minutes later, Jonathan left the group and came over to join me. I introduced him to Rothworth and we all exchanged pleasantries for a few more minutes before Rothworth excused himself to go get another drink, asking if we'd like one. We declined with thanks, and he left us alone by the mantle.

"So how did it go with Evan's writing friends?" I asked.

"Great!" Jonathan said, his face brightening. "That tall one is Phillip Tanner—he writes the Grant Moss detective series. I've read them all. The other is Charles Beeman...he won a couple of awards for his last book...*The Ghost of Years,* it's called. I was embarrassed that I haven't read it, and told him I would pick up a copy as soon as I could. They were both very nice guys. I'll try to introduce you later, if you'd like. I was really impressed."

Again, though, I knew full well Evan Knight's attentions to Jonathan were based on more than his being a nice guy. But I was happy for Jonathan's opportunity to meet people he admired.

We went back out to the patio for another drink before, as Jonathan suggested, hitting the buffet table. Jake, Jared, and the guy Jake had been talking to in the pool were nowhere to be seen, and there seemed to be several more guys wandering around without their clothes. Evan was just walking away from the bar, his shirt unbuttoned to display a very nice set of pecs and a forest of chest hair.

Watch it, Hardesty, a mind voice cautioned. *You don't even like the guy.*

Yeah, well, my crotch responded, paraphrasing an old standard gay joke, *I didn't come here to fuck personality.*

"You about ready to come in the pool?" Evan asked as he passed.

"In a minute," I said.

"Shall we?" Jonathan asked. I noticed that he'd given Knight's impressive torso a rather lingering glance.

"If you want," I said.

I saw that there were several chairs around the pool with clothes on them.

"Don't you want something to eat first?" I asked.

"Not if we're going swimming," Jonathan replied. "It can wait."

Very un-Jonathan, I thought, but we detoured to one of the few still empty chairs and began taking our clothes off. Odd, I'd done this a hundred times in the past without a second thought, but now that I was with Jonathan...

You don't want other guys to see him naked, a mind voice observed casually.

Well, damn it, I realized it was right. I didn't.

But you don't mind them seeing you? the voice asked.

That's different, I thought defensively.

Oh, yeah? Like how, for example?

Get over it, Hardesty, the voice said. *You are* not *Tarzan. Jonathan is not Boy. He's* not *your possession. You don't own him.*

It was right again, of course.

We undressed and walked over to the edge of the pool, where seven or eight guys were splashing around, or doing underwater laps, or floating on their backs. Jonathan stuck one foot in. "Nice," he said. "Come on!" and he dived in. I followed.

I must admit, it was a lot of fun. Jonathan insisted on ducking me every chance he got, and we got into a couple underwater scuffles. We weren't even aware of the other guys around us until all of a sudden we came up for air, laughing, and Evan Knight was there right in front of us.

"Enjoying yourselves?" He asked. He was able to touch bottom, and was standing right in front of Jonathan. I saw him staring at Jonathan...and not at his face. "Ah," he said with a big smile, "*very* nice! Just as I remember it."

*   *   *

It was as if somebody had just kicked me in the gut...hard.

"*What the...?*" I heard myself say.

Jonathan looked quickly toward me, his face a study in mortification. "I..." he started to say.

"Oh, oh...sorry," Knight said, his tone making it perfectly clear that he was no such thing. "No offense. But I *knew* I knew you from somewhere. It wasn't until after you'd left the other day that I remembered from where. We met at Hughie's quite a while ago...you've changed so much I didn't recognize you at first. You've really filled out nicely. Dick must be treating you right." He reached out his hand under the water, and Jonathan stumbled quickly backwards.

He still looked stunned, and then I was afraid he might start to cry.

Knight looked at me, his face a mask of fake concern. "Hey, I'm really sorry if I opened any closet doors," he said, his eyes shifting back to Jonathan. "I rather thought that might have been how you met Dick, too. No shame in being a hustler, especially if it pays off."

I'm not sure quite what happened next. All I know is that there were little clouds of red in the water and Evan Knight was holding both hands to his face and a trickle of blood was running down one arm and dripping from his elbow into the water. I grabbed Jonathan by the arm and we waded to the steps at the end of the pool and got out of the water. There wasn't a sound to be heard, except music coming from the house. I wasn't aware of anyone or anything—just a bunch of statues standing around as if frozen in time.

I grabbed our clothes and we padded through the house, dripping water across the carpet, and walked out the door, stark naked.

We stopped only long enough to put on our shorts and pants, then padded barefoot and shirtless to the car. I pulled my keys out of my pants pocket and started the engine.

As we pulled out into the street, Jonathan, staring straight ahead, said: "I'm sorry, Dick. I'm so sorry. I didn't remember him! I swear, or I'd never have gone over there."

I reached over and put my hand on his still wet leg. "Don't worry about it," I said. "But don't be hurt if we're not invited to Evan Knight's next party."

I grinned at him, and after a moment, he grinned back.

* * *

Jonathan, Joshua, and Craig had gone off to services at the M.C.C. and I was on the couch reading the paper when the phone rang.

"Dick! It's Jared. You sure know how to liven up a party!"

"Well, thanks," I said. "I do what I can. We had a heck of a time explaining to our babysitter why we came home soaking wet, though."

Jared laughed. "I can imagine. Too bad you left before the party got really interesting."

"A good time was had by all, I assume?"

"Oh, yeah! Remember the doorman and his dressed-alike buddy?"

"How could I forget? You don't see bodies like that every day." I had an immediate second thought on that one. "Well, you and Jake do every time you look in a mirror, but for the rest of us...Anyway, don't tell me you and Jake..."

"Both of 'em—singularly and together. Talk about 'double your fun!' It was quite a night."

"Gee, I'm really sorry we missed out," I said. Most of me was kidding, but my crotch was sincere. I really *did* miss the "good old days" every now and then.

"Well," he continued, "I just wanted to check and see if you were okay. I never did find out exactly why you popped Knight, but I'm sure he deserved it."

"He did. Trust me."

"I do," he said. "So we'll see you next Saturday at Steamroller Junction. About what time?"

"9:30 okay? I'll try to pick up the tickets tomorrow. We can meet out front."

"9:30's fine. See you there."

* * *

One thing having a 4-year-old boy around the house does is to make you pretty careful what you talk about and when. Neither Jonathan nor I mentioned the party all day, what with both Joshua and...until early afternoon when we dropped him off at home...Craig always within earshot. Craig was obviously very curious about the party and asked several questions about who was there, what went on, etc.—we'd given him a story about the lawn sprinklers having turned on just as we were leaving, but he was too smart to buy it, I'm sure. The idea of going to a large party where everyone was gay was something of a fantasy for him and I suspect the knowledge that some of those parties can turn into minor or major orgies would have been more than his already overcharged-hormone-driven libido could take.

As we were leaving the apartment to take him home, he asked if he could borrow a book he'd been reading the night before after Joshua'd been put to bed. I noticed it was one of

Evan Knight's books: *Fate's Hand*. We said of course.

"I don't remember that one too well," I said as we left the apartment. "Which one is it?"

"It's about this gay guy and his lover who get drafted in the war and then get separated, and what happens to them and..."

That's right, I thought, *remembering. The protagonist's name was...uh...Ted, and the sailor's name was...Scott.*

I did a quick mental double-take. *Scott?*

* * *

It wasn't until Joshua was asleep and we were in bed ourselves that Jonathan brought up the subject of the party at Evan Knight's.

"I *really* didn't remember him," Jonathan said. "I guess I tried hard to put all those guys I tricked with out of my head. I'm so sorry to have embarrassed you."

I pulled him to me. "I wasn't embarrassed—I was pissed at him for mentioning it."

We lay there quietly for a moment and then my Scorpio got the better of me. "Can I ask you...if this whole mess hadn't come up and he kept pursuing you, do you think you might have been tempted?"

He didn't say anything for a time, then said: "Well, tempted, sure. He was really nice to me, and he flattered me and made me feel important—not that you don't, of course, but...I guess I knew all along what he wanted but, well, it was just sort of like a game, and it was exciting. But I guess he thought because I used to hustle, I still did. He made a couple passes when we were alone together while Evergreens was working on his yard, but they weren't serious gropes or anything, so I just thought he was playing around, like Jared and Jake do with me."

"So you wouldn't have..." I let my question trail off, angry at myself for even mentioning it.

He snuggled closer. "Let me ask you," he said: "Have you ever been tempted since we got together? Be honest."

I shrugged. "Well, yeah. Like we talked about the other day, I'm only human. I never followed through on any of it."

"And I'm only human, too," he said. "But what makes you think you're stronger at resisting temptation than I am?"

Point taken.

* * *

I wasn't sure exactly how long T/T would be in town and I really wanted to talk to him alone, if I could. The last time we'd seen him, he'd just come in for a one-night gig for Steamroller Junction's opening, and he'd joined the gang afterwards for a drink. But I wanted to ask him about Taylor Cates, and murder doesn't exactly fit into general having-a-drink-together conversation.

Monday morning, while waiting to hear from Dave Witherspoon, I called William Pearson's office and asked to speak to him. He came on the phone a moment later.

"Good morning, Mr. Hardesty. What can I do for you?"

"I was wondering if you might have a number where I could reach Teddy Wilson? I really would like to talk with him about Taylor Cates, and I don't know how much time he might have while he's in town."

"Not very much, I'm afraid," Pearson said. "He's flying in specifically to do the show, then returning to Atlanta Sunday afternoon. I'm expecting a call from him any minute now, as a matter of fact, to go over some last minute logistical details. If you'd like, I could ask him to call you."

Good timing, Hardesty!

"I'd really appreciate that," I said—and meant it. "And let me give you my home number in case he's not able to get back to me until this evening."

I gave him the number, thanked him again, and we hung up.

No more than ten minutes later, the phone rang. It was Dave Witherspoon.

"Ah, thanks for calling, Mr. Witherspoon," I said. "Did you have a nice trip?"

"It's Dave, please," he said. "And we had a wonderful time. We both needed to get away. Cancun is one of our favorite places!"

Cancun? I thought. Now that was interesting. I'd rather assumed the purpose for the trip might have been a job interview. Not many people can afford to take a vacation to Mexico right after they'd been fired.

"So I've heard," I said. "So will you be available to get together today for a few minutes, then?"

"Sure," he said. "I've got to be in The Central later this morning. You want to meet at Coffee & for lunch?"

"That's be fine," I said, looking at my watch. "Noon?" I suggested.

"Noon it is," he said. "My lover will be with me...I'm sure you don't mind."

"Not at all," I said. "How will I recognize you?"

"Well," he said, "unless there's more than one black and white couple in the place, it shouldn't be too hard."

I laughed. "No problem," I said. "See you at noon."

* * *

Part of me really wanted to return to the Burrows and dig further into Morgan Butler's papers, although exactly what I could expect to find in there that might have any direct application to Taylor Cates' death, I had no idea. But for some reason, I'd really become fixated on a man I'd never known and who was long-since dead. Why? For a change, my inner voices were silent.

I also wanted to call Glen O'Banyon to see what if anything I could find out about Collin Butler, but I didn't want to tie up the phone. I certainly couldn't see any remotely serious connection between Collin Butler' grievances against the Burrows and Taylor Cates' death, but that didn't make me any the less curious as to how it might affect the Burrows' future, despite McHam's assertion that it wouldn't have much of an effect one way or the other. I still wanted to know more about it.

Just as I was ready to leave the office, the phone rang.

I picked it up on the second ring. "Hardesty Investigations," I said.

"Is this the world famous private investigator and my very favorite Dick in the whole world?" the immediately-recognizable voice asked.

"Teddy!" I said enthusiastically. "I'm glad you called."

"Now honey, you know if I'd have had your number before, I'd have been callin' you just about every day, just to say hello." There was only a slight pause, then: "Bill Pearson tells me you want to talk to me about Taylor."

"Yeah, as a matter of fact, I do," I said. "I'm trying to find out everything I can about him from people who knew him, and I understand you and he were friends."

There was a long sigh from the other end of the line, and a longer pause. "Oh, that poor baby," he said after a moment.

"I always thought of him as a kid brother—not that I didn't have five of my own, but none of them's worth the powder to blow 'em to hell. But Taylor...I'd be happy to tell you anything I can."

"I understand you're not going to be in town more than a day," I said.

"That's right, honey. I have to be back in Atlanta Sunday night. I've got another two weeks here at Priam's Palace before I move on to Chicago, then Palm Springs, then...well, I do keep myself busy. No moss growin' under this girl's shoes."

I laughed. "So it seems," I said, then had an idea. "Is anyone picking you up at the airport here?" I asked.

"No, I usually take a cab."

"Well, I'd be happy to pick you up. We could talk on the way into town."

"Well, darlin', aren't you sweet? A true gentleman! That would be real nice of you. Delta flight 444 at two o'clock."

"Great," I said. "I'll see you then."

There was a pause, which I expected preceded a "Good bye," but instead I heard:

"That fall that killed Taylor...it wasn't an accident, was it?"

That caught me a bit by surprise, wondering why he might think so, but I didn't want to get any further into it until I could talk with him in person, face to face.

"I'm still not sure," I said. "But I'll find out."

CHAPTER 6

Well of course T/T was far from stupid, and having any p.i. want to talk with him about a friend who recently died in a supposed accident would give him a clue that somebody suspected something out of the ordinary. But I wondered if he might have had another reason for his comment.

I made a note to call Glen O'Banyon's office when I got back from lunch with Dave Witherspoon. I did want to know more about Collin Butler, more for my own curiosity about the Butler family dynamics than out of any thought that Butler might be involved in Taylor's death. Normally, I probably would have just called him myself, but since he was already an open enemy of the library, I didn't want to give him any more fuel for his drive to have the Butler papers removed.

And I realized as I left the office to head to The Central that I still hadn't talked with Evan Knight, Zachary Clanton, or Marv Westeen about what they might know about Taylor Cates. Of the three, the only one I thought really might have some idea of what was going on with Taylor was Evan Knight.

And why in hell did I keep thinking of *Fate's Hand*?

I was tempted to try to contact either Clanton or Westeen next, but realized I'd just be forestalling the inevitable, and that I might as well get Evan Knight out of the way first. I felt fairly sure that my having punched him out at his own party and in his own swimming pool might make approaching him on Taylor's death just a tad awkward, and I probably shouldn't have done it. But it sure seemed like a good idea at the time. And while I might have chosen a more private time and place to punch him, I wasn't about to apologize just to get him to talk to me. Well, I'd work it out somehow.

* * *

Coffee & is one of those places which really has little to recommend it other than its location: in this case on the main drag in The Central. Its "it's okay" food and service were matched by its almost total lack of what some people call "ambience." But because of where it was, it was always busy.

I'd have been, as usual, early, had it not been for a slight confrontation between a bottled water truck and a city bus which caught me in the middle of the block and held up traffic for a good ten minutes. When I walked into the diner, I spotted a black guy and a white guy sitting across from one another at a booth looking at menus. The black guy looked up as I came in, said something to his friend, then gave me a heads-up nod. Trusting this was not merely an across-the-room cruise, I went over. "Dave Witherspoon?" I asked, not sure which one might actually be Witherspoon.

"Hi," the white guy said, scooting over to make room for me to sit. "I'm Dave. This is Ryan."

I shook hands with both of them and sat down. A cute young waiter I'd seen before appeared with menus, a place mat and a set of silverware wrapped in a paper napkin, which he set in front of me. "Coffee?" he asked, and I nodded.

"So what can I tell you about Taylor?" Witherspoon asked as the waiter went off to get my coffee.

I like a guy who gets right to the point.

"I understand you two didn't get along too well," I said, deciding to follow his lead.

Both Witherspoon and his friend...Ryan...grinned, and Witherspoon shook his head. "I'm afraid not," he said, and didn't wait for me to ask why, "and it wasn't just all about working together at the Burrows. We all went to Mountjoy," he continued. "I transferred in from Eastern at the start of our sophomore year...that's when I first met Taylor and Ryan. Unfortunately Taylor was dating Ryan at the time, and when Ryan and I got together, Taylor never forgave me. He never gave up on trying to get him back, either."

Now that was an interesting comment, I thought, but before I had a chance to follow up on it, Ryan stepped in.

"I don't know why he took it out on Dave," he said as the waiter returned with my coffee. "I was going to break off with Taylor anyway. It wasn't Dave's doing." He looked at Witherspoon and grinned. "—though I have to admit, Dave came on pretty strong. He sees something he wants, he goes for it. Taylor was always a little too serious for his own good. He never said much, but you knew there was an awful lot going on inside him."

The waiter...uh...waited until Ryan finished talking before asking if we'd like to order. I hadn't even looked at the menu, but ordered an olive-burger and fries, and when he had all three orders, he left.

"I understand you were hired first," I said, and Witherspoon nodded.

"Yes, I'd started sending out resumes the last quarter of our senior year. I sent one to the Newberry in Chicago, and Irving McHam must have seen it, because I got a letter from him saying he had been hired to head the new Burrows library—I hadn't even heard that there was going to be one. But he said he would be needing catalogers, and would be interested in talking with me. So when he arrived in town, about two months before the transfer of material from the Burrows estate to the new facility, he hired me, and I started immediately. Then, just before the actual move, they started hiring more catalogers, and that's when Taylor showed up. He wasn't happy that I'd been hired first, and I'm afraid I never let him forget it just because I knew it bugged him. I wouldn't have done it if he hadn't been such an arrogant prude. He was always talking about how rough a childhood he'd had and how hard he had worked to overcome it. Hell, my dad worked in the coal mines, so Taylor didn't hold the patent on working hard to overcome obstacles."

"So what did you know of Taylor's personal life?" I asked. "Friends, enemies, lovers?"

Witherspoon sighed. "Friends, very few. I really don't know of any close friends, other than a guy from his old neighborhood…a pretty successful drag queen…"

"Teddy Wilson," I interjected.

He looked at me, a bit surprised. "Yeah, Teddy Wilson. Taylor bragged about knowing him all the time. But other than him, I don't know of anyone. Taylor wasn't exactly the easiest guy to like. No lovers, though he did date Evan Knight a few times, I understand. Enemies? Well, apparently he thought I was one, but I wasn't, really."

"Did you blame Taylor for losing your job?" I asked.

The waiter arrived and we were silent until he'd put down our orders and left.

"Well, I wasn't happy about it, that's for sure," Witherspoon said, picking up the conversation where it had left off. "Taylor confused having a superiority complex with being a perfectionist, and he was always sucking-up to Irving, so I wasn't surprised when he reported me."

"Exactly what did you do?" I asked, though McHam had already told me he had taken papers home with him. I wanted to get Witherspoon's version of the story.

I took a bite out of my olive-burger while Witherspoon answered my question.

"We were swamped with work as you can imagine," he said, "and we just couldn't keep up with it all. Taylor resolved it by never going home except to eat and sleep. As for me, the only way I could do it was to take some papers home with me every now and then to work on there. Ryan wasn't too happy about my working so much, but it had to be done. Actually, nearly every cataloger there has done the same thing, but I was the only one to get reported for it."

"I understand you were cataloging Jerromy Butler's papers, and those of his son."

"Mostly Jerromy Butler," Witherspoon said. "I'd started on him even before the move. I had just started working on Morgan Butler when the ax fell, but I hadn't gotten very far. And it didn't help that for some reason Taylor became fascinated with the guy. He was constantly going through his stuff every chance he had: lunch hour, coffee breaks, whenever I wasn't actually working on it. We had some pretty heated run-ins on that. He wanted to do the cataloging, and I wouldn't be surprised if he got me fired so that he could."

"Did you say anything to McHam about it?"

He took a bite of his sandwich and waited until he'd swallowed before answering.

"No," he said at last, "I wouldn't give Taylor the satisfaction. It was just another of his cheap-shot ways of getting back at me for Ryan."

He paused again, to take a sip of coffee and wipe the corner of his mouth with his napkin.

"Did you happen to notice anything unusual about Morgan Butler's papers?" I asked on a hunch.

Witherspoon shrugged. "Like what?" he asked, then continued before I had a chance to say anything. "Unlike Taylor, I tried to concentrate just on the cataloging and not to be distracted by what was in the papers themselves."

"So you didn't get any impression from Morgan Butler's letters that he might have been gay?"

He shrugged again. "You couldn't prove it by me," he said. "I wasn't looking for anything like that anyway. I know he wrote a lot of letters to somebody named Scot, but as I said, unlike Taylor I just didn't have the time to do more than my job, which was to skim them for general content and write down the basic information—date written, to whom sent, and maybe a brief note if there seemed to be anything of particular historical interest or importance. I can't remember there being any of either."

"I didn't read every one of them closely myself," I said. "but I got some definite gay vibes from what I did read. Nothing conclusive, I'll admit, but enough to set me wondering."

"Well," he said as I took the last bite of my olive-burger, "I guess sometimes we don't see what we're not looking for."

He had a point.

The waiter returned with more coffee, which we all refused, and left to add up our tab.

"How is your job hunt coming?" I asked.

"It's over," he replied. "I'm going back to the Burrows. Irving called me at home when we got back last night and offered me my job back. I'll be on probation for a while, but I can handle that. It's pretty obvious they really need me."

"Congratulations," I said. Odd how things work out.

Lunch was just about over, and while I knew I'd undoubtedly have more questions for Witherspoon, I wanted to take some time to sort out some of the things we'd touched on in our conversation. So we small-talked through the last of our coffee, divided up the bill when the waiter brought it, and left—my first having left the door open for possible future contact and questions.

* * *

Not one to waste time, I began the mulling process on my way back to the office. McHam had described Witherspoon as being 'laid back' and that was certainly the impression he gave. But I found it a little hard to imagine his being so casual about the whole thing. His comments about Taylor having kept trying to get Ryan back, of Taylor's being a 'suck-up,' of having Taylor want to take away one of his projects, and then being fired as a direct result of Taylor's having gone to Irving McHam all would have resonated with me a lot more strongly than they apparently did with him. I'm pretty sure if I'd been fired because of a 'suck-up' running to my boss, I'd have been a lot more pissed than Witherspoon had indicated he had been. But I guess it all worked out for him, since he now had his job back.

As soon as I got back to the office, I called to leave a message for Glen O'Banyon to ask him to call me when he could. And then I stood there, phone in hand, wondering just what I should do about Evan Knight. I definitely wanted to talk with him, but...oh, what the hell, the worst he could do would be to hang up on me. I put the phone back on the cradle long enough to look up his number, then picked it up again to dial.

The phone rang four times, and then: "Evan Knight." And since it wasn't immediately followed by an "I'm not in right now," I guessed I had the real thing.

"Evan, this is Dick Hardesty," I began. I didn't wait for a response before saying: "I'm calling in regards to my investigation into Taylor Cates' death and am talking with everyone associated with the Burrows. I wondered if we might get together to talk about it."

There was an uncomfortably long pause, then: "I suppose. I have nothing to hide."

Hide? I wondered. *Who said anything about hiding anything?*

"I wasn't suggesting you did," I said. "But the Board wants me to look into every angle in order to be completely sure Taylor's death was accidental."

"Why would anyone think otherwise?" he asked.

"Again, just covering all bets," I said.

Another long pause. "Can we do this over the phone?" he asked.

I didn't know whether he thought I might decide to punch him again, or what, and I really wasn't overly enthused about the idea of seeing him again, but I had no doubt that he knew considerably more about Taylor Cates than any of the other board members, so while a phone conversation with them was sufficient, I wanted to be able to watch Knight's reactions while I talked to him.

"I think we should talk in person," I said. I was pretty sure we both would prefer it to be on neutral territory. "We could meet for coffee somewhere."

Yet another pause. Obviously, he wasn't any more thrilled with the whole idea than I was.

"I think I'd prefer a drink," he said. "You want to make it today?"

"The sooner the better," I said.

"Okay, how about four o'clock at the Carnival?"

"That'll be fine," I said. "I'll see you there."

I hadn't been to the Carnival in ages. It was a nice businessman's-type bar that I used to go to frequently when I lived nearby. I was very glad he hadn't suggested Hughie's.

* * *

I called Evergreens to leave word for Jonathan that I might be a little late getting home. It was about two o'clock, and I had the strong urge to go by the Burrows. Dave Witherspoon's subtle jibe that maybe I was seeing something that wasn't there had gotten to me. And for some strange reason, I suddenly wondered if the letters I had gone through were all the letters there were? What if some of them were missing? How would I possibly know?

I made a quick call to the Burrows to ask McHam if it was okay for me to stop by, and he agreed…though with just the right amount of hesitation to let me know he hoped this wasn't going to become a habit. He told me I could go directly to the cataloging room and he'd tell them to be expecting me.

* * *

I made it to the Burrows by about 2:30, figuring I'd have an hour before I had to leave for the Carnival.

Janice was there at the same table surrounded by what looked to be the same boxes. I picked up Box #12-A and carried it to the far end of the table. Removing the lid, I took the yellow notepad and began looking through it. There were about four and a half pages of closely spaced writing, the last three and a half in handwriting different from the first. Dave Witherspoon's first, then Taylor's, I assumed. Just, as Witherspoon had explained, a list of dates followed by the name of the person to whom the letter was written and an occasional comment or two regarding any specific references of possible historic interest.

Okay, so if some letters were missing, comparing the list to the letters from the box should show it—at least up to the point the cataloging had reached when Taylor died. A quick thumb-through, comparing the dates of each of the letters to the entries in the notepad showed that every single one of them was there; no letters without a corresponding date on the list, no dates on the list without a corresponding letter. Damn. I noted that beside each of Witherspoon's entries there was a small check mark, and I'd wager Taylor had gone over every one of Dave's entries to verify its accuracy.

The catalog list ended with a letter on February 22, 1953—further back than I'd started reading the first time, actually. I pulled out the remaining letters in the box, being careful to keep them in order.

All right, Hardesty, one of my mind voices—the one in charge of general impatience—said: *just exactly what in the hell are you doing? You're spending all this time on a dead guy and some maybe-missing letters from decades ago. Exactly what do you think you're looking for? What possible bearing could it have on Taylor Cates' death?*

It does, my gut told me. *Trust me.*

Like a dog unwilling to let go of a bone, I ignored all the letters not to Scot and started reading the ones that were. Maybe I could pick up some indication that some letters were missing. I wished Scot's letters to Morgan—if there had been any, and I'm sure there were—had been saved. It would have been easier to pick up a sense of flow. I tried to keep my mind objective, but was pretty sure my eye would have picked up some key words if they were there. Nothing. Just that elusive whatever. Sentences like: "I was thinking of that little restaurant we found in the hills above Genoa, next to the bombed-out church. Remember how the owner's wife went to the garden and henhouse behind the place to get us fresh eggs and vegetables for that fantastic omelette?..." were really totally innocuous on the surface: but why did I insist of finding something underneath? I'm sorry, but I don't think many straight guys would remember things like that—or mention them to a straight buddy if he did.

I only had a chance to read about five or six letters, spaced over a period of several months, before I glanced at my watch and saw it was time to go. Carefully replacing the letters I'd removed, I laid the notepad on the top and closed the lid. I carried the box back to Janice, thanked her, and left.

But instead of walking out the front door, I found myself climbing the steps to the main floor and going to the general fiction section of the stacks, where books were listed alphabetically by author. Sure enough, they had all of Evan Knight's books. I picked up *Fate's Hand* and opened it, turning quickly through the pages until I found what I was looking for. It didn't take long. The character's name wasn't, as I remembered it, 'Scott'. It was 'Scot'. One 't'.

* * *

I arrived at the Carnival at about ten 'til four, early as usual despite having made a quick swing by Steamroller Junction to pick up our tickets for the Hospice benefit. Though I'd not been to the Carnival for a long time—since way before I met Jonathan, I now recalled—it hadn't changed all that much. Happy hour started at four, and since it got a lot of after-work businessmen who weren't off work yet, there were very few people in the place. No sign of Evan Knight, so I took a stool at the far end of the bar where I could keep my eye on the door. I ordered a Manhattan and had just paid for it and taken my first sip when I saw Evan walk in. He saw me and came over, not smiling. He took the stool next to me, and neither one of us offered to shake hands.

He all but ignored me until he'd placed his drink order, then turned to me. "So what do you want to know about Taylor Cates?" he asked.

Right to the point. Good. I thought. Apparently he wasn't going to mention the night of the party, and I certainly wasn't.

"How did you meet?" I asked.

The bartender brought his drink and he took a swig before setting the glass down. He was sitting facing straight ahead, his forearms on the bar, and only turned his head far enough toward me to answer. "Well, this whole thing with a separate library for the collection sort of caught me off guard. I was on a long vacation in Europe, and when I got back it was all a done deal. The final plans were being made to transfer Chester's collection from the estate to the new library. Apparently some members of the Board felt a little guilty about not having included me in the planning, so they asked me, since I'd done some cataloging for Mr. Burrows, if I would take over the preliminary recruiting and screening of applicants for the library staff. Irving McHam had already hired one, but it was clear he just couldn't do everything. I was glad to help.

"I contacted Mountjoy's library sciences department—that's where McHam had found the first cataloger he hired—and they referred me to the Placement Bureau. I gave them my address for the submission of resumes, and one day less than a week later there was a knock at my front door, and I opened it to find Taylor standing there. He was so eager to get the job, he brought his resume over in person. You have to give a guy like that credit."

I nodded. "So you started dating him, then?" I asked, hoping I sounded non-accusatory.

He looked at me out of the corner of his eye and gave me a suppressed smile. "I'd hardly consider it 'dating,'" he said, "but we did get together a couple of times. As I said, he was really eager to get the job."

Gee, I thought, *if you can move that semi out of the way, I think I'll be able to read between the lines, here.*

"So what else did you know about him?" I asked.

He shrugged. "Not much. He had a pretty rough childhood, I gathered, and while he had a scholarship, he still had to work hard to make it through school. He had a lot of ambition and he was willing to do whatever it took to get ahead."

I took another sip of my drink. "Meaning?" I asked.

"Meaning nothing," he said. "He was a pretty serious guy, but he gave me the impression that once he set his mind to something, he kept at it until he got it. That's one of the reasons I put in a good word for him with Irving McHam, and I was right: Taylor was a damned good cataloger and worked his tail off."

Well, it sounded like a convincing story.

"So that was it as far as your relationship was concerned?" I asked.

He looked at me and cocked his head slightly. "That was it," he said. "And I hardly think our contacts could qualify as a relationship. We both got what we wanted, and that was all there was to it." Apparently realizing how that last sentence might be interpreted, he hastened to add: "He wanted a job, I wanted to help the Burrows get a qualified staff."

"Did you have many contacts with him after he got the job?" I asked.

"Other than running into him a couple of times at the library, not that I can remember," he said.

"At the time of Taylor's death, he was working on the papers of Morgan Butler," I said. "I understand you'd done some preliminary work on them, too, when they were still at the Burrows' home." I actually didn't know that as a fact, but I was following a hunch.

"Butler? Yes, I seem to recall I did some work on them. Several others, too."

"Do you remember finding out anything particularly interesting about Morgan Butler?"

He had both hands around the base of his glass on the bar, and began turning it around, slowly. "Nothing particular that I recall. Like what?"

"Like Morgan Butler's possibly being gay?"

The glass continued to turn. "No. Nothing like that. Of

course I didn't have time to read every single letter. Where did you get that idea?"

"I didn't get it…Taylor did. He approached McHam about it. I looked through some of the letters, but I couldn't find anything other than vibes that he might have been."

Knight shook his head, hands still twirling his glass. "I really wouldn't know about that…and what difference would it make if he were?"

"Point," I said.

He noticed me looking at his hands and immediately picked up his glass for another long swallow, putting the glass back on the bar and folding his hands.

"What did you think of Morgan's manuscripts?" I asked.

"I didn't read them," he said.

"But you looked through them?" I asked.

"Just cursorily," he replied.

"I was curious as to what you thought of them," I said, "one writer of another."

"As I said, I didn't look at them too closely. I had a lot to do. The writing seemed…competent, as I recall. It's been a long time…several years."

"Not too long before your first book came out, if I remember right."

"I don't remember," he said. "But you're probably right. As soon as I found a publisher for *A Game of Quoits*, my first book, I stopped doing cataloging for Mr. Burrows."

"Interesting coincidence," I said, "but a lot of Morgan's letters—the ones with the gay vibes—were to a guy named Scot. One of the main characters in *Fate's Hand* is named Scot."

He looked at me with no expression. "Wow, imagine that," he said. "I wonder how many books have characters named Scott?"

I looked at him closely. "Spelled with only one 't'?" I asked. "Not many, I'd think."

I couldn't really tell in the artificial and dim light of the bar, but I swore I saw him flush for just an instant as he stared into his drink. Finally he turned to me, the flush replaced by a look of what I can only describe as defiance.

"How about that?" he said, his voice tinged with contempt. "I guess it is a pretty small world after all."

"So where did you come up with it?" I asked.

"Well," he said, reaching for his drink, "obviously I must have picked it up subconsciously from Morgan Butler's letters," he said. "I was working on *A Game of Quoits* at the same time as I was cataloging the Butler papers. I guess I liked the name and used it in *Fate's Hand.*"

He picked up his drink and drained it, then looked at his watch.

"Look," he said, "I've got an appointment, and I've really got to go. Are we about through here?"

I nodded. "Yeah," I said. "I appreciate your time. Thanks."

He got up from his stool, took a bill out of his pocket and laid it on the bar, sliding it forward with his empty glass.

"Okay," he said. "And I think you're wasting your time on this Taylor Cates thing. He fell down the steps, he died. Too bad, but life isn't always a mystery novel. Accidents happen."

And with that, he turned and left the bar.

I sat there for a few more minutes, nursing the last of my drink and going over the just-finished conversation. He had a perfectly logical explanation as to why one of his books' characters was named Scot with only one "t". But why, then, had he flushed when I brought it up...if he indeed had flushed at all? Maybe I had just expected him to flush, so assumed I saw a flush when there was none.

I was aware that my mind...like one of those guys making balloon animals at a kid's party...was busily doing something that I couldn't quite recognize yet.

Well, I knew it would show me whenever it was ready. In the meantime, I finished my drink and headed home.

* * *

First thing Tuesday morning I called Marv Westeen. I didn't expect that he'd be home, and I was right. There was a machine, though, so I left a message, including my home number in case he didn't get home until later. I could have called McHam and ask if Westeen had a work number, but decided I could also ask Glen O'Banyon when I spoke to him.

I next tried the number for Zach Clanton, and the phone was answered by a woman: "Clanton residence."

"Is Mr. Clanton in?" I asked.

"May I ask who's calling?"

I told her, adding I believed he might be expecting my call.

"Ah, Mr. Hardesty," whoever it was I was talking to said. "Zachary did mention that you might call, and asked that you leave your number and he'll get back to you."

"Thank you, Mrs. Clanton," I said, taking a chance that it was indeed Mrs. Clanton I was talking to. Since she had referred to 'Zachary' instead of 'Mr. Clanton' I felt fairly confident it probably wasn't the nanny or housekeeper. "Do you have any idea when that might be? I have a rather full schedule today." I lied, but she didn't have to know that, and I didn't want to feel obligated to sit around the office all day just waiting for a call.

"He's golfing at Birchwood this morning," she said, "and should be home around eleven. I'll have him call you when he gets in."

"Thank you," I said again. "I'll expect his call."

We exchanged goodbyes and hung up. *'Golfing at Birchwood,'* eh, I thought. So much for him worrying about where his next meal was coming from—the Birchwood Country Club was the most exclusive in the city.

I'd just finished my second cup of coffee and filled in the last blank on the crossword puzzle when the phone rang. I glanced at my watch: 10:15...too early for it to be Zach Clanton.

"Hardesty Investigations," I said, dropping the pen into my open top middle desk drawer and closing it.

"Dick; Glen." From the sounds in the background I guessed he was at court. "Want to join me for lunch? I gather you have some questions for me."

"Yeah, I do," I said. "I've got a call in to Zach Clanton, who his wife says is playing golf until about eleven—he's supposed to call me then. And I left a message on Marv Westeen's machine...I didn't have a work number for him."

"Ah, sorry," O'Banyon said. "Marv's been devoting all his time to the Hospice Project. The whole thing is more or less his and Bill Peterson's baby. Marv's set up an office in his home, but there is a separate phone line for it. I've got it in my book, and I'll get it to you at lunch, okay? Twelve fifteen at Etheridge's?"

"Sure," I said. "See you there."

William Pearson had mentioned the Hospice Project as the reason T/T was coming into town, but I was impressed to learn that Marv Westeen was a driving force behind it. AIDS was still taking a horrific toll in the gay community, and too many of the seriously ill really had no place to go. A hospice was a relatively new concept, but a terrific idea whose time had definitely come.

I was really hoping to hear from Zach Clanton before I had to leave for lunch, and once again luck was with me. At 11:20 the phone rang.

"Hardesty Investi..."

"This is Zachary Clanton returning your call," the definitely-all-business voice said, cutting me off.

"Thanks for calling, Mr. Clanton," I said. "I was won..."

"I assume you're calling about the accident at the Burrows," he said, "and I can save us both some time by telling you I know nothing whatever about it."

Gee, thanks for the heads-up, I thought. *I was afraid I was going to have to try to figure that out all by myself.* I was more than a little irked at being cut off twice in mid-sentence.

"So you didn't know Taylor Cates?" I asked.

"Never met him, wouldn't know him if I saw him," he said. "And frankly, I think this whole thing is a waste of time and money. It was an accident. The police have accepted it as such. Period."

"Uh," I said, "I'm afraid it's not quite as simple as all that. Cates' death may well have been an accident, but the majority of the Board members want it looked into, just in case, and that's what they've hired me to do."

"Yes, I know," he said. "So do you have any specific questions for me?"

He had me there. "Nothing specific at the moment," I admitted. "I'm just in the process of contacting all the members of the board to find out anything I can about Taylor Cates or the circumstances of his fall—what he may have been doing in that particular part of the cataloging area at that time of night, for example."

"I have no idea," he said. "But my opinion remains that it was an accident and that trying to make something out of nothing is an enormous waste of time and money. Just how long do you intend to drag this thing out?"

While I was tempted to try to reach through the phone lines and grab him by the throat, I kept calm. "I've been hired to determine if Taylor Cates' death was an accident or not," I repeated. "As soon as I make that determination, it is up to the board to decide what to do next, if anything."

"Uh huh," he said. "Well, there's nothing I can tell you."

"I understand you were opposed to the entire idea of the Burrows library, is that correct?"

"That's no secret, obviously. I couldn't see going to all the time and expense of creating an entirely new library from scratch when there are already more than enough well established and well qualified research libraries out there to handle it."

"What do you know of the collection itself?"

"Very little. I'm not particularly a bibliophile, and the subject matter is, frankly, of little interest to me."

"So you're not aware if anything in the collection might be sufficiently controversial to warrant someone's possibly taking action to prevent its becoming public knowledge?"

He snorted. "Hardly! Who cares what's in a bunch of old books? If they've been published, they're public record already."

"I understand there are a number of unpublished manuscripts as well," I said.

"Yes," he said, "and I'll bet most of those were unpublished for good reason…like being a bunch of crap, for example. My uncle would take anything from anywhere as long as it had the word 'homosexual' in it. I'd wager they could take fully 3/4 of the stuff in that collection and pitch it into the trash and nobody would either notice or care."

"So why are you on the board?" I asked.

"Well, somebody had to be there to exercise some fiscal restraint," he said. "If it were left up to my cousin and some of the other board members, they'd have spent every cent of the bequest and then some."

"What do you know of Collin Butler's attempts to have his grandfather's and father's papers removed from the collection?"

"Not much. I…his father's papers, you said? I didn't even know his father had any papers—Collin's never mentioned them."

"You know Collin Butler?" I asked, somehow a little surprised that he might.

"Yes. Known him for years. We played golf together this morning, as a matter of fact." He paused for just an instant. "All I know is that he just wants his grandfather's papers turned over to Bob Jones University, and I can certainly understand his wishes. It's a much more fitting place for them."

"I understand he's threatening a suit against the Burrows to have them removed," I said.

He sighed. "Yes," he said. "Well, the Butler papers are only a very small percentage of the entire collection and certainly not worth going to court over, in my opinion. But I can understand Collin's wanting them back. It is a great source of embarrassment to him to have his grandfather's—and from what you've now told me, his father's—name associated in any way whatsoever with anything hinting of homosexuality. Jerromy Butler was of the old school, and while he made financial arrangements for his wife, he left everything else to Morgan. I wouldn't be surprised if Morgan's bequeathing his father's papers to the Burrows collection wasn't some sort of payback."

"Payback?" I asked.

"Yes. Jerromy Butler had little use for anything or anyone who did not see things the way he did, and sons and fathers often disagree. I'm sure Jerromy made Morgan's life more than a little miserable.

"Anyway, Collin is a graduate of Bob Jones, and is hoping for a seat on their Board of Trustees. The only reason he hasn't already filed suit is because he doesn't want to stir up a lot of controversy at this point in time. I've asked him to let me see if I can convince the board to give the papers up voluntarily. I certainly can't see being dragged into court and incurring huge expenses just to keep one man's writings. But they're being obstinate, and I'm afraid Collin's patience is wearing thin. I can't blame him. "

"Would it be so terrible just to leave them where they are?" I asked. "I mean, in this day and age…"

"They're his," he said. "He wants them. He's entitled to them. But if you're somehow implying he'd push somebody down a flight of stairs to get them, you're out of your mind."

Actually, I hadn't been implying that at all…at least not consciously. And even while it might be an interesting thought, it was also more than a little unlikely that pushing one employee down a flight of steps might convince the Burrows Foundation to give up the papers.

CHAPTER 7

By the time I'd hung up with Zach Clanton, I just barely made it to Etheridge's by 12:15. Being across the street from City Hall, the place was crowded, as always, with lawyers, clerks, and office personnel of the City Building on their lunch hour, but fortunately Glen O'Banyon apparently had a permanently-reserved table and I was surprised to see he was already there.

"Well, this is a first," I said as I slid into the booth, reaching across to shake hands.

"Just got here," he said. "Court got out a few minutes early, which happens about once in every ten blue moons."

The waiter appeared with coffee and a menu—O'Banyon already had his. "I'll be back in a second," the waiter said, and moved off to another table.

We small talked for a minute or two until the waiter came back to take our orders: though we'd talked a bit about it when we met at Hughie's, O'Banyon was curious as to how Joshua was doing and how Jonathan and I were dealing with being de-facto parents.

When we'd ordered, O'Banyon sat back and said: "So how's the investigation going? Anything at all to indicate it was anything but an accident?"

I shook my head. "Nothing definite, but there's an awful lot of tiny arrows pointing in that direction. Maybe it's just an occupational hazard that I always lean toward the 'foul play' scenario, but this just doesn't feel 'accidental' to me."

"So what did you want to ask me?" he said.

"I just talked to Zach Clanton…which is why I was almost late…and found out he knows Jerromy Butler's grandson, Collin. I'd been wondering about him and was wondering if you had any idea just how badly he wanted to get back his grandfather's papers."

"He's pretty adamant about it, obviously. Zach's doing everything he can to keep Butler from going to court, but the interests of the library have little to do with it. I'm afraid Zach still sees the Burrows as an annoying financial drain from his own pocketbook. He's been trying to convince the board to simply give in and return the papers."

The waiter brought our food, and as we ate I filled O'Banyon in on my conversation with Clanton, and also on

what I'd found out about the strong possibility that Morgan
Burrows might himself have been gay.

He looked rather surprised. "Really?" he said. "I had no
idea."

"And from what Zach Clanton said, it appears that Collin
Butler isn't even aware that his father's papers...or some of
them, anyway...are in the collection."

O'Banyon wiped the corner of his mouth with his napkin,
then replaced it in his lap. "Interesting," he said. "I wonder
what they're doing there?"

"Excellent question," I said, suddenly wondering why I'd
never asked it myself. "I've gone through a lot of them, but
only concentrating on the letters he wrote to a service buddy
named Scot, and I didn't see a single direct reference to
homosexuality. The ones I skimmed through, to other people
including his parents, are totally bland: no real emotion on
any subject. I hadn't realized that until just this moment."

If Morgan *was* gay, giving his papers to a collection devoted
to gay history would be pretty clear evidence he was trying
to say something about himself to posterity. And I was also
beginning to suspect that there were more papers than were
currently in the collection. But if that was true, where were
they? What had happened to them?

"Well," I heard O'Banyon saying as I pulled myself back
to the moment, "if Morgan Butler was gay, I wonder if his son
knew about it?"

"Another good question," I said. "Off the top of my head,
I'd think it was pretty unlikely. If Morgan was gay, he was
pretty firmly locked in the closet. I'm sure he never would have
told his parents—most certainly not his father—or his wife.
And Collin was only four years old when Morgan died."

O'Banyon pursed his lips and nodded. "From what I know
of Collin Butler, he takes after his grandfather as far as his
views on gays. He'd really have a hemorrhage if he suspected
his own dad was a *pre*-vert!" He grinned.

"You've met him?" I asked.

The grin turned into a wry smile. "Yes, a couple of times.
The firm's done some legal work for him, but our few meetings
have only been in a business context. He strikes me as being
wound pretty tight. I just recently did something for him, as
a matter of fact."

"But he knows you're on the board of the Burrow's
Foundation, of course?"

He nodded. "I'm sure he must, but he's never mentioned it, and he's apparently comfortable with separating his need for my legal services from his efforts to get the Butler papers returned."

"I really think I'd like to talk to him at some point."

"About what?" O'Banyon asked.

"I'm not sure, exactly," I said. "But I'd really like to know how much he knows about his father. My gut tells me that Taylor Cates' death is related to Morgan's work at the Burrows, and since Taylor had been working with the Butler papers when he died..." I shook my head and sighed. "I don't know, it's probably nothing, but..."

"Well, I'm expecting a call from Collin on the matter I just finished for him, and I suppose I could ask him if he'd be willing to talk to you."

"I'd really appreciate that," I said.

O'Banyon was quiet a moment, then said: "Actually, I gather Morgan Butler and Chester Burrows were close friends at one time. Mr. Burrows was not always a recluse—he began withdrawing just about the time of Morgan Butler's death." He paused and raised an eyebrow. "Hmm," he said, "do you suppose...?"

"Now, wouldn't *that* be a kick in the pants?" I said. "And it just goes to support the strong impression I got from reading between the lines of Morgan's letters."

We both concentrated on our lunch for a minute or so until O'Banyon said: "Well, all this is damned interesting, but where does it leave us on the question of Taylor Cates' death?"

I sighed. "As far as concrete evidence, nowhere. As far as being more and more convinced that it wasn't an accident...well, there's just too many little ducks *not* in a row, here. I can't escape the feeling that something odd was going on. I still haven't talked to Marv Westeen, and I want to talk with Teddy Wilson when he comes into town, and then I want to spend a little more time at the Burrows. The one thing I'm sure of is that Morgan Butler is somehow a key piece in the puzzle. As soon as I've done that, I'll have a better idea of where Morgan Butler's piece falls."

The waiter came by to see if we needed more coffee or wanted dessert, and we declined. Removing our plates, he disappeared, leaving us to finish our coffee.

"Well, if there is anything more you need of me, just ask," O'Banyon said.

"Like you had any doubt?" I said, and we exchanged grins. The waiter returned with the bill, and I reached into my back pocket for my billfold, but O'Banyon waved me down. "You can get the next one," he said, taking a wallet from his jacket pocket.

We finished our coffee and left, exchanging our goodbyes on the sidewalk in front of the restaurant.

* * *

I'd intended to head back to the office to try and reach Marv Westeen again to set up a meeting. He was the last of the people on my contact list, and I suspected that he had closer ties to the library and the collection than the other members. But I found myself once again heading toward the Burrows Library. I did stop for gas along the way, and called Irving McHam to be sure my coming by was okay. I didn't expect him to put up any objection—I was, after all, working for the board—but considered it a matter of courtesy, since he did run the place, and I really didn't want to get too much in the way.

He'd told me to just go to the cataloging room when I arrived, which is what I did.

Janice was at her same table, but I noticed she seemed to be working on a different set of boxes. She told me the cataloging of Butler papers had been completed, and they'd been moved to the stacks.

"Did you want both boxes?" she asked.

"If you would," I said.

She smiled and said: "Why don't you have a seat over there…" indicating a smaller, empty table beside the door…"and I'll have someone get them for you."

I was perfectly capable of getting them myself, but of course I realized it was all just a part of the security policy, and when I saw Janice approaching a guy just emerging from another area of the stacks and realized it was the cute redhead I'd seen upstairs a few days before, I didn't mind at all.

She spoke to him and he looked over at me and smiled, and I nodded and smiled back. Then she returned to her table as he went in search of my request. A minute or so later he came over carrying two new and newly labeled boxes. He was wearing a short sleeved shirt and I noted that carting heavy boxes filled with paper did wonders for the biceps. He placed them on the table in front of me and smiled again... *nice smile,* my crotch observed...and handed me a clipboard with a 4x6 card on it.

"If you'll just sign here," he said, reaching into his shirt pocket for a pen.

I signed and handed the clipboard and pen back to him. He looked carefully at my name. "Dick Hardesty, huh?" he said, his face breaking into a grin.

"That's me," I said.

"I'll bet," he replied.

I usually hate it when people see my name as a double entendre, but I was willing to make an exception in his case.

"If you need anything else, just let me know," he said.

"I'll do that," I said

Oh yeah, do that! my crotch said eagerly.

When he'd gone, I opened the box with the correspondence and carefully began going through the letters, from the very beginning. There must have been 300 letters in all, the bulk of them starting when he was in the navy: there were a considerable number to his parents and several other people in his life, but the first letter to Scot was not until September 3, 1945, apparently right after Morgan had been discharged, and continuing sporadically up until his death—maybe only 30 letters in all, over a nine-year span. Scot had apparently remained in the military, mostly overseas from what I could tell, but there were references in the last few letters to "adjusting to the real world" and "you'll find civilian life..." indicating he may have been getting out of the service. Though all the letters were dated, none included the addresses to which they'd been sent, and I had no idea of what Scot's last name might be. I carefully re-read the letters I'd gone over the first time I'd looked at them, trying to find...something. And in one I did find a sentence which read: "It must be part of the McVickers charm." So Scot's last name was McVickers! I'd almost missed it. But now that I had it, what difference did it make?

Again, all the letters to Scot were pretty innocuous on the surface. But as I read, I became more firmly convinced that what was in the box did not represent all the letters Morgan had written. There were several sentences along the lines of: "as I said in my last letter" or "as I told you," referencing subjects which, on going back, were not *in* previous letters. And if Scot were indeed overseas much of the time, it's unlikely that they could have been in contact by phone. I double-checked the chronological log started by Dave Witherspoon, continued by Taylor Cates, and apparently finished by Janice. Every letter logged, no letter missing. Damn!

I'm sure most people would simply assume any other letters, if there indeed were any, had been either thrown away or lost somehow. But I didn't buy that idea: anyone who would go to the time and effort to make carbon copies of handwritten letters obviously wanted to preserve them as a part of himself. His letters were a reflection of himself, and Morgan Butler didn't strike me as the kind of man who would be casual about something so important to him.

I had glanced through a couple of the letters he'd written to his wife and parents, and while I couldn't put my finger on it, there was definitely a different...*feel*...to his letters to Scot. Damn! Did I think Morgan Butler was gay just because I...for God knows what reason...*wanted* him to be gay? Just because a guy writes another guy doesn't mean he's gay. Something was missing.

That belief was strengthened by two other sentences, buried within separate letters, which again almost skipped notice but somehow caught my eye. One, in June of 1947, said: "...I find writing is becoming more a compulsion than a hobby," and the other, in September of 1952 said: "...up until three again last night, writing."

'Writing' ? I thought. *Writing what?* The few articles and short stories I'd found? There were only two manuscripts in the box, and one of them only went to Chapter 9. Even if he was a very slow writer....

After I'd finished reading and replaced all the letters, I opened the second box, took out the unfinished book manuscript and began reading. Other than the writing style, I hadn't particularly been impressed with what I'd skimmed through on the completed one, the *Scarlet Letter* take-off. So I concentrated on the second book...the one he'd not finished...and found myself pulled into the story almost immediately. The writing was sparse but powerful, and the story gripping. Unlike the characters in the first book, the characters here were real and honest. The story followed an unnamed young sailor from the time of his induction through a bomb attack on his ship off the coast of Italy, where the book suddenly ended. And it included, most interestingly, a strong subplot of his developing friendship with another sailor. I could clearly see where it was heading.

Something was taking shape in the periphery of my mind's eye. I couldn't see it clearly...yet...and straining to see something that can't be seen is an exercise in frustration, so I forced myself to just let it drop. I knew I'd see it when I was ready.

I looked at my watch and saw it was 3:25. Jeezus! I had just barely enough time to get back to the office to check to see if Marv Westeen had returned my call and make it home at my regular time.

Unfortunately, I didn't get a chance to see the redhead again. I merely told Janice I was finished and had to leave, and she gave me a blank 3 x 5 card for me to mark and initial my time out, then told me to just leave the boxes there and she'd see to it that they were returned to the stacks.

* * *

Sure enough, there was a message from Marv Westeen on my office machine, saying he could see me at his home at 9:30 the next morning, if I'd care to come by (I would) and leaving his address. I dialed his number, thinking he might be there, but got his machine and left a message saying I would see him at 9:30.

That done, I picked up the phone book and looked under "McVickers." I knew it was a one in a million chance that there'd actually be a Scot McVickers listed, and I had absolutely no reason to think he might even have been from this area...he was someone Morgan knew in the service. He could be anywhere in the country. Anywhere in the world. And he might not even be alive now.

Five "McVickers" listed. No "Scot". None even with an "S." Oh, well. I put the phone book back in the drawer, tied up a few loose ends around the office, and left for home.

Joshua met me at the front door with an 8x10 black-and-white photograph. "Look what I got, Uncle Dick!" he said.

I took it from him and, while Jonathan was coming in from the kitchen with a watering can for his plants, I took a look at it. Joshua stood about six inches in front of me, the tips of our shoes nearly touching, staring up at me as though I were a redwood. It was a photo taken apparently in the back yard of his Happy Day daycare, and was of the staff and the kids...the two owners, the Bronson sisters, and their helper (holding the youngest of the kids) standing, the rest of the kids sitting on the grass in various stages of inattention. All but Joshua, of course, who was looking directly into the lens and grinning. What a ham.

"Can you see me?" Joshua asked anxiously.

I knelt down just as Jonathan came over, and stared intently at the photo, my brows furrowed, looking back and forth between Joshua and the picture. "Why, no, I can't," I said. "But who is that handsome big boy right there?"

"That's me!" Joshua said, laughing delightedly.

"Well, so it is!" I said, scooping him up and getting to my feet for our traditional group hug. "You're getting so big I hardly recognized you!"

"One of the mothers is a professional photographer," Jonathan said as I set Joshua back on the floor. "She's got a studio—the name and address is stamped there on the back. I think we should have her take a photo of the three of us, don't you?"

A 'family portrait'? one of my curmudgeon-y mind voices scoffed. Jeez, Hardesty!

"I mean," Jonathan continued, talking rapidly as he always did when he anticipated some sort of negative reaction from me, "you said yourself Joshua really is growing fast, and we don't have hardly any photos of the three of us together, and…"

"Okay, okay," I said, I think catching him a little by surprise. "Call her and make an appointment. Try for a Saturday, though."

He grinned, gave me a quick hug, and went to water his plants while I went into the kitchen for my evening Manhattan.

* * *

Marv Westeen's house was a classic two-story, early 1900s affair with a full open front porch across the entire front, complete with a porch swing and hanging baskets of flowers. Very pleasant, though not at all pretentious for an heir to a sizeable fortune. There were three cars parked in the driveway, and I assumed they belonged to volunteers with his Hospice Project office.

I rang the bell, and a moment or so later, the door was opened by a 40-something guy I recognized from the Burrows' opening as Marv Westeen.

"Hi, Dick," he said, pushing the screen door open to let me in. "I hope you don't mind my calling you Dick—I don't think we were ever formally introduced the night of the opening."

I took his extended hand and shook it. Nice, firm grasp.

"Dick's fine," I said. "In fact, I prefer it."

He led me through the small entry foyer into the living room.

"Would you like some coffee?" he asked. "I just made a fresh urn for the gang."

"Sure," I said. "That would be nice."

He smiled. "Come on into the kitchen."

From an open door apparently leading to the basement I heard several voices.

"I've converted my basement rec room into an office," he said, with a heads-up nod toward the open door. "We're doing phone follow-ups to our most recent mass mailing."

He took a cup from an open cupboard above the coffee urn and poured me a cup.

"Cream? Sugar?" he asked.

"Black, thanks," I said.

He handed me the cup, then picked up a half-full cup beside the urn and topped it off.

"Shall we go into the living room, or do you mind sitting at the table?"

I grinned. "I spent most of my childhood at the kitchen table," I said, moving to it and pulling out a chair. "The living room's for 'company.'"

When we were seated, he rested both his forearms on the table, both hands around his cup.

"So what can I tell you?" he asked.

I took a quick sip of my coffee—I'd come directly from home and hadn't had my usual office 'fix'—before answering.

"Anything you know about Taylor Cates, for starters," I said.

"Not all that much," he said. "I talked with him several times during the transfer of Uncle Chester's collection from the estate to the library, and then several more times while the collection was being set up for cataloging. Nice enough guy, though not exactly a life-of-the-party type. Very serious, very concentrated on what he was doing."

"Any idea why anyone might want him dead?" I asked.

He shook his head. "Sorry," he said. "I know he didn't get

along with Dave... Witherspoon..., one of the other catalogers, but I'd hardly think that would be any reason he should end up dead over it."

"But you think his death wasn't an accident," I said, again not making it a question.

He shook his head. "I really don't know," he said, "but considering the circumstances, it seems like it may well not have been."

"Did you know anything about his personal life?" I asked.

Again a head shake. "Nothing."

"I understand he dated Evan Knight a couple times," I said.

He took a sip of coffee before replying. "I'm not surprised," he said. "Evan tends to date just about every good looking young man he comes in contact with, and I did get the impression that Taylor might not have been averse to taking an opportunity to advance himself."

I had my coffee cup about halfway to my lips, but stopped it in mid air. "Meaning?" I asked.

He shrugged. "Meaning nothing, really, I guess," he said. "But as I say Taylor appears to have been a very ambitious young man with a strong drive to succeed. I understand from Evan that Taylor showed up at his door shortly after the job listing was posted at Mountjoy, and knowing Evan...well..." he let the sentence trail off, but I had no doubt where it would have gone had he completed it.

"What's your relationship with Evan Knight?" I asked.

He took another sip of coffee before answering. "I've known him for a number of years," he said, "ever since he started working for Uncle Chester."

"And do you get along okay?" I asked.

"Oh, yes. I really like Evan, I guess. Our personalities and lifestyles are too different for us ever to have become real friends. His moral compass wobbles a bit when it comes to his crotch, and he's pretty much an opportunist. But he really was devoted to Uncle Chester, and he watched out for him as best he could. I'll always be grateful to him for that."

I was curious: "Had he been a writer before he started working for your uncle?"

He looked at me. "Interesting question. I really don't know. I'd never heard him speak of it that I can recall. But I guess a lot of writers play it pretty close to the vest. The first I knew of it was when his first book came out, and the rest, as they say, is history."

"But he kept working for your uncle?"

"Yes. As I say, Evan was really devoted to Uncle Chester. He cut back on his hours pretty dramatically to devote more of his time to writing, but he was with Uncle Chester to the end. That's one reason I was a little surprised when I learned he'd tried to talk Uncle Chester out of bequeathing the collection to what is now the Burrows Library."

"He did?" I asked, surprised. "Any idea why?"

He sighed. "Well, Evan agreed with Zach that it would be better to have the collection go to a more established institution rather than to a private foundation."

"Well, perhaps," I said, "but if it had gone to a university somewhere, it might have tended to get lost in the maze of other collections."

"Exactly!" he said. "Uncle Chester was always very much a loner, driven by his passion for his collection. It was his life. The Burrows is a tribute to that life which would have been diluted in a larger environment."

I had another thought about Evan's possible motivations. "It's none of my business," I said, "but I was wondering if your uncle included Evan Knight in his will?"

"Oh, of course," he said casually. "Somewhere in the neighborhood of $100,000 as I recall."

Nice neighborhood, I thought. But it was a set sum, unlikely to be affected by the $1,000,000 bequest to the Foundation for the library. I could see Zach Clanton's objections to the Burrows Library based on its possible direct effect on how much Zach would walk away with, but with Evan, it was less clear. Maybe it was just his personal feeling, and if so he was entitled to it. But as a gay man, I'd have thought Evan would have been all for the collection staying within the gay community.

"And how do you and Zach Clanton get along?" I asked.

He shrugged. "We're cousins," he said. "We get along, but we've never been what you would call 'close.'"

"I understand he's something of a homophobe," I said, and noted his look of surprise.

"Oh, I wouldn't say that, really," he said. "He just lives in a different world. Always has. He's really had very little exposure to gays, other than through Uncle Chester...who never talked about his homosexuality in front of Zach...and me. And now, being on the Foundation's board...well, the members are all respectable businessmen, so Zach is hardly being thrown naked into a pit of screaming queens. He has no reason to be a homophobe." He paused a moment and gave a small smile. "But then I guess a lot of straights don't need a reason."

He took another sip of his coffee and looked at me. "May I ask what all this has to do with Taylor Cates' death?"

Good question. I heaved a sigh. "Well, I'm trying to get as complete a picture as I can of *all* the circumstances surrounding Taylor's death. I try to consider everything objectively, but there are just too many subtle hints and indications that it was more than an accident. The cause of death was the fall, but the reason he fell is what I'm trying to find."

"And have you?" he asked.

I was quiet for a moment, then said: "I feel I'm getting close. It's fairly obvious that there is somehow a direct link to the Burrows other than it's being where he died. Figuring out exactly what that link might be is the hard part. But the more I learn about the dynamics of the place, both on and beneath the surface, the closer I come to having an answer."

"And I hope you find it," he said. He finished his coffee and indicated my cup with a nod of his head. "Would you like more coffee?"

I recognized it as an exit cue. "Thanks, but no," I said. "I really should let you get back to work. How is the Hospice Project going, by the way?"

"Very well," he said, getting up from his chair and reaching across to take my now-empty cup, which he carried with his to the sink. "The Steamroller Junction benefit should put us over the top for our projected goal."

I got up, too, and pushed my chair back into place against the table. "That's great," I said, and meant it. "I admire you for your efforts, and I'm sure the benefit will be a huge success."

He turned and walked with me to the hallway leading to the front door. "It's a job that needed to be done," he said. "I assume you'll be there?"

"I wouldn't miss it," I replied.

We reached the door and shook hands. "Thank's for your time," I said.

"My pleasure," he said, and I left.

* * *

I'd just finished lunch (a tuna salad sandwich with coleslaw and a carton of milk from the diner downstairs) when the phone rang.

"Hardesty Investigations."

"Hi, Dick. Glen here. I talked to Collin Butler this morning and told him you might want to talk to him. He wasn't exactly sure why, but he says it will be okay for you to contact him if you really need to."

"Great!" I said. "Thanks."

"Any new developments at all since last we talked?" he asked.

"Well, one, sort of," I said. "I'm convinced that some of Morgan Butler's papers are missing, and I found out the last name of the guy I suspect he was involved with was McVickers. But where he might be and how I might contact him, I have no idea. I took a chance and checked the phone book here, and he's not listed."

"Hmm," O'Banyon said. "What did you say his first name was?"

"Scot," I said. "With one 't'."

"Well, I'll be damned," he said. "The Scot I knew spelled his with only one 't', too. Do you suppose…?"

Bingo!

"I'd sure like to find out!" I said. "Do you know where he is now? How can I get in touch with him?"

O'Banyon sighed. "Well, if it *is* the same Scot McVickers I knew, unfortunately you can't," he said. "He died several years ago."

Damn! It was as if he had slammed the oven door on my souffle. I went from elation to depression in a heartbeat.

"But his lover is still alive," O'Banyon continued. "Wayne Powers. We still see each other every now and then. He might be able to tell you if it's the same Scot."

My souffle was back on the rise. "He's here in town?" I asked. "Is he in the book?"

"Yes on both counts," he said. "He lives on Blackhawk Ave. I don't know the number off-hand."

"That's okay," I said. "I'll find it. Thanks again, Glen. You're a lifesaver."

"I do what I can," he said, then: "Ah, I've got another call coming in. Good luck with Wayne."

"Thanks," I said, and we hung up.

I immediately pulled the phone book out of the drawer and looked up Powers, Wayne…328 Blackhawk Ave. Reaching for a pen and a blank sheet of paper, I wrote down the address and number, then dialed it.

No answer, no machine. I copied the number on the bottom of the sheet, tore it off, and put it in my billfold...I'd try him when I got home.

So—another major step forward: Wayne Powers was gay so Scot McVickers had been gay, which pretty much confirmed, in my mind anyway, that Morgan Butler had been gay, too.

And now that I had a possible link between Morgan Butler and Scot McVickers, maybe I might be able to fit a few more pieces into the puzzle.

* * *

Wednesday being Jonathan's class night, I stopped on the way home to pick up some fried chicken—one of Joshua's favorite meals since he could eat it with his fingers. Well, most of it. We drew the line at the mashed potatoes and gravy.

After Jonathan had gone off to school and while Joshua alternately played on the floor and watched TV, I pulled one of Evan Knight's novels—*Chesspiece*—from the bookcase and began reading. Like *Fate's Hand* and *A Game of Quoits*, I'd read it before, and enjoyed it. But that was before I knew Evan Knight and now I was going over it from a slightly different perspective. Knowing what an asshole he was, I was fully prepared to hate the book on second reading. But I didn't. It drew me in as it had the first time. Set in an unnamed city, as I realized were all of his books, in the early postwar years, it evoked a very real feeling of the time—or what I understood of the time. His protagonist, Stan Ledder, was discreetly but obviously gay, as befit the period in which the book was set. As in the other books, the relatively few sex scenes were so well set up that they could leave most of the details up to the reader's fertile imagination without detracting from the impact.

I suddenly was aware that Joshua was being very—and very uncharacteristically— quiet, and I looked up sharply from the book to see him lying on his side on the floor, one arm around Bunny, sound asleep. Glancing at the clock, I saw it was 9:10! Jonathan would be home any minute, and would be less than happy to know I hadn't put Joshua to bed yet. I hurriedly got up from the couch and went over to pick Joshua off the floor.

"Come on, tiger, it's time for bed," I said as I scooped him up.

"No it isn't," he said sleepily.

There was no way I could give him his bath, put him in his pajamas, and get him into bed before Jonathan walked in, so I decided to forego the bath and took him directly into his bedroom. Helping a groggy four-year-old undress and get into his pajamas was something of an adventure, but we managed. Lucky for me he was too sleepy to demand a bedtime story, and I'd just closed his door—as always leaving it open a crack—when Jonathan came in.

"Sorry I'm late," he said. "I was talking to the instructor after class."

We hugged, and I said: "Building brownie points for a better grade?"

He grinned. "Hey, it can't hurt!...Joshua behave himself while I was gone?"

We walked to the sofa and sat down. "I'm thinking of nominating him for sainthood," I said. "I doubt he'll make it, but it's worth a shot."

He noticed *Chesspiece* on the coffee table.

"Aha!" he said. "Another Evan Knight convert in the making?"

"Well, I have to admit, it is pretty absorbing," I replied.

He leaned forward to pick up the book. "You know, I really admire writers," he said. "They make up whole different worlds. And one of the things I find fascinating about Evan's books is that he doesn't talk at all like he writes."

"What do you mean?" I asked, though it instantly struck me that, from what few words I'd exchanged with Evan Knight, Jonathan was right.

"Well," he said, "I've talked to him quite a bit, and he doesn't really talk at all like the characters in his books talk. The words he uses and the way he expresses things—they're just so...different between what he writes and the way he is."

"I'd imagine that's the way it is with a lot of writers," I said.

"Maybe," he said. He was thumbing through the pages and stopped at one point and grinned. "Did you get to this part, yet?" he asked.

I leaned toward him to see what part he was referring to.

"Where he gets seduced by the gardener in the greenhouse?" he asked. "I really liked that part. Subtle, but you can read between the lines pretty easily. I like sexy parts."

I put my hand on his leg. "So do I," I said with a grin. "I

haven't gotten there yet, but *you're* a gardener, sort of, and with all these plants around here, this is almost a greenhouse. And I'm eminently seducible. Wanna show me what happens next?"

He put the book down, got up from the sofa, and held out his hand. I got up, turned out the lights, and followed him into the bedroom.

CHAPTER 8

I felt a little guilty, Thursday morning, that I hadn't tried to reach Wayne Powers the night before, so I tried as soon as I got to the office, even before making coffee. No answer. The more I thought about the case, the more I wanted to talk with him, to see if he could shed any light on Scot McVickers' relationship with Morgan Butler and, by extension, on the missing letters and what might be in them. I assumed Powers and Scot had gotten together sometime after Morgan's death, so I couldn't be sure that Powers would know anything at all about it. Some guys don't like to bring up past loves to current partners.

Okay, I know that it seems I was going in two different directions at once here. I was supposed to be concentrating on whether Taylor Cates' death was an accident or not. But if it wasn't an accident, I'd have to find out who did it and why, and the 'why' kept snapping me back to Morgan Butler.

The thoughts that had been flitting around the periphery of my mental vision were becoming much more clear, and certain pieces of the puzzle were showing themselves to me, as if saying:"I go *here*, stupid!" I sat at my desk drinking coffee—I hadn't even thought about reading the newspaper yet, which was very unlike me—and going over the pieces of what I knew, comparing them with the pieces of what I suspected.

Morgan Butler was a writer, and from the looks of at least his unfinished manuscript, a darned good one. But I'd bet the farm that what was in the Burrows collection was not everything he'd written.

Well of course there were more manuscripts, one of my mind voices observed casually. *You've just been reading one.*

Of course! How stupefyingly dense could I have been? How could I not have seen it the first time I came across the two manuscripts left in the collection? Why didn't I catch on the minute I checked the spelling of 'Scot' in *Fate's Hand*? Of *course* there were more manuscripts! And they were being published with Evan Knight's name on them!

Evan Knight had worked for Chester Burrows. He had ready access to everything in the collection. He had to have come across Morgan Butler's papers and found the manuscripts and simply stolen them! Who was to know? Who could prove it even if they suspected it? How could *I* prove it? Morgan Butler was long dead and it's probable that the only person he ever told about his writing was Scot, who was also now dead. He certainly wouldn't have told his homophobic father, or admitted his homosexuality to his wife. (Was she still alive? I'd have to check.)

With all the principals involved either definitely or most likely dead, Knight had gambled—at excellent odds—on Morgan's having been so uptight about anyone finding out he was gay that he not only would never have tried to have his books published, but probably would not even let anyone else see them. Except, perhaps, Scot McVickers…if I were right about what I suspected between him and Scot.

I knew next to nothing about Morgan Butler, but I sensed from his letters—and I was positive, now, that a lot of *them* were missing, too—that he was the kind of guy who, especially given the times in which he lived, was locked in the closet by circumstances. Writing would have been the only way he had to set himself free.

And no wonder the books bearing Evan Knight's name portrayed the sense of time so clearly. It was Morgan's time, not Knight's!

I'd realized from the start that Morgan put his own papers in with his father's as part of his bequest to the Burrows as a way to preserve as much of his inner self as he could—he made carbon copies of handwritten letters, for God's sake! And knowing Chester Burrows' collection centered on the subject of homosexuality, it was also Morgan's way of finally coming out to the world. The fact that none of his papers currently in the collection even mentioned the "G" word was another strong indication that they weren't all there.

And following that nebulous string of conjectures, Taylor Cates' death became more clearly the center of the whirlpool. Since Taylor had been working on the Butler papers at the time of his death, perhaps he somehow figured it out. Irving McHam had said Taylor was particularly animated just before his death.

Would/could Evan Knight possibly have found out or suspected that Taylor knew something and resorted to murder to keep his secret?

Talk about building air castles! Speculation isn't fact.

But if there were a key to converting speculation *to* fact, the one living person who might have it would be Wayne Powers. A long shot, but….

* * *

Patience, I've often said, is not one of my greater virtues, and I was more than a little frustrated by the fact that it was, at the moment, my only option. There was nothing more I could do until I talked to Wayne Powers and, the coming Saturday, to T/T when I picked him up at the airport. If I got nothing from those two contacts, I was really going to be up a creek.

I left the office a little early and was sitting in the living room reading *Chesspiece* when Jonathan and Joshua got home. I could tell from the fumbling at the lock that Joshua had insisted on opening the door himself, and I had to admit he was getting better at it, though it still took several seconds. As usual, I'd been so caught up in reading that I'd lost all sense of time. Plus the fact that I had been reading with the new perspective provided by my new certainty that *Chesspiece* had been written by Morgan Butler and not by Evan Knight. As I read, I couldn't understand how I didn't pick up on it sooner. It *fit* what little I knew of Morgan Butler: I felt, admittedly perhaps in hindsight, that I could recognize a definite similarity in writing style between the books Evan Knight had published as his own and the unfinished manuscript and more casual of Morgan's letters at the Burrows.

I could be wrong, I suppose. But I knew I wasn't.

The door opened and Joshua raced into the room, of course leaving the key in the lock for Jonathan to remove. I put the book on the coffee table and got up for our group hug.

"We're going shopping!" Joshua announced happily as I was in the process of picking him up for the hug.

"We are?" I asked, having no idea what that was all about.

We completed our hug and I set Joshua back on the floor before Jonathan said: "I called June Schramm…she's the mother from Happy Day I told you about who has the photo studio…and got us an appointment for 11 Saturday. I figured we could get Joshua something nice, and maybe I could pick up something to wear for the benefit Saturday night. And you and Joshua really should get a haircut, and…"

"…and I've got to pick T/T up at the airport Saturday at 2," I interrupted, following him into the kitchen. "When are we supposed to get all this done? It's already Thursday."

"Easy," he said, reaching into the cupboard for my Manhattan glass and a jelly glass for Joshua's newly-favorite pre-dinner libation, cherry Kool-Aid. "I'll take Joshua to the barber on the way home tomorrow—he may not like it, but he's going. You can meet us there or maybe go sometime during the day...that'd save us a little time—then I'll treat us to dinner at Cap'n Rooney's, and we can go to Marston's to look for clothes...they're having a sale."

He'd kept talking as he took ice cubes, the pitcher of Kool-Aid, and a coke for himself out of the refrigerator, and I listened while I got out the bourbon and sweet vermouth for my Manhattan.

"Got it all figured out, eh?" I said.

He looked back over his shoulder with a very serious expression and said: "Hey, I'm more than just a pretty face, you know."

I reached out with my free hand and grabbed him by the back of the neck, giving him a quick squeeze. "Modesty being your only flaw," I said, and we both grinned.

"Where's my Kool-Aid?" Joshua demanded from the kitchen door.

* * *

Immediately after we finished dishes, I went to the phone and dialed Wayne Power's number, which I hoped I'd memorized since I left the piece of paper I'd written it on at the office.

"Hello?" a male voice said after the second ring.

"Wayne Powers?" I asked.

"Yes...?"

"Mr. Powers, my name is Dick Hardesty, and I understand you knew a Scot McVickers."

There was only a slight pause before: "Yes, I knew Scot. He's been dead several years, now."

"I know," I said, "and I'm really sorry for your loss. I'm a private investigator, and Glen O'Banyon told me you might possibly have some information on one of Mr. McVickers' friends from a long time back...Morgan Butler."

A definitely longer pause. "I'm afraid I can't help you," he said, but the tone of suspicion in his voice told me differently. "What, exactly, are you trying to find out?"

"Well, it's all a bit complicated," I said, realizing just how true that statement was. "But let's say it's something of a 'family' matter. I wonder if it might be possible for us to meet and talk for a few minutes person to person."

"By 'family' you mean…" he began.

"Yes," I assured him. "I'm gay; I know Scot was gay, and I'm pretty sure Morgan Butler was gay, too. As I say, it's all too complicated to go into over the phone, and I really would like to meet with you at your convenience. I gather you work during the day?"

"I'm retired," he said, "but I do volunteer work for the AIDS Hospice Project. I'm not going in tomorrow, though—I'm having some electrical work done here on the house. I suppose if you'd care to come by around eleven or so, we could talk for a bit."

"That would be great," I said. "I really appreciate it."

"You have my address?"

"Yes…328 Blackhawk Ave., right? I'll see you there at eleven. And thank you."

"So," Jonathan said when I'd hung up, "you can get a haircut during the day, then?"

"I really need one?" I asked.

He gave me a raised-eyebrow look. "You need one," he said. "Really. Trust me."

* * *

I went in to the office Friday morning just long enough to check the mail and the answering machine, read the paper, do the crossword puzzle, and drink a couple cups of coffee before heading out for a haircut—a close look in the mirror while shaving had convinced me that Jonathan was right—before my meeting with Wayne Powers.

Powers' house was in an older part of town of basic, solid, American middle class homes built between the World Wars. 328 Blackhawk Ave. was a comfortable, story-and-a-half bungalow with a well-kept lawn and a tradesman's van—this one belonging to Jorgensen's Electric—in the drive. I parked on the street and walked to the small, pilastered porch. I rang the bell and waited. When there was no response, I rang it again. I was about to try a third time when the door opened by a pleasant looking guy in his late 50s or early 60s, balding, with a short mostly-grey beard.

"Mr. Hardesty," he said, pushing the screen door open. "I'm sorry, I was in the basement with the electrician and didn't hear the doorbell. Please, come in."

He stood partly aside, still holding the screen door open, as I entered, to be greeted enthusiastically by a large brown retriever.

"Andy," he said by way of introduction as I bent over to pet him...Andy, not Powers...and rub his ears. "Ferocious beast, as you can tell," Powers said."Would you like some coffee?" he asked as he closed the door. "I just made a fresh pot for the electrician and was going to have some more myself."

"That would be nice," I said. "Thanks."

He and Andy led the way to the kitchen, where Powers pretty much re-enacted the same coffee-offering ritual I'd gone through at Marv Westeen's.

"Cream and sugar?" he asked.

"Black is fine," I replied.

He opened a cabinet drawer and took out a couple of coasters, then gestured back down the hall in the direction we'd just come. "We'll probably be more comfortable in the living room," he said, again leading the way.

When we were seated, me on the couch, Andy directly in front of me demanding attention, and Powers on a chair facing me across a large, round coffee table, he smiled and said: "Now, what's this all about?"

Without going into too much detail I told him I'd been hired by the Burrows Library board of directors to investigate the possibility of some documents—specifically those of Morgan Butler—having been removed from the collection without authorization. I explained that I'd read those of Morgan's letters which were still there, and that I'd immediately sensed a special bond between Morgan and Scot McVickers.

I asked if he knew anything at all about their relationship.

He cupped his coffee in both hands, holding it just about at chin level, and looked into it as if it were some sort of crystal ball, then looked up at me and nodded.

"Yes," he said with a small smile. "Morgan was the love of Scot's life," he said softly. "Please don't get me wrong. Morgan had died two years before Scot and I met, and we were together more than twenty years, so I had no reason at all to be jealous. We were devoted to one another, but Scot never stopped loving Morgan, and I understood."

Not knowing exactly what sort of response to make to that, I plunged ahead. "Scot was in the service at the time Morgan died, am I right?" I asked. "I recall one of Morgan's later letters to Scot—he kept copies of all his letters—referring to Scot's getting out of the military?"

He nodded. "He was leaving so that he and Morgan could be together. But Morgan was married, as I'm sure you know. From what I understand, Morgan was totally dominated by his father...I'm sure he married—and I suspect had a child—only at his father's insistence. I can imagine how thoroughly miserable he had to have been, having to pretend to be something and someone he was not. One of the reasons Scot had reenlisted in the navy was because Morgan got married. It nearly ended their relationship. Scot obviously didn't approve, and he was angered by Morgan's refusal to stand up to his father. But he could never break it off entirely, and he hoped Morgan would eventually gather the courage to defy his father and end a marriage that was causing both him and his wife endless pain. And the fact that they had a son together made it even harder on both of them."

He took a long sip of his coffee. "Morgan seemed to be moving in that direction, so much so that Scot decided to leave the service and come back home to be with him. And then Morgan's father died suddenly, and Morgan began talking about leaving his wife so that he and Scot could be together. Scot hoped his presence would give Morgan that final measure of courage he needed. But..." he paused, looking again into his coffee.

"But Morgan killed himself," I said, completing his sentence for him. Andy nuzzled my knee with his head, and I reached out to pet him.

Powers nodded. "I don't think Scot ever fully understood just how conflicted Morgan was. His father had ruled his life in ways I'm sure few people could understand. Morgan loved Scot. He wanted desperately for them to be together. But to defy his father, even after his death...to go against everything his father stood for...well, he apparently, at that last terrible moment, took the only way he could see to relieve all the pressures."

There was no hint of any of this in the letters in Morgan Butler's file except for that single letter referencing Morgan's love for his son. I was frankly surprised that Powers knew so much about Morgan, and said so. "Did Scot discuss all this with you?" I asked, thinking that he would have been more than a little insensitive if he had.

He shook his head. "Oh, no," he said. "Scot never said very

much about his relationship with Morgan at all...I could tell it hurt him even to think of it, and he respected me far too much to let me know how strongly he felt about Morgan. But I knew, and after Scot's death, I found Morgan's letters...."

Yes! I thought, explosively.

"Everything's in there," he continued, "including that last, terrible note..."

"Note?" I asked.

"Yes," he said. "His last words to Scot. It was in effect a suicide note. And by the time Scot got it, it was too late."

I felt as if I'd just stuck my finger in a light socket.

"And you still have them?" I asked, even though he had just said he did.

He nodded.

I had to keep my eagerness under control, but it wasn't easy. "Did the letters mention Morgan's other writing?" I asked.

He leaned forward to put his coffee cup and the coaster on the coffee table.

"Oh, yes," he said. "He said many times that writing was his way of hanging on to his sanity. He used writing to create a world that couldn't exist for him in real life. He apparently wrote constantly... novels, I gather, but I'm not sure what type or how many. He said he could never dare to even try to have them published because, while he didn't come right out and say so, I got the impression his protagonists were based upon his secret self, and quite probably gay. Actually, I find it very interesting that Morgan never once used the word 'gay' in a single one of his letters. He didn't have to, of course, but I found it odd that even with Scot he was so uptight about it. Maybe he did in his writings, but I wouldn't know."

"He didn't send any of his writings to Scot?" I asked.

"No," he said. "I'm sure Scot would have loved for Morgan to have shared them, but he understood. Morgan was undoubtedly afraid they might somehow fall into someone else's hands and his true self would be exposed. Even in his letters, except for that last note, he tries so hard not to let his true feelings show, but they certainly wouldn't fool anyone with even an ounce of perception."

"And Morgan's being so uptight didn't bother Scot?" I asked.

Powers smiled. "Oh, I'm sure it did," he said. "Scot was always totally comfortable with his own sexuality. But he understood Morgan, and he didn't have to be told how Morgan felt about him. He was quite good at reading between the lines."

"Why did you save them, if I may ask?" I said.

"Because Scot saved them," he said. "They were important to him, and he kept them despite Morgan's frequent instructions to destroy them immediately after reading them. He was so afraid someone might find out about who he really was. Terribly sad, really. But for me to dispose of them when Scot couldn't would be…well, you know…."

I knew, and that knowledge made my next question a bit of a gamble. "Would you allow me to see them? They may hold a key to what I'm looking for."

He was silent for a long moment, and then sighed. "No one else has ever seen them," he said. "And of course I'd never show them to anyone who wasn't…" He didn't say *gay,* but he didn't have to. I understood, and just nodded. "But if you think seeing them might somehow be helpful to you, of course."

"Would you prefer I read them here, or may I take them with me?" I asked.

He smiled. "There are rather a lot of them," he said. "You can take them with you, but…"

"I'll take good care of them," I interjected, "and will get them back to you as soon as I've read them."

He smiled. "I'd appreciate that," he said, then looked at me rather sadly. "I hope you understand…"

"I do," I said. "Completely."

"Would you like me to get them for you now?" he asked.

"If you don't mind, please," I said. "I don't want to take up too much of your day."

"Time is one thing I have plenty of," he said, as he got up. "If you'll excuse me a moment, I'll be right back."

The minute he left the room, my mind started racing so fast my thoughts were stumbling over each other in anticipation. Exactly what I expected the letters to tell me, I had no idea, other than perhaps to somehow provide incontrovertible proof that the books Evan Knight published under his own name and profited handsomely from had actually been written by Morgan Butler. How that confirmation would lead me closer to knowing whether Taylor Cates' death was not an accident, I wasn't sure. The obvious link/conclusion would be that Taylor Cates had somehow found out what Evan was up to, and Evan had killed him to keep his secret.

But why, then, hadn't Evan simply have disposed of all of Morgan's papers? Why just leave a relative few? Probably to hedge his bets. He couldn't be sure that there weren't other records somewhere that would show Morgan Butler donated his own papers with those of his father's. And in case anyone did know that Morgan wrote, he left the two manuscripts: the completed one apparently wasn't that good anyway, and the unfinished work, though showing a lot of potential, wasn't that far along that Evan could have finished it himself.

My attention was snapped back to the present when Powers re-entered the room with a small hinged metal box which he set on the coffee table in front of me. He took a seat beside me on the couch and pushed the small button which opened the box. There had to have been well over a hundred letters in there, all neatly opened and laid flat, each one paper-clipped to its envelope.

"September 3, 1945 to August 12, 1953…the day before Morgan killed himself," Powers said.

We were both quiet for a moment until my next question made me break the silence.

"They met in the service, then?" I asked, and Powers shook his head as he closed the lid of the box, which made a small, metallic 'click' as it locked.

"No," he said, "actually they'd gone to high school together. Scot was something of what they call a jock nowadays, and Morgan apparently had a crush on him but never did anything about it—there's a joking reference or two to it…veiled, of course…in a couple of the letters. I became quite good at reading between the lines, too."

He smiled and looked at me. "Interesting, isn't it, that I find comfort in the words of someone I never met…someone who loved Scot as much as I did?"

"Did Scot make copies of the letters he sent to Morgan?" I asked, and Powers laughed.

"Oh, no!" he said. "Scot wrote everything in longhand and just dashed it off. He'd never have taken the time to even think about making a copy. And I'm quite sure Morgan would never have dared to keep them, much as I imagine he would like to have." He paused and his face grew serious. "I suppose that's another reason I keep Morgan's letters. I see Scot through his eyes, and it reaffirms my own memories of him."

"Mr. Powers?" a male voice called from somewhere in the house...I assumed the basement. "I'll be right there," Powers called back, rising from the couch. I echoed his movement. "Well, I really should go," I said. "I very much appreciate your cooperation in all this, and I'll have the letters back to you in a day or so, if that's all right."

Andy, who had been lying quietly on the floor with his head on his paws, his eyes moving back and forth between Powers and me as we talked, also got up, ready to perform his duty as guardian and escort.

Powers reached down to pick up the box and hand it to me. "Take your time," he said. "It's not as though I read them every day. Just call when you're finished. I'm home most evenings."

He and Andy walked me to the door, where I exchanged a handshake with Powers and gave Andy one last ear-tussle, and left.

* * *

I spent the afternoon at the office reading the letters Morgan Butler had written Scot McVickers those many years ago, and it was as if I were looking over Morgan's shoulder as he wrote them. Though I was intensely curious about that last letter in particular, Scot had kept them in chronological order, and I forced myself to read them in the order they were written. I could sense Morgan's intensity and, under it, his love for Scot. The whole relationship was there—at least Morgan's version of it. It just took careful reading—including Morgan's desperate attempts to explain, without actually saying what he obviously meant, why he had gotten married. Under the bluster was the regret, and the stern hand of Jerromy Butler.

These weren't the treacly love letters of some moonstruck teenager. The words "I love you" never appeared. Powers was right...Morgan tried very hard not to let his feelings show, but they were clearly there, just beneath the surface. When he wrote of Scot, or reminisced about some shared experience, there was an almost palpable sense of longing, and I got the impression of someone terribly lost for whom Scot was his only contact with a world he wanted so badly but felt he could never have. Maybe it was just me reading what I wanted to read into them. But I doubted it.

I must admit I'd been a little puzzled by how two guys apparently so much in love could have tolerated being apart for so many years. But in the letters there were references to several meetings during Scot's annual leaves—including one meeting in New York. The letters leading up to each reunion were filled with barely muted anticipation, and those after with fond re-tellings of incidents during their time together, and an almost tangible sadness. How Morgan managed to hide the true nature of these meetings from his father—and later his wife—I had no idea, but he did it, and I took an odd comfort in the knowledge that their affair was not totally without the opportunity to hold each other.

One thing was for sure: there were many more letters to Scot than were now at the Burrows, and the gay undertones were far stronger than any of the letters left in the collection. Obviously the letters still in the Burrows collection had been carefully culled to remove anything that might give anyone the idea that Morgan Butler was gay.

August 12, 1953
Scot:
Never forget that I love you, now and forever. Forgive me.

Morgan

I sat staring at those sixteen words while the romantic in me ran roughshod over my emotions. I felt an overwhelming sense of sadness...for Morgan, for Scot, and for some strange reason, for myself.

But when I finally pulled myself back to reality and started reading them again, it struck me how few of them I could recall having seen in the Burrows files. I was looking carefully for something, and I hadn't a clue of what that something might be. But somewhere in the back of my mind, I knew.

It was nearly three thirty. Getting time to go home. Still...I'd know what it was when I saw it and cursed myself for having been distracted the first time through. And then I found it:

"I had a dream last night about the night we got lost in the fog on our way back to the ship. We were so drunk we couldn't see straight. And then that little old lady suddenly appeared by that ornate fountain—remember?

—and she didn't say a word but just pointed? How could she know where we were going? But she was right, and we got back to the pier just in time for the last liberty boat. You swore she was a ghost, and I just laughed at you. I should have known better. And I never forgot it, obviously."

I left the office early and headed home. I'd arranged to meet Jonathan and Joshua at the barber shop so we could go clothes shopping directly from there, but I had to go home first. I couldn't wait to see if I was right.

The minute I walked into the apartment, I went directly to the bookcase and took out *Chesspiece*, thumbing quickly through the pages, looking for...

Aha! Page 97:

"The fog was so thick I couldn't see ten feet in front of me and, apparently having taken a wrong turn coming out of the bar, I had no idea where my hotel might be. Nothing like being drunk in a strange town and not knowing where you are. I continued walking, looking for something familiar, and I suddenly made out an ornate fountain on a sort of island in the middle of the street. As I got closer, a little old lady appeared out of the fog, and pointed to my left. She didn't say a word, and I hadn't asked her anything. I don't know how she could know what I wanted, but I staggered off in the direction she indicated, and within two blocks found my hotel. I swear to this day she must have been a ghost."

Got'cha, Knight!

CHAPTER 9

Okay, I had him. Now what was I going to do with him? Being able to prove he had stolen another man's work was one thing; proving he had anything to do with Taylor Cates' death was another. It was pretty obvious, to me at least, that Cates had somehow made a connection between the manuscripts that *should* have been in with Morgan Butler's papers and the books Evan Knight had published as his own. But how could Taylor have known? From the letters still in the box it would be very difficult to figure out. And what about the missing letters? Had Taylor taken them? Not likely. My first guess was that Evan had removed them when he stole the manuscripts: there were just too many gay undertones and references in them to writing and the time Morgan spent on it. Neither of the manuscripts left in the collection had a gay theme, as the books Knight stole did—though the unfinished work was, I felt, heading there. Knight had to leave *some* letters in the file, so he left only the ones he thought wouldn't tip anyone off, and probably destroyed the rest. But then how had Taylor figured it all out?

The phone's ringing pulled me back to reality, and I glanced at my watch: nearly 5:00!! Damn! I was supposed to have been at the barber shop fifteen minutes ago!

I hastily picked up the phone.

"Hardesty Investigations," I said, though I was pretty sure who was on the other end of the line.

"Hi," Jonathan said. "My name's Jonathan. Remember me?"

"I'm sorry, Babe," I said. "I was just on my way out the door. I got tied up."

"Yeah," he said, "I figured that. Joshua's done with his haircut, so why don't you just meet us at the mall? There's a Grandma's Kitchen a couple doors down from Marston's, and we can go eat first. I'd say we could hold off until after we shop, but Joshua's already doing his 'starving child' number. He's a natural for Broadway."

"Takes after his Uncle Jonathan, obviously," I said. "See you there in about 15 minutes. Wait for me in front of the restaurant, okay?"

We hung up and I left the office.

* * *

Saturday morning Joshua helped Jonathan make scrambled eggs—I don't think they started out that way—for breakfast, then we took our time getting ready for our appointment at the photo studio. Jonathan had insisted we buy Joshua a sport coat and a white shirt and bow tie, and I must say he looked great in it. I was struck by how much he looked like his dad, Samuel, who, with his mother Sheryl, kept guard over him from a photo near the boy's bed. Jonathan frequently commented on the resemblance, and I knew it brought him a lot of both comfort and pain.

At Jonathan's insistence, we took along two sets of clothes: one set for a formal "portrait" type shot with coats and ties, and one for a more casual, "family" group shot. "This is something we'll want to have forever," Jonathan said. "We might as well do it right." I guess he was right. We wore the casual set to the studio lest Joshua find some way to get his new sport coat wrinkled or dirty. And, of course, Joshua insisted that Bunny be included in the festivities.

The shoot went surprisingly well, and Joshua confirmed Jonathan's assessment of a possible future on the stage or silver screen by playing to the camera like a pro. His only moment of rebellion came when the photographer suggested that perhaps Bunny might like to be absent from one or two of the variety of shots she took.

We were in and out in less than an hour.

Even so, we just had time for lunch before I had to leave for the airport to pick up T/T. I hated to stick Jonathan with the other Saturday chores, and I knew he would have liked to come to the airport with me—as of course would Joshua, had we mentioned the word "airport" in his presence—but Jonathan understood that this was more business than pleasure trip and Joshua's being there would be a distraction. So he arranged to go to the laundry and do a few more Saturday-type errands while I was gone. He also said he'd call the gang to coordinate what time we were to meet at Steamroller Junction for the benefit.

* * *

I got to the airport at a little after 1:30 and was relieved to note on the schedule board that Delta flight 444 was due to arrive on time, Gate 5. I bought a cup of coffee and wandered toward Gate 5 to wait. No matter how often I go to airports, the almost palpable air of anticipation always impresses me. I suppose that's true in any place devoted to comings and goings of large numbers of people: bus stations, train stations, boat docks. Even if you weren't going anywhere, you could pretend.

Sure enough, at 1:55 there was a flurry of activity outside the window, and the large, graceful form of a 727 glided majestically up to the ramp, which moved out to greet it. I wondered, as I always did, how planes managed to look like they were either brand new or just freshly washed. Maybe the clouds do that to them.

I allowed my mind to idle away in neutral until the doors opened and, like an uncorked bottle of champagne, the passengers began flowing into the terminal. Hugs and handshakes and hurryings, clothes bags flung over shoulders, kids in tow. All teetering on the brink of confusion but not quite crossing over. And then through the swirl of people I saw T/T approaching, like a yacht through a bay full of fishing boats.

He was in his full Teddy Wilson mode—a large, pleasant-looking overweight black man who was just another face in an airport-terminal crowd. Few if any hints of the flamboyant Tondelaya O'Tool, his larger-than-life drag-queen persona. I moved forward toward him, and as he spotted me his face broke into a huge grin and he flung his arms wide in a "come to mama" motion, nearly hitting a cute college-type who expertly ducked out of the way and kept going.

"Well, honey-chile, I do declare" he said as we exchanged a hug, "you just keep gettin' sexier and more handsome every time I see you!" He looked around at the surrounding crowd. "Why, where's that delightful boy of yours? Jonathan, right? You got him tied up to the bedpost at home?"

"Long story," I said and, as we began moving toward the baggage area, I filled him in.

For someone who was only going to be in town for two days, it looked like he'd brought more luggage than Jonathan and I, combined, had taken on our two week visit to New York. There were two huge garment bags, a suitcase, another suitcase, and two large hat boxes. "A lady's got to look her best," he explained.

It wasn't until we were in the car and heading into town that I had a chance to broach the subject of Taylor Cates and his death, and not being able to think of a clever or subtle way to segue into it, I just enjoyed T/T's endless string of stories and experiences on the road and waited for a chance to jump in when I could. Luckily, I didn't have to.

Suddenly, his mood changed, and he turned to look at me. "So what did you want to know about Taylor?" he asked.

"Anything you can tell me," I said. "What kind of guy was he?"

T/T sighed heavily. "He was a fine young man, darlin'," he said. "Like I told you on the phone, I knew him since he was just a tiny little thing. His daddy was dead, and it was just him and his mom. She worked cleanin' house for a rich old white lady during the day and as a cook in a diner at night. They lived next door to us on Freemont Street near Summit, and you know what kind of area that is. It wasn't easy for either one of us. I was only a teenager myself, and I didn't have many friends—fat, gay black kids in the ghetto seldom do. Taylor wasn't fat, but he was gay. I swear I don't know how we got out of there alive.

"Anyway, Taylor used to follow me around while we were still kids. I guess he needed a man in his life, and I was as close to it as he had. We both had one thing in common: we wanted to get out of the world we were born into, and we both did, though in different ways. The good Lord looked after us both, and Taylor was blessed when that white lady his momma worked for helped him get a scholarship to college. She was a fine woman. Her own son had died, and she just sort of took Taylor under her wing."

"Any chance that she's still alive now?" I wondered aloud. "I might like to talk with her, if she is. Do you remember her name, by any chance?"

T/T thought a moment, then sighed. "Right on the tip of my tongue," he said, "but I can't think of it for the life of me. I don't imagine she could still be alive…she was pretty up there in years. Her grandson's still around, though, I'm sure, and I'm sure he could vouch for Taylor's character, if you think it needs vouchin'."

I grinned. "It's not a matter of vouching for anything. It's just for me to get a better idea of what other people might have known about him that you don't. Do you recall the grandson's name?"

He shook his head. "Same last name's hers," he said. "Dang! Why can't I remember it?"

"Well, if you do, could you let me know? It probably doesn't matter, but I would like to check out every possible angle, if I could."

"I'll do that, darlin'," he said. He was quiet a moment, looking out the window, then continued. "That boy worked his tail off to make somethin' of himself, and he did! I was so proud of him when he told me he'd got a job at such a fancy place."

"Do you know of anyone else I might contact about him?" I asked. I was really curious about what sort of person Taylor Cates may have been. What little I'd heard had varied with the person I was talking to.

Still looking out the window, T/T said: "Not really, darlin'. He didn't really have many friends. He was quiet. Real quiet until you got to know him, and not many people did. He fought so hard against his ghetto days that I'm sure some people thought he was uppity. He had his own way of lookin' at things, and sometimes he could be a little...well..." he glanced at me out of the corner of his eye and grinned "...uppity."

"Did he ever tell you about people he worked with, who he was dating, that kind of thing?"

T/T shook his head. "Not too much. Like I say, he was pretty quiet. I do know he didn't get along with one of the guys he worked with...a 'David' somebody, I think. Taylor took his work *very* serious, an' he felt this David didn't. He didn't like that at all."

"Did he ever say anything specific?" I asked.

"Huh-uh. I could just tell every time he mentioned that boy's name it was like he was suckin' on a lemon."

"How about people he was seeing?"

He looked at me. "I don't think he had much of a social life," he said. "I do know he was seeing some writer dude for a little while, but nothin' ever came of it."

"Did he say why?" I asked.

He sighed. "No, and I didn't press him. Taylor didn't take to bein' pressed."

"Did he mention anything about his work? Something he may have found out in the course of his cataloging?"

T/T pursed his lips and knit his brow. "Well, now that you mention it, he did give some hints that he knew somethin' that would surprise a lot of people, but he never said what it was. I could tell he was pretty excited about it, though...as excited as Taylor ever let himself get."

I thought a moment, not quite sure if I should risk

somehow insulting T/T, but decided I had to take a chance. "This is maybe an odd question," I said, "but do you think Taylor might have been capable of blackmail?"

T/T's eyes opened wide and he pulled his head back in surprise. "*Blackmail?*" he asked, shocked. "Oh, Lordy, no! That boy was as honest as the day is long. What in the world would ever make you ask a question like that?"

"Sorry," I hastened to say. "It's just that if Taylor's death was not an accident, there had to be a reason for someone to kill him. He worked in a place that probably has a lot of secrets buried in all those research materials, and I wondered if maybe he found something that could be used to blackmail someone."

T/T looked a little mollified, but still obviously unhappy over the perceived attack on his friend's character. He shook his head solemnly. "Well, if he *did* find somethin' like that, he never would have used it for blackmail. Never in a million years. He was a good boy."

His voice cracked just a bit on that last sentence, and I realized perhaps for the first time just how much Taylor had meant to him.

"I'm sure he was, Teddy," I said, hoping to reassure him. "But it's my job to look at every possibility, no matter how remote."

T/T reached over with one large hand and patted me on the thigh. "I know, darlin', I know," he said. "You just find out what happened to him, okay?"

"I will," I said. "I promise."

* * *

I dropped him off at his hotel and headed home, first offering to take him back to the airport for his return flight—he'd expressed a real interest in meeting Joshua, and I knew Joshua's fascination with airports and airplanes, so.... He also said he'd join the gang after the show for a drink, which would give the rest of the guys a chance to say hello.

So what had I learned from him about Taylor? Not all that much, really. I realized that T/T's firm denial that Taylor might be involved in anything even hinting of blackmail might understandably be colored by their long friendship, but I tended to believe him. Which meant that the mental picture I'd been forming of Taylor as an opportunist was probably wrong. So if blackmail didn't enter the picture, what else did?

I kept flashing back to the missing letters and what I would stake my life on were missing manuscripts as well, and the answer as to who had taken them was obvious: Evan Knight. Somehow, Taylor had caught on to what Knight was up to, and Knight had killed him. Now all I had to do was prove it.

* * *

By the time I got back to the apartment, Jonathan had everything under control. Jared had called to suggest we might all get together for dinner at Napoleon before the show, and Jonathan had contacted the other guys to set it up. He'd also called for reservations for 7:00. I was impressed, especially when I compared him to the Jonathan I'd first met. He'd come a long way, and I was proud of him.

Craig came over around 5. We hadn't expected him until 6, but I knew he enjoyed being around "older" gay men: i.e. adults. Being a teenager isn't easy, and being a *gay* teenager is rougher still. The fact that he was out to his parents took a great burden off him, but still…he didn't feel he really belonged with most of his peers—he was only out to one or two close friends at school. For the most part, he just played the game and, like many gay teens, resented it but realized the consequences of being totally out. And he was still far too young to fully participate in the gay community. He was very curious about the benefit and I could tell he would have loved to go but, at 16, there was no way. The Metropolitan Community Church had just initiated a series of monthly dances and "socials" for teens, and Craig was looking forward to going to the first one, scheduled for the following weekend.

I gave Craig some money to run down to the local fried chicken outlet two blocks away and pick up dinner for himself and Joshua—Jonathan had already laid in a supply of milk and fruit, plus chips and pop for Craig for after Joshua was in bed.

* * *

Dinner at Napoleon was, as always, great. We were there early enough so that shuffling a couple tables around to seat all eight of us wasn't a problem. The great thing about being with friends is that you can totally relax and just be yourself. We talked about nothing of any great importance, and laughed a lot. Jared and Jake, especially, took great delight in teasing

Tim over the fact that Phil was featured in a new ad campaign for Spartan briefs, for which he was a top underwear model.

"What's it like to have your lover be a j.o. fantasy for every gay guy in the country?" Jake asked.

I resisted pointing out that so were Jared and Jake for anyone who'd ever seen them in *their* briefs

"Yeah," Jared said, "I went to take a look at it in Jake's copy of MenStyle, but the pages were stuck together."

Jake grinned and nudged Jared with his shoulder.

"Uh-huh," Phil said, obviously embarrassed.

"Hey, let 'em look," Tim said.

We actually got through the entire dinner without my being asked, mentioning, or even thinking about Taylor Cates' death. As I said, a good evening.

* * *

We arrived at Steamroller Junction shortly before 9:30, and the place was already fairly well packed. I was glad to see the crowd was a good mix of men and women, and a broad cross-section of ages. Dance bars never seemed to change much: same blaring music—probably different songs, but who could tell?—same pounding beat so strong that even the deaf could dance to it with ease; same strobes and flashing lights, and the same adrenaline-charged atmosphere. There was a live band in honor of the benefit, but the overall effect was the same.

I could also sense that Bob Allen was, as always, more than a little uncomfortable with the large crowd and I understood totally. The horrendous Dog Collar bar fire was ancient history for those who hadn't been there, but for me, who had been walking up to the place when it began, and especially for Bob, who had actually been inside....

We ordered our drinks, then maneuvered ourselves around the edge of the room toward the stage, positioning ourselves near an exit. Old habits die hard. And, as usual, Phil, Tim, Jared, Jake, Mario, and Jonathan headed onto the dance floor, leaving Bob and me—the only non-dancers in the group—to guard the drinks. Since the music was too loud to make normal conversation possible, we just watched the dancers. To me there's nothing sexier than a good male dancer. I was glad this was a benefit and not a regular mostly-guys night when the shirts would start coming off as the evening progressed. I don't think my crotch could have taken it.

Around five minutes 'til ten, the band finished a number and the DJ took over while the band moved their instruments to the back and side of the stage. Our gang left the dance floor to retrieve their drinks—Jonathan drained his coke in one long series of gulps and went off for another. At exactly ten o'clock, the DJ switched on the "show" music, and the evening's m.c.—the same incredibly androgynous lesbian as had m.c.'d the last show we'd seen at the Steamroller—came on to start the evening. She introduced William Pearson and Marv Westeen as heads of the Hospice Project and organizers of the benefit, who in turn spoke of the importance of the Hospice to the gay community, which was still being ravaged by AIDS. This was to be one of the first hospices in the country specifically for AIDS patients, and each of them pointed out that in addition to the need to help our own, AIDS was beginning to cross over into the heterosexual community, and that the Hospice would be open for all. "*We* will not politicize," Pearson said, "and *we* will not discriminate." They left the stage to unanimous applause.

The m.c. then announced the lineup of the evening's performers, which included a top-ten-album female pop singer who, though straight herself, was noted for her support of gay causes. There was also a gay stand-up comic who I'd seen on a couple of TV comedy club shows, and Cree and Dunn, two cute male folk-singers everyone assumed to be lovers, who had a large following in the gay community. And, of course, T/T, who had gotten his start in the local drag bars and gone on to be one of the most popular drag stars in the country. He, not surprisingly, was scheduled for last: if anyone could end the evening on a high note, it was T/T.

There's something about minorities that those in the majority can never quite understand or appreciate: the sense of…well, almost euphoria…that comes with being totally surrounded by your own people in a positive, upbeat setting. Each successive act built the crowd's energy level, which was allowed to let off some pressure during the 15 minute dance-break intermission, only to build again when the second half started.

By the time it was T/T's turn, there was enough emotional electricity in the room to light up a couple city blocks.

We had worked our way as close to the stage as we could get and still be relatively close to an exit. And when the m.c. announced: "Ladies and gentlemen and everyone in between, let's hear it for our own Tondelaya O'Tool!" and a spotlight suddenly swept through the crowd to the front entrance where the doors swung open (we couldn't see more than the tops of the doors, since the entire crowd was between us and the front), the crowd went wild. It took fully two minutes for T/T, flanked by four hunky Steamroller bartenders and bouncers clearing the way, to move through the crowd to the stage, waving, blowing kisses, and bestowing benedictions on old fans. She passed close enough to us to spot us and, zeroing in on Jonathan, she gave him a big grin and a wink, and a slow, languorous lip-licking motion. Jonathan blushed furiously but was of course delighted.

It wasn't until he mounted the stage that we could fully appreciate the visual effect: he was a vision in pink—wearing a dress I'm sure he found in a store catering to the kind of high school prom dresses featured in 1960s musicals. But on him, it worked.

He said a few words about the importance of the benefit, and how glad he was to be back "home" among so many of his old friends, then launched into his set of classics—"You gotta see Mama Every Night," "Bill Bailey Won't You Please Come Home," "Proud Mary," and the one number I always associated with T/T because he used to seem deliberately to direct it to me and my ex-lover Chris whenever we were in the audience: the really down-and-dirty "The Butcher's Son" (*"I'm not the butcher, I'm the butcher's son, but I'll give you meat until the butcher comes..."*). And he did it again, staring direct and hard at both Jonathan and me two or three times in the course of the song.

It brought the house down as always, and the crowd wouldn't let him leave the stage until he did "A Good Man is Hard to Find."

When the show was over, the m.c. made another brief appearance to encourage donations and continuing support for the Hospice Project, then turned the evening over to the live band.

While the rest of our little troupe returned to the dance floor, Bob and I waited near the rear stage entrance from which we knew T/T would be emerging. He'd told us he'd join us for a drink, and about twenty minutes later, T/T in his Teddy persona came out from backstage.

"Honey," he said, after working his way slowly through a cluster of fans to us, "would it be too much trouble if we went someplace else for that drink?" he asked. "I'd truly like to set myself down and relax."

Bob and I managed to flag down the rest of the crew, who all came over to exchange greetings, handshakes, and hugs with T/T, and after a minute or two of discussion, we agreed to take a run out to Griff's, a really nice piano bar not too far from The Central. None of us had been there in a while, and it would give T/T a chance to revisit one of his—and my—favorite places.

T/T excused himself to go backstage to make arrangements to pick up his things in the morning before Jonathan and I took him to the airport. That accomplished, we formed something of a flying wedge in front of T/T in order to plow through the crowd toward the door. It still took nearly ten minutes, interrupted nearly every step by Teddy's stopping to exchange hugs and best wishes with fans. At last we reached the relative calm of the bar area in front of the main room entrance doors and, finally, left.

* * *

As we'd hoped, Guy Prentiss—who knew every song from every Broadway and Off-Broadway musical since 1929—was playing, and of course he called a never-reluctant T/T to join him for a number of songs. We sat around listening attentively during his sets and talking and laughing during his breaks. During one of his breaks, Guy came over to join us. He and T/T were old friends and Jonathan was as mesmerized by listening to them swap stories as he was by their performing.

But as all good things must come to an end, so did the evening. We wound up closing the bar at 2 a.m....something I'd not done since I'd met Jonathan. By the time we'd taken T/T back to his hotel and gotten back to our apartment, it was close to 3 a.m. I knew we'd probably pay for it in the morning, but it was well worth the price. And maybe the nicest thing of all was that I hadn't given one minute's thought to Taylor Cates, Morgan Butler, or the Burrows Library.

* * *

True enough, Sunday was a bit hectic. Craig tried to keep Joshua under as much control as possible to allow us to sleep a bit longer, but it wasn't long before Joshua was banging on our bedroom door with the announcement that "It's time for

Sunday School!"

We pried ourselves out of bed in time for Jonathan, Craig, and Joshua to make it to church on time, and rather than reading the paper as was part of my Sunday morning ritual, I went back to bed for an extra hour's sleep.

T/T's flight back to Atlanta was scheduled to leave at 3:20, which gave us enough time to do our breakfast-out routine. I was dressed and waiting when the Three Musketeers returned. Craig was beaming from ear to ear, and obviously excited about something.

"Is it okay if we go to the Cove again for breakfast?" Jonathan asked.

The Cove was where we'd eaten the last time Craig babysat, and where Craig had been smitten by one of a group of gay kids his own age.

"Sure," I said. "Any particular reason?"

"Craig's got a boyfriend!" Joshua announced happily, then ran off, shrieking with laughter, as Craig growled and made a fake lunge at him.

"That was fast," I said when things quieted down.

Craig looked mildly embarrassed, but his excitement overcame it.

"Remember those kids Craig's age we saw at the Cove?" Jonathan asked. "Well, one of them was at church and he apparently recognized Craig and came over to tell him the same group was getting together again at the Cove after church. Apparently one of his friends—the one Craig was checking out—took a liking to Craig and…well, you get the picture."

I got it. *Oh, God! To be 16 again!* I thought.

* * *

Breakfast went well—especially for Craig, I'm sure. The same four teenagers were there when we arrived, sitting, not coincidentally, I surmised, at a table rather than in a booth. Though there were two or three empty tables, we took the one beside them. We all exchanged casual greetings as we sat down, Jonathan taking special care to seat Joshua between himself and me, with Craig taking the seat closest to the other teens. While Jonathan and I looked at the menu, Jonathan making a valiant effort to keep Joshua distracted by pointing at each item and reading it aloud to him, Craig and the other teens made tentative forays into conversation, exchanging information on their schools: three of the others went to Iversen, one went to East, and Craig to Columbus. Jonathan and I were largely invisible, which didn't bother either of us. It was too much fun watching—surreptitiously, I hoped—the bonding and courting rituals of teenage males.

The other table had finished eating long before we did, but sort of hung around until the waiter came and cleared away the dishes, leaving them with little excuse to stay. I felt a little like I was watching either a scene from Romeo and Juliet or a part of my own past. Three of the guys were more than ready to go, but the fourth—Craig's new friend, whose name I gathered was Bill—was obviously reluctant. But finally they got up to leave, Bill looking back frequently as they stood at the cash register.

"Oh, go give him your number," Jonathan urged, and Craig looked hesitant.

"You think I should?" he asked, his eyes still locked on Bill.

"Do you want to?" Jonathan asked.

"Well, sure," Craig admitted, still hesitant.

"Then...?"

Needing no further prodding, Craig got up immediately and hurried after the group, who were just walking out the door.

"Jonathan Quinlan, boy Yenta," I said with a smile.

"What's a Yenta?" Joshua asked.

* * *

We took Craig home, then stopped at a pay phone to call T/T and let him know we were on our way.

He was waiting in front of the hotel as we pulled up, his suitcases by his side, but no garment bags or hat boxes. I got out of the car to open the trunk, while Jonathan changed to the back seat with Joshua—stopping in transit to exchange a greeting and quick bear hug with T/T, who got in front. He immediately turned around in his seat to greet Joshua.

"I do declare, Jonathan, this must be the handsomest boy-chile God ever put breath into! What's your name, chile?" he asked, though of course he already knew and just wanted to engage Joshua directly.

"Joshua," the boy said, wide-eyed. He had been staring intently at T/T since we drove up. I realized he may well never have seen a black man up so close—Jonathan had said once that his home town in northern Wisconsin had no black families, and there were no black children at Joshua's day care. T/T twisted around to extend one large hand into the back seat. "Well, Joshua, it's a pleasure to meet you." Joshua, of course, was delighted by the attention, and at only a little urging from Jonathan leaned forward to take and shake T/T's hand.

T/T opened his eyes wide. "Why, chile, with a grip like that I'll just bet you're goin' t' be a football player when you grow up!"

"I'm going to be a fireman and a cowboy when I grow up," Joshua announced with the total surety of a four year old.

"Well, if my ranch ever catches on fire, you'll be the first one I'll call," T/T. said, grinning.

I'd managed to follow the conversation as I put T/T's bag in the trunk, and when I climbed back into the driver's seat, T/T turned his attention to me.

"Could you be a real lamb and swing by Steamroller so's I can pick up my other bags?" he asked. "I meant to go over this mornin', but I slept in. When you get to be my age, you need all the beauty rest you can get."

"Come on, Teddy, you're not a day over 25," I said.

He reached over to pat me on the leg, then turned to look at Jonathan. "Honey, you ever get tired of this man, you call me right away, hear?"

Jonathan grinned. "Fat chance," he said, "but I'll keep it in mind."

*　*　*

We picked up T/T's garment bags and hat boxes at Steamroller Junction, and headed for the airport. The trip was uneventful, much of it taken up with Joshua, with T/T's encouragement, regaling T/T with his adventures, real and imagined.

We arrived in plenty of time, and found a parking place not too far from the terminal. T/T and I took the garment bags and suitcases, while Jonathan carried one of the hat boxes and held Joshua's hand until we got into the terminal. Joshua had insisted on "helping" and with T/T's approval, was given the lightest of the hat boxes, neither one of which was very heavy.

"You know, Dick," T/T said as we walked behind Jonathan

and Joshua toward the terminal, "I've been thinking of that nice white lady's name, and it just won't come to me." He sighed. "Well, they say the mind's the first thing to go..."

"That's okay, Teddy," I said. "If it comes to you, just let me know the minute it does."

"Well, then, honey, expect a call some mornin' around 3 a.m. That's when I usually wake up rememberin' somethin'."

T/T's plane was late, so he insisted on taking us—well, primarily Joshua—to the snack bar for ice cream, thus moving himself up several places on the list of Joshua's favorite people. When we'd finished, T/T insisted we head for home rather than sit around and wait, but we had nothing better to do, and Joshua was, as always, enthralled with the planes.

We stood at the windows, talking—Joshua taking great care to call our attention to every landing and take-off in his line of vision with undiminished enthusiasm.

After half an hour, T/T's plane pulled up to the gate, and we watched as the plane emptied and then waited until they announced boarding. T/T gave us all a big hug, including Joshua. Then, with promises to keep in touch, he walked down the passageway and was gone.

Joshua insisted we wait until the plane was backed from the gate and began taxiing to the runway. "Bye, Teddy!" he said, waving in the certainty that T/T was watching him and waving back.

When the plane disappeared around the corner of the terminal, we convinced Joshua it was time to go, and we headed home.

* * *

While the weekend had given me a most welcome respite, the minute I woke up Monday morning, my mind shifted back into gear. As I sat at my desk doing the crossword puzzle, I was thinking of Evan Knight and what I was going to do—or be able to do, for that matter—about him. While the threat of being exposed for stealing another man's work might possibly be a motive for murder, I found it a bit of a stretch, especially since I couldn't think of any way to *prove* conclusively that Knight's books were in fact Morgan Butler's. From everything I knew of Morgan, writing was an intensely private thing: not even Scot McVickers, apparently, had ever read his writing.

What struck me as really weird was this oddly strong...connection...I felt with Morgan Butler. Where it came from or why I had no idea. Our lives couldn't have been more different, and maybe that was a part of it. The more I learned about him, the more empathy I felt for the guy. Having been gay all my life, I couldn't comprehend what it must be like to live locked in a closet, when all you had to do was turn the knob. But I wasn't Morgan Butler.

On the one hand, it was clear that although Morgan was so securely imprisoned in his closet he probably never could have found his way out, much as he wanted to, I could easily see that his writing—particularly his books—would provide a form of escape. I realized I was doing an awful lot of speculation with little to really go on, but there was something about Morgan Butler I instinctively identified with. Don't ask me what, but I felt I really knew this guy.

To me, anyone who kept carbon copies of handwritten letters felt a strong need to leave written evidence that he had lived. So, again to me, it was logical for him to keep a copy of his letters—even handwritten ones; once a letter without a copy leaves the writer's hand it is, unless the recipient decides to keep it for some reason, for all intents and purposes lost. But by making a copy, Morgan could be assured his words would also stay where he could preserve them—which was obviously his intent in leaving them to the Burrows. I clearly saw it as a somehow sad but understandable bid for immortality. He had his son, of course, but I don't think that was the kind of posterity Morgan really wanted.

I've always suspected that for many writers, books are a more sure form of posterity than children. Books live longer than sons or grandsons, or great-grandsons, by which time all personal memories of the line's founder are largely lost. But words can last forever and are a direct and personal link to the writer.

Then why did I think Morgan *hadn't* made copies of his books? Well, for one thing, writing in a spiral notebook would have made making copies pretty cumbersome, unless he tore out every other page, and there was no evidence of that...only the last notebook of the second manuscript appeared to have had any pages missing. And since Morgan's last note to Scot had been on spiral notebook paper, I'd bet it was torn from the unfinished book.

So fucking sad! my mind said, but I forced myself not to

pursue the thought any further.

Maybe, again, I was projecting way too much of myself into him, but it struck me that Morgan also may well not have made copies because he really didn't need to; he had no intention of their leaving his possession while he was alive. Letters are by their very nature intended for someone else to read. I didn't think Morgan ever intended for anyone else to see his books...at least not in his lifetime. He probably felt they revealed far too much of a side of his life he had to keep hidden. And I felt sure that if he would have shared his books with anyone on earth, it would have been with Scot. But from what Wayne Powers had indicated, apparently he had not.

I thought again how sad it was that people have to hide part of themselves even from the people they truly love. Even Morgan's letters to Scot were largely guarded.

No, if I was right, his books were his way—the only way he felt he had—to set his soul free...and he wouldn't even allow that to happen until after he was dead. I'm sure he took comfort in knowing they would be there long after his death. And perhaps he harbored a hope that they might eventually be published.

So, again, there were probably no copies of his books. The originals were enough. But now they were gone.

Then why would Evan Knight go to the trouble of killing Taylor Cates or anyone if he had the only copy of the book(s) in his possession? And if I were him, I'd have destroyed the original immediately after copying it. Evan may be a bottom feeder, but he wasn't stupid. He knew Morgan made copies of his handwritten letters. If the other manuscripts —and there was no doubt in my mind that there were other manu- scripts—were also written in spiral notebooks he may very well have assumed, as I did, that making a copy would be next to impossible. But he couldn't know for sure. And neither, I knew, could I.

Even if Morgan had made copies, that Taylor Cates may somehow have found them struck me as nearly impossible: Evan had access to the entire collection long before Taylor came along. And Taylor was only working with the materials brought over from the Burrows estate. Evan had undoubtedly taken the time to remove the bulk of Morgan's letters to Scot—and with them any overt clue of Morgan's being gay. Surely he would also have taken the time to check for copies of the manuscripts.

But if there were, despite all my neat conjectures, by any possibility copies of Morgan's books, there was only one person who might know where they were: Collin Butler, Morgan's son. And if Collin had read them, it probably wouldn't take him long to have figured out his dads' secrets.

I was increasingly tempted to try to contact Collin Butler to resolve the question, but I was more than a little hesitant to do so. I understood Collin was, like his grandfather before him, a rabid homophobe, and I do not suffer homophobes gladly. I wondered again just how much Collin Butler knew about his father. And I wondered, too, just what Collin thought of the father who had in effect abandoned him when he was no older than Joshua is now. Did he have any idea what drove Morgan to it? How could he?

Still, if I was to figure out what Taylor Cates could have known or found out to have Evan Knight kill him, I couldn't overlook the possibility, however remote, of there being copies of the manuscripts, and that Taylor somehow found out about them.

* * *

As so often happens, my dilemma about whether or not to contact Collin Butler was resolved by the ringing of the telephone which, since I'd been so immersed in my thoughts, startled the hell out of me.

"Hardesty Investigations," I said, putting the receiver to my ear.

"Dick, Darlin', it's Teddy," the unmistakable voice said.

I was totally surprised, but pleasantly so, to hear from him. "Teddy!" I said. "You made it back safe and sound, obviously."

"That I did, sugar. Like I told you, I do my best rememberin' when I'm asleep, and sure enough, I dozed off on the plane, and when I woke up I remembered the name of that nice white lady who helped Taylor get his scholarship. Her name was Gretchen Butler, an' she lived in a big ol' house on Crescent Drive. I still can't think of her grandson's name, though, but as soon as I do I'll call and tell you."

He didn't have to. I knew the name already. "His name's Collin," I said.

CHAPTER 10

I managed to get through the rest of the conversation with Teddy, who seemed duly impressed with my detecting skills, and confirmed that the grandson's name was indeed Collin, though my mind was of course off at a full gallop in several directions at once. We hung up after a mutual exchange of affection and good wishes and shared pleasure at having had the chance to get together.

The minute I hung up the phone, I reached for the phone book. And there it was: Butler, Collin, 7273 Crescent Drive. He apparently still lived in his grandmother's house, and I briefly wondered if she were by any chance still alive.

I dialed the number and waited, not having a clue as to what I was going to say if he were actually there. But I was pretty good at winging it, and I was too impatient to sit down and write out a list of questions first.

"Butler residence," a woman's voice—too young-sounding to be the grandmother—the wife?...the maid?...answered.

"Is Collin Butler in?" I asked.

"He's at work. May I take a message?"

I still no idea who I was talking to, but I guess it didn't matter at the moment. "Yes, if you would," I said. "My name is Dick Hardesty, and I'm with Hardesty Investigations." I gave her my number and asked if she would ask him to return the call.

"I'll do that, Mr. Hardesty," she said, and we exchanged good-byes and hung up.

There's nothing so intriguing as a newly opened can of worms, and to have learned that Taylor Cates knew the Butler family merely reconfirmed my suspicion that Taylor had somehow made a link between Morgan Butler and Evan Knight. I still had no idea exactly what the link might be, but perhaps Collin Butler just might be able to provide a significant piece of the puzzle.

* * *

I hung around the office a little later than normal in case Collin Butler might return my call, but he didn't, so I headed home. Jonathan was planning to stop by the photographer's to pick up the proofs on his way home and I'd volunteered to stop at the store to pick up a few things, including a jumbo box of Crunchy-Os, Joshua's current cereal of choice. Either it was a very big box with very little cereal in it, or the kid was packing it away like a truck driver...the last box we'd gotten had lasted less than a week.

I beat them home by only five minutes or so, just long enough to put most of the stuff away and fix my Manhattan. When I heard the door open, I pulled out Jonathan's Coke and a poured a small glass of Kool-Aid for Joshua.

Jonathan's enthusiasm over the pictures had rubbed off on Joshua, who insisted we sit down and look at them immediately after our group hug. There were about 24 shots in all: about eight each of the three of us in casual and less-casual clothes, and another eight of Joshua alone. I always hate seeing pictures of myself, but I had to admit these were pretty good. We'd decided we'd get an 11x14 of the three of us, another 11x14 of Joshua dressed up, two 8x10 (one for Jonathan's dad—Joshua's grandfather—and one for us) and a dozen wallet-size of one of Joshua in his regular clothes for sending to relatives in Wisconsin. Of course I made the mistake of asking which one of himself Joshua liked best. "All of them!" he said. Let's face it, the kid's a ham.

* * *

I brought the box with Morgan's letters to work Tuesday, intending to swing by Wayne Powers' place after work. I'd called him the night before to verify that he'd be home, and after my morning coffee/paper/crossword ritual, I couldn't resist the temptation to pull them out and read them one more time, to see if there might have been anything I'd missed. Each time I read them, Morgan became more real to me and the more strongly I felt his situation. He clearly knew, I think, that he was doomed: a life sentence of self-imprisonment in his closet with no chance for parole. Yet the door was locked from the *inside* and I could tell he knew it. God, I felt for the guy. And my empathy was mixed with not a little anger. *Just open the damned door, fer chrissakes!* my mind all but yelled at him across the years. But he couldn't, and we both knew it.

Sigh.

I couldn't be quite certain if, with each reading, I was getting better at reading between the lines or if I was just subconsciously putting in things I wanted to be there, but I really didn't think it would be too difficult for anyone with an ounce of savvy to see Morgan's love for Scot.

I looked closely for other instances, similar to the lady-in-the-fog incident, that I could tie directly to one of his...excuse me, one of Evan Knight's...books. But I couldn't. I determined to go back and read all the books again, carefully, to see if anything rang a bell from the letters. I was sure Wayne Powers would give me access to the letters again if I needed to check anything specific.

Just as I was finishing the last of the letters, the phone rang.

"Hardesty Investigations."

"Dick Hardesty?" the male voice asked.

"Yes," I said, hoping this might be the call I was waiting for. "Can I help you?"

"This is Collin Butler." Four words crammed with no-nonsense. "You called my home yesterday. My attorney had mentioned you."

"Yes, I did, Mr. Butler," I began. "I was..."

"What is it you want?" he asked.

Well let me finish a sentence and maybe you'll find out, I thought. *Oh, well...* I recognized a good-offense-is-the-best-defense ploy when I heard one.

"I understand you knew a Taylor Cates," I said.

"Well, you understand wrong," he said. "I've never heard of him. What has any of this to do with me?"

"Actually, this might go back a few years," I said. "Taylor's mother worked for your grandmother at your home on Crescent Drive. I understood that you knew him at that time."

There was a slight pause then. "Taylor Cates. Negro. Yes, I remember him now. And it's been more than 'a few' years. He was one of grandmother's projects."

"Projects?" I asked.

"Yes. Grandmother became an unregenerate liberal after the death of my grandfather, always taking on lost causes, helping the 'downtrodden'. Wasting both her time and her money on ingrates."

"So, how was Taylor a 'project'?" I asked.

"Taylor's mother was Grandmother's cleaning woman, and he was constantly here with his mother. While she worked, he read. We have an extensive library, thanks largely to my late grandfather, and Taylor read everything he could get his hands on. All with Grandmother's approval and encouragement. She even let him wander around in our attic where there were even more books."

And manuscripts? my mind voices asked.

"When was the last time you saw him?" I asked.

"He was at Grandmother's funeral. There was quite a contingent of Negroes at the cemetery—the service was by invitation only—and I recognized him there."

"Were you aware that he died?" I asked.

"No, I wasn't," he said. "And I still don't know why you're calling."

"Actually, I am looking into Taylor's death, and I had some questions about your father."

"My father is dead." he said with no trace of emotion. "He has been dead for many years. I can see no possible connection with whatever it is you are looking for."

"Well, it's a long story, I'm afraid," I said. "I was wondering if we might get together for a few minutes at your convenience and I can explain."

"Mr. Hardesty…" his voice reflected a weary impatience "…I am a very busy man and while I have no idea what your object is in contacting me, I simply have no time to indulge you."

"But if you…" I began.

"I really must go," he said. "Good-bye."

And there was the click of the receiver being hung up, followed by a dial tone.

Well, that was fun, I thought as I put the phone back on its cradle.

Still, I felt I'd confirmed quite a bit even though I hadn't learned anything new. Taylor having spent a lot of time at the Butler house, for example, and having had access to not only the library but to the attic where, I'd imagine, copies of Morgan's books—assuming now that there *might be* copies—would most likely have been kept.

Collin's complete lack of emotion when he mentioned his father rather puzzled me. I got no clue from it as to what Collin Butler either knew or felt about his father's death. Perhaps he knew nothing, or did not choose to know. He was only four when Morgan died. It's quite possible he didn't even remember him. I'm sure that's one of the reasons Jonathan was constantly telling Joshua stories of Sheryl and Samuel, and how much they loved him and of how they were always watching over him from heaven. It seemed to comfort both Joshua *and*

Jonathan. At least Joshua would grow up knowing his father loved him and had not left him willingly.

But Collin Butler was largely a cipher. I was curious as to how Collin's mother had reacted to Morgan's death. Did she feel betrayed as well as abandoned? What had she told Collin about his father, and the circumstances of his death? Was *she* still living?

I know, I know...Taylor Cates. I had to stay focused on him, though the pull to learn more about Morgan was nearly overwhelming, and I had no idea why.

I was more than a little frustrated by not having had the chance to ask Collin Butler what, if anything, he might know about his father's writings, and I determined to let things rest for a day or so and then try to contact him again. The most he could do would be to hang up on me...which, gathering from the tone of our just-completed conversation was a very real possibility. But faint heart ne'er solved fair murder mystery.

I guess it all boiled down to this: if Morgan Butler had made copies of his manuscripts and if I could somehow get my hands on them, it would be not only conclusive proof that Evan Knight had committed plagiarism and fraud, but that the police might be convinced to open a complete investigation into the likelihood that he was responsible for Taylor Cates' death.

But... my mind said...and damn I hate *"But"s...if Taylor had indeed come across Morgan's books somewhere in the Butler house...again, the attic would be the most likely place...and had read them, don't you suppose he would have made the connection the minute he read 'Evan's' books?*

Good question. But that's assuming that 1) copies of Morgan's original manuscripts existed; 2) Taylor had read them at the Butlers'; 3) he had also read them when they were published under Evan's name; and 4) that he somehow had figured out what was going on. It's possible that Taylor never read 'Evan's' books, though I can't imagine dating a writer without being curious about what he'd written.

If all those assumptions were valid, why hadn't Taylor then said something to someone? Perhaps he did...to Evan Knight, either in the form of a blackmail attempt (despite what T/T had said about his honesty) or in an incredible display of naivete which then got him killed.

But "if"s and assumptions don't hold up very well in a court of law. And a house of cards built on and of assumptions is a pretty flimsy house indeed.

* * *

I left the office around three, but what should have been a fifteen minute drive to Wayne Powers' home took nearly 40 minutes, thanks to a burst water main which had turned a major intersection into a lake and backed up traffic in all directions. We were finally diverted through a residential area, but even there the narrow streets held everyone down to a crawl.

Andy, standing just inside the closed screen door, greeted me with a frenzy of tail-wagging and butt-wiggling. I knocked and heard Wayne's voice call: "Come on in: it's open. I'm in the kitchen." Making sure I had the box of letters securely under one arm, I knelt to give Andy a proper head-and-body rub 'hello', which was received with great enthusiasm and a demand for even more attention. Dogs and people are a lot alike sometimes. We then proceeded through the living room to the short hallway to the kitchen, Andy leading the way.

Wayne was standing at the sink, dish towel in hand, just drying the last of a small stack of plates which he then put into the cupboard to his left.

"Coffee?" he asked with a smile.

"If you're having some," I said. "I could go for a cup."

He opened a door under the sink and draped the dishtowel over the edge. Then, reaching back into the cupboard, he took out two large mugs, which he set on the counter.

"Black, right?" he asked as he poured the coffee.

"Right," I said, and he just nodded.

"Have a seat," he said, indicating the kitchen table with a nod of his head. I carefully put the box of letters in the center of the table, then pulled out a chair and sat down.

He handed me one of the cups, then sat down himself.

"So," he said. "Did you learn anything?"

I took a sip of my coffee before answering. "Mainly just a verification that most of Morgan's letters to Scot are missing from the Burrows' papers."

He shook his head. "How very strange. I wonder why that might be?"

"I think I have a pretty good idea," I said.

"Do you think it has anything to do with Morgan's being

gay?" he asked. "Who would care after all these years?"
"Trust me," I said. "There was a good reason."
He merely shrugged.
"Do you do much reading?" I asked. It was an out-of-the-
blue question, but Wayne took it in stride.
"Oh, yes. Especially since Scot died."
"Have you ever read Evan Knight?" I asked.
Wayne smiled broadly. "Of course!" he said. "He's one of
my favorite authors; I've read everything he's written. He has
a character named Scot: did you know that?"
As a matter of fact, I did. "Yes," I said. "I was reading *Fate's
Hand* just the other day."
"Wonderful characterization and sense of time," he said.
"Amazing how I identify with his writing so strongly."
Amazing, indeed, I thought.
"Did Scot ever read any of Knight's books?" I asked.
Wayne's enthusiasm dimmed slightly, and I was afraid the
question may have brought him down, somehow. "No," he
said. "He died before Knight's first book came out. Scot was
an avid reader, and I'm sure he would have enjoyed them."
Oh, I'm sure he would, a mind-voice said.
Time for another subject change. "Do you know if Scot ever
had any contact with Morgan's son?" I asked.
Powers took a sip of coffee and set his mug on the table
before responding.
"No, he never did."
"You're sure?" I asked, and he nodded.
"I'm sure," he said. "I asked him myself, once, but Scot said
that Morgan was rather like the moon, with two distinct sides:
the one he let Scot see and the one he didn't. Collin...was a
part of the side of Morgan that Scot never knew, and he sensed
that Morgan didn't want him to know. So he respected what
he felt would have been Morgan's wishes."
"And you've never seen him, either?"
He shook his head. "Not that I'm aware of. I've only seen
a picture of him, with Morgan, taken shortly before Morgan
died."
A picture? my mind asked.
"A picture?" I asked aloud. I realized that I had never seen
a picture of Morgan Butler, let alone his son. I was instantly
curious on several levels. "Do you still have it, by any chance?"
Powers gave me a small smile. "Of course I do," he said.
"Again, it was Scot's, and I would never throw anything of his

away."

I wondered why, if Morgan wanted to keep his...other side...private even from Scot, he would have given Scot a photo of himself with his son. But before I had a chance to ask, Powers answered.

"It was included with one of the last letters Morgan ever wrote Scot. The only way I know which letter is because Scot had paperclipped It to the letter and envelope. The letter itself doesn't mention it, which I felt was very odd. But I realize now, especially in light of his last letter, that he knew what he was going to do and wanted Scot to have something to remember him by...as if Scot would ever need anything to remind him. I suppose it was probably the last photo Morgan had taken, and perhaps Collin just happened to be in it. I don't know."

"Could I see it," I asked, "if it's not too much trouble?" I was hoping that it would not be.

"Of course," he said. "It was just a small snapshot, but Scot had it blown up to an 8x10, though he'd put it away when he met me. As I've said, Scot was very considerate of my feelings. He knew I knew how much he loved Morgan, but he never wanted to rub my nose in it, as it were."

He started to get up from the table, but I hastened to say: "No, you don't need to get it right this minute. Later will be fine."

"That's all right," he said. "It will only take me a moment."

Andy was obviously ambivalent about Powers' leaving the room: he wasn't sure whether he should follow his master or stay in the kitchen to keep a close eye on me lest I try to make off with the silver—or perhaps just in the hopes of getting a bit more attention from me. He apparently opted for the latter and, as soon as Powers had gone, got up and came over to nudge my leg with his head.

Wayne returned a few minutes later carrying a framed 8x10 photo and a smaller snapshot, unframed, which he set on the table in front of me.

"This is what Morgan sent," he said, indicating the smaller photo. "Scot had it blown up and framed after Morgan died."

The photo was of an expressionless but rather handsome man with intense eyes—it was impossible to determine their color since the photo was in black and white. A young boy, around Joshua's age, apparently standing on the chair in which the man was seated, rested his head on the man's right shoulder and stared into the camera with the same impassivity as his father.

I realized that while I'd had absolutely no preconceptions as to what Morgan Butler looked like, my mind instantly recognized it as unquestionably him.

"I'd thought several times," Wayne said as he returned to his chair and sat down, "about perhaps sending it—the original, that is—to Collin Butler. It must have been very hard for him growing up without his father. But I didn't know how it would be received, and I certainly didn't want to intrude into his life."

"Well," I said, "I can't speak for him, of course, but if I were in his position, I'd be delighted to have it. It's a snapshot, which means Scot's blow-up is quite probably the only other copy in existence."

I was silent a moment, trying to phrase my next question. Talking about an intrusion into someone else's life…but finally I just let it out.

"I've been meaning to have a face-to-face talk with Collin," I said, "but I didn't know exactly how to go about approaching him. I was wondering if you might allow me to give this to him…if you don't need it yourself?"

Wayne smiled. "Certainly," he said. "Scot would want for him to have it."

We took our time finishing our coffee. I knew I was going to be late getting home, but I was absorbed by Wayne's stories of Scot. At one point he got up from the table and went to bring me a photograph of Scot taken about the time the two of them had met. It was clear Wayne still worshiped him, and from listening to his stories and looking at Scot's photo, I could see why.

"He was a very handsome guy," I said, and Wayne smiled wistfully.

"Yes, he was, wasn't he?" he said. "I was very lucky to have found him, and to have had him as long as I did."

I of course had no idea how it must feel to lose a lover like that, and I didn't allow myself to go anywhere near thinking about what I'd do if something were to happen to Jonathan.

To forestall the possibility of doing so, I glanced at my watch. "Well," I said, "I really should get going. Thank you for the photo, and I'm sure Collin Butler will appreciate it."

"I hope so," he said, as we both got up from the table, Andy immediately rising to his feet in anticipation of doing escort duty.

Both Wayne and Andy walked me to the door. I thanked

Wayne again for all his help, and especially for the photograph. We shook hands and I bent to give Andy another vigorous body rub, and left.

* * *

Jonathan and Joshua had planned to stop by the photographer's on the way home to drop off the proofs we had selected, so I had a few minutes when I got home to fix my Manhattan and settle down again with *A Game of Quoits*. We had four of Evan Knight's...*No, damn it!* my mind corrected sternly: *Morgan's!*...books: *Fate's Hand*, which Craig had borrowed, *A Game of Quoits*, *Chesspiece*, and *Eye of Newt*. Knight had indicated there was another one forthcoming, and I wondered just how many more there might be. He was smart enough to space them out. I also wondered what he'd do when they were all published? Well, that sure as hell wasn't my problem. With luck he'd be in jail by then.

* * *

Wednesday morning I called Butler's home again, and the same—I assumed—woman answered the phone.

"This is Dick Hardesty," I said. "I spoke with Mr. Butler yesterday, but would you ask him if he could call me again? I have something I think he would like to have."

I gave her my office number again and, just in case, my home phone. She said she would relay the message, and I thanked her and hung up. I hoped his curiosity would prompt him to call despite his obvious reluctance to talk with me.

* * *

No word from him by four, so I just locked up the office and went home. It was Jonathan's class night, which meant that Joshua and I would be left to our own devices again. Being alone with Joshua was becoming easier as time went on. I didn't feel the need to constantly find things to fill up the time—four year olds generally find enough to keep themselves busy without having a schedule laid out for them.

Because we'd had to renege on our last plans to go to Joshua's favorite restaurant, Cap'n Rooney's Fish Shack, we made a point of going as soon as they got home, again taking both cars so that Jonathan could go directly to class after dinner.

Joshua occupied himself, when we got home, with a new coloring book and crayons we'd gotten the night we went to the mall for his new clothes. I settled down with the last chapter of *Chesspiece*, and when I'd finished it, I went to the bookcase for Knight's…Morgan's, damn it!…*Eye of Newt*. When I returned to the couch, Joshua brought his coloring book over to show me his latest work: a bright orange-and-red fire truck with firemen in purple fire gear spraying yellow water on a green house burning with pink flames. Pretty impressive, and I told him so. He was getting really good at staying within walking distance of the lines.

Seeing I had *Eye of Newt* in my lap, Joshua wanted me to read it to him. An adult murder mystery with a gay detective wasn't exactly in the same league with *The Littlest Tractor* or *Lemon Pizza*, but it's the reading that matters, and the sound of the words and the bonding. I opened the book as Joshua snuggled closer so he could pretend to be reading along. I traced the words with my finger as I read:

Ledder always felt more comfortable at night. Days were always too distracting. Telephones, people, sirens, horns. No, nights were better. Time to think clearly….

Joshua stuck with it for a little more than a page, then scooted down off the couch and ran into his room to show Bunny his drawing.

The phone rang just as I started Chapter 2, and I quickly put the book aside to answer it.

"This is Collin Butler. You told Martina you had something for me? I must have misunderstood. Since we've never met, I have no idea how anything you have could be relevant to me."

Okay, Hardesty, walk carefully, here, a mind-voice cautioned.

"I came across a photograph of you taken with your father, and I thought you might like to have it. Since it's a snapshot, I'm fairly sure you may not have seen it before, and I don't imagine you have many photos of you with your dad, since you were so young when he died."

"I have *no* photos of myself with my father and don't recall any ever having been taken. Just how did you come across it?" His tone was a mixture of suspicion and defensiveness, but I could also tell he was curious.

"It belonged to an old friend of your father's…a navy

buddy," I said. "It's a long and rather involved story, but it centers around your father and some of his missing papers and..."

"Papers?" he interjected. "What papers? I have absolutely no idea what you're talking about."

"Which is precisely why I hoped we could have the chance to meet in person to discuss it. I can explain everything then."

Everything? a mind voice asked. Don't promise what you can't deliver.

"Who are you working for?" he demanded.

I didn't want to go there, but it was a logical question.

"I've been hired by the Burrows Foundation to look into some missing papers...your father's among them."

"My father had no papers," he said flatly. "You mean my grandfather's papers, which the Burrows Library has illegally confiscated."

Oh, God, I was afraid this was going to happen. Try to head it off while you can, Hardesty.

"I can assure you, Mr. Butler, that this has nothing whatever to do with your grandfather or your dispute with the Burrows. And if you'd just give me the chance to..."

He cut me off again. "Oh, very well," he said, his tone making his displeasure clear. "Tomorrow, one o'clock at my home. I'll give you fifteen minutes."

I felt rather like Oliver Twist, standing in front of Mr. Bumble with an empty bowl in his hand, asking for more gruel.

"That's very kind of you," I said, taking great care not to let my sarcasm show. "I'll see you at one tomorrow, then."

I had Joshua safely bathed, pajama'd, in bed, read to (*The Popsicle Tree*, his favorite), prayers said ("Now I lay me down to sleep. I pray the Lord my soul to keep. And if I die before I wake, I pray the Lord my soul to take. God bless mommy and daddy and Uncle Jonathan and Uncle Dick and everybody. Amen.") and he was asleep before Jonathan got home.

* * *

I took some time Thursday morning, after my coffee/paper/crossword ritual, to sit back and think about exactly where I was...or wasn't...with the case, starting with the Burrows' opening night and Taylor Cates' death. Taylor was found at the foot of a metal staircase at the back of the cataloging room, with no apparent reason for being in that part of the building. Was it possible that he had somehow turned off the alarm to let his killer—and I was certain at this point that there had been a killer—in for some reason? Too far-fetched. I was grasping at straws, and I knew it. The theft of Morgan Butler's book manuscripts, and by whom, wasn't in question. They had been taken by Evan Knight long before Taylor Cates died.

And while I was leaning pretty heavily toward Evan Knight as the killer, I realized that I have been known to be wrong once or twice before when it came to being sure who'd done what to whom. There were still a lot of the puzzle pieces that just didn't fall into place yet.

The missing letters, for example. Evan may well have gone through them and taken any that might have hinted at the existence of the manuscripts or of Morgan's being gay. Possible. He had no way of knowing that Scot had kept all the originals. But I'd seen the originals, and nowhere in them were there references to Morgan's writing *books*...only to writing. There were a few anecdotes and memories of things Morgan and Scot had shared together which were somewhat similar to incidents I remember from the books, but only that one specific, nearly word-for-word link between *Chesspiece* and Morgan Butler's letters. I could see Knight's taking that one. But why all the others? I suppose it's possible Knight took most of the letters referring to writing so that people wouldn't get too curious about what Morgan wrote. But hell, lots of people write. I couldn't imagine why Knight would have particularly cared about whether anybody found out about Morgan's being gay or not—those clues were nebulous enough as it was.

But if Evan Knight didn't take out all the missing letters, who did? And why?

Okay. Let's say Taylor did it. I'm sure he'd read all of 'Knight's books'—and if Morgan had made a copy and somehow left it/them in his father's attic, chances would have been good that Taylor'd read them as a kid and made the connection the minute he saw them published under Knight's name. Or if there were no copies of the manuscripts, he may well have come across the little-old-lady-in-the-fog letter—if Knight hadn't taken it first—and tied it definitely to *Chesspiece*. He may have confronted Knight over it, and it got him killed.

I realized, too, that my meeting with Collin Butler was really less about solving the crime than about satisfying my curiosity about Collin's knowledge of and feelings toward his father. Being nosy just comes naturally to me, and I'd developed this inexplicable sense of connection to Morgan Butler. It was as if I somehow wanted to...what?...make things right for him? Maybe to give him in death the completion he never achieved in life.

* * *

I went downstairs to the diner in the lobby for an early lunch—they had a good corned beef hash special on Thursdays—and then walked across the street to the parking lot to pick up my car for the drive to Collin Butler's. As I was pulling out of the lot between two parked vans flanking the drive so closely I couldn't clearly see the oncoming traffic, I was nearly clipped by a shiny new Datsun 280zx. That alone was enough to get my adrenaline pumping, but what really got my attention was the glimpse I got of the driver: the guy looked exactly like Dave Witherspoon.

I pulled into the wide driveway at 7273 Crescent Drive—no street parking allowed—at exactly five minutes to one, having spent ten minutes driving idly up and down the neighboring streets to avoid being early. One of the city's original wealthy neighborhoods, the streets were lined with large, elegant homes built in the early years of the century by the city's more prosperous businessmen.

The Butler residence was surrounded by a tall wrought-iron fence around a spacious manicured front lawn flanked by ornate flower beds that all but shouted: "Professional Gardener."

Climbing the wide front steps , I crossed the broad front porch to the imposing beveled-glass double front doors and rang the bell. After a moment, the right-hand door was opened by a tall woman in a dark grey dress. No makeup, her greying hair pulled back.

"May I help you?" she asked, pleasantly enough but with no smile.

"I'm here to see Mr. Butler," I said. "My name is Hardesty."

"Yes," she said. "Please come in."

I followed her across the highly polished oak floor, past the sweeping balustered stairway which smelled slightly of lemon oil, noting a cavernous living room to our left and formal dining room to the right. I somehow got the impression that when Collin Butler was a child, he did not have to depend on a paper route for his spending money. She rapped lightly on a closed classic-paneled door just behind the stairway and opened it without waiting for a reply. She stood aside as she held it open for me, and closed it behind me when I'd entered. The room—the study/library obviously—was lined with glass-fronted bookcases. Between two tall windows, the top quarter panels of which being beautiful floral-patterned stained glass, the lower three-quarters being clear beveled glass, was a large but comfortable looking desk, and behind the desk sat a man about my age whom I recognized immediately from the snapshot I was carrying in my shirt pocket. Collin Butler was the spitting image of his father and it gave me a very odd feeling.

He did not get up as I entered. I walked over to the desk and extended my hand across it. He leaned forward to take it, then motioned me to a wing-back chair to the right and in front of the desk. To one side of each window was a portrait: on the left, a dour-looking man with a bible cradled in his right arm. I recognized him from somewhere as being Jerromy Butler; on the left a regal-looking woman I assumed to be his grandmother, Gretchen Butler.

"I appreciate your seeing me," I said as I sat down, and his response was a mere flicking of one hand, which reminded me of a king acknowledging the allegiance of a courtier.

"And what of this photograph?" he said, obviously intending to stick to the fifteen minute time-frame.

I reached into my pocket for the photo and half rose from my chair to hand it to him, then returned to my seat. He studied the picture for what seemed like an eternity without looking up.

"You look very much like your dad," I said at last, which seemed to pull him back to the moment.

"Really?" he said casually. "I don't see it." He set the photo on the desk in front of him, almost reluctantly, it seemed. "So exactly how did this come into your possession, again?"

"Indirectly from a friend of your father's," I said. "They served in the navy together and remained close"—I watched him for any reaction to the word—there was none—"until your dad's death."

While "close" had elicited no response, "death" produced a flicker of…something …across his face.

"I appreciate your bringing it to me," he said. "I have very few photographs of my father. My mother found them too upsetting. She never recovered from his death, I'm afraid."

"Is she still living?" I asked.

He nodded. "Yes, she remarried when I was seven and is living in Florida with my stepfather, who officially adopted me after they married."

"But you kept your father's name," I said.

He looked at me expressionless. "It was my grandfather's name," he said.

There was a rather awkward pause until he said: "So exactly what is it you expect me to give you in return?"

Normally, a remark like that would have pissed me off royally. But I let it pass. "I don't expect anything in return," I said, which of course wasn't true and he knew it. "Except perhaps a little information," I amended. "I was wondering if you might know anything of your father's writing."

He raised an eyebrow slightly. "Writing? What writing? And what 'papers' were you referring to when you said the Burrows has some of my father's papers? And some of them are missing?"

"Your father, from what I've learned, was a talented writer who never allowed his books to be published. I have reason to believe someone stole his manuscripts and a number of his personal letters. I was wondering if you knew if there might be any copies of his manuscripts somewhere?"

"I know of no manuscripts. I had no idea he wrote at all," he said. "But you see why I cannot trust my grandfather's writings to a place like the Burrows Library, especially if their security is so lax that they cannot even keep what they have. His papers deserve far more respect than they can receive where they are. They will be much better off at my alma mater."

"Bob Jones University?" I asked, though I knew.

"Yes. It is a much more fitting place for them than...the Burrows." His tone left little doubt as to what he thought of the Burrows Library.

"And your father's papers?" I asked, curious as to what his reaction might be.

"I expect them to be returned as well," he said, "even though I was not aware they existed until you mentioned them."

"You would give them to Bob Jones as well?"

A look of mild distaste crossed his face. "My grandfather was a prominent figure in the religious movement. He was an important man. A leader. A visionary. My father was...not. The University would have no interest in them, I'm sure." "Then you would leave them at the Burrows?" Again, I was watching his reaction. "Of course not!" he said, making no attempt to hide his contempt. "I do not intend to have the Butler name in any way associated with such a place."

"Were you aware that Taylor Cates was cataloging your father's papers at the time of his death?"

"I had no idea," he said. "What does that have to do with anything?"

"Coincidence, perhaps," I said. "But I believe his death was related to your father's missing papers in some way, in spite of the fact that he was working on them for only a short time before he died."

Butler looked taken aback. "So you're telling me that just anyone wandering around that...place...has ready access to my family's private papers? That's outrageous!"

"It isn't that bad," I said. "There was as far as I know only one other cataloger working with them. Taylor took over from Dave Witherspoon, the original cataloger. To the best of my knowledge, no one else worked with them. They are really quite professional at the Burrows."

My explanation did little to change his mood.

A grandfather clock somewhere chimed the quarter hour. Butler, still agitated, looked in its general direction and said: "Our time is up. I'm expecting a call from Bob Jones University any moment."

I was in no hurry to leave. "I understand you are up for seat on their Board of Trustees," I said.

"I have no idea how you might know that," he said, "but yes, I am. It's a great honor and I've worked very hard for it."

"Well, I wish you luck," I said.

He looked at me dismissively. "Thank you," he said. "Now, if you'll excuse me..."

I got up from my chair, and he remained seated.

"Thank you for your time," I said, stepping over to extend my hand again. He took it and gave it a cursory shake.

"Mrs. Barlow will show you out," he said.

He must have had some sort of buzzer on his desk, for the door opened and the same woman who had met me at the door appeared.

As I followed her into the foyer, I heard a phone ringing.

CHAPTER 11

Thinking back over our meeting as I drove back to the office, the one thing that struck me about Collin Butler was his seemingly total lack of a personality. I'm sure he had to have one, but he certainly hid it well. He reminded me, in a way, of Morgan's letters to Collin's mother and grandfather: efficient, but almost perfunctory. The only emotions I had witnessed in him seemed to be variations on displeasure. The Butler name—his *grandfather's* name, that is—was obviously very important to him, as was his anticipated appointment to his alma mater's Board of Trustees. But I wondered if, like his father, he might not have an awful lot going on beneath the surface which he would or could not allow himself to express. I still didn't know if there might be a *Mrs.* Collin Butler, though I certainly didn't get even the most remote hint that he might be, like his father was before him, locked in a closet.

On reflection it also occurred to me that, while Collin strongly resembled his father and was therefore a very nice looking man, I didn't find him the least bit sexually attractive. I hadn't really thought much before about the relationship between sex appeal and personality, but I realized that for me, at least, there was a definite link. Odd how the mind works.

It was pretty obvious, too, that Collin Butler really didn't know very much about his father, and from what he said about his never having seen photos of himself with Morgan, that said quite a bit. He may have been lying about not knowing about Morgan's writing, and that he didn't know about any of Morgan's manuscripts, but I tended to believe him, especially since I'd pretty much come to the conclusion, even before I went to see Collin, that Morgan hadn't made copies. But I had to check. And I was fairly sure that, considering the gay nature of the books and Collin Butler's reported homophobia, that if Collin did know about them, he'd have reacted to my question a little more defensively.

I wondered again just how much Collin might know about his father's death, or the reason for it. I thought of that terribly sad last note Morgan had written Scot. What a waste! What a waste!

* * *

And suddenly I found myself heading not for my office but for the Burrows. My mind was doing it again…it knew something I didn't, and it wasn't telling me exactly what it was. But I knew it had something to do with Morgan's last notebook….

I did not bother stopping to call ahead to let Irving McHam know I was coming or, when I got to the library, going up to his office. Instead, I went directly downstairs and rang the bell to the cataloging room. I saw, through the wire-meshed glass of the door, Janice glance toward me and turning to say something to someone else. A moment later, the cute red-head came to the door and opened it.

"Well hello, Dick Hardesty," he said with a big grin.

Any other time, my crotch and I would have been delighted that he remembered my name, but I had no time for that at the moment.

"I need to see Morgan Butler's papers," I said as he held the door open for me and closed it behind me. "Box 12-A," I added.

"Sure," he said. "I'll go get it. You can use that table over there." He nodded toward a small empty table next to the one at which Janice was working on a stack of manila folders. She smiled, nodded a hello, and went back to her work.

While I waited, I looked around the room for Dave Witherspoon, but didn't see him.

"Is Dave here today?" I asked Janice.

She stopped writing on her note pad and looked up. "No," she said, "He was here this morning, but left a little after noon. He had a doctor's appointment."

And I suddenly remembered the shiny new Datsun 280xz that had almost hit me as I pulled out of my parking lot at work. I wondered if I had been right, and it *was* Dave Witherspoon who was driving. If so, I wondered how he could afford a new car and a trip to Cancun on a cataloger's salary.

The red-head brought the box and set it on the table, handing me a sign-in sheet and a pencil. "Now that we're getting organized," he explained.

"I'll just be a minute," I said as I signed the paper and returned the pencil to him.

"Shall I wait?" he asked with a more-than-slightly sexy smile.

Please do! my crotch said, ignoring my resolve to get to what I'd come in for.

"If you'd like," I said. "As I say, I'll just be a minute."

I opened the box, pulled out the notebooks, and went quickly to the last one. Opening it to the last page, I studied the small strip of paper left where the page had been torn out. Sure enough, there wasn't one torn strip, but two! *Morgan had made a copy of his farewell note!* He'd sent the original to Scot...so *where was the copy?* Probably removed with the other letters, and probably by Evan Knight.

I put the notebooks back in the box, closed the lid, and took the pencil the red-head handed me with another smile. I signed the check in/out sheet and gave the sheet and the pencil back to him.

"Is there anything else I do for you?" he asked.

"Not right now, thanks," I said, getting up from the table, and I was so preoccupied that not even my crotch picked up on it until I was halfway up the stairs.

* * *

The very idea that someone might make a copy of their suicide note really got to me, but then from what I knew of Morgan Butler, I guess I shouldn't have been surprised. The question was, where was it now? Would Morgan have torn it out of the notebook and put it with the other copies of his letters? For some reason, I doubted it. This wasn't *like* his other letters, for one thing. It was the most revealing thing Morgan Butler ever wrote about himself. No, I had the strong feeling that he would have left the note right there in the notebook. His novels were a secret part of himself; I believed Morgan would have wanted his final note to be the coda to his secret life. Evan found it and took it, like he had taken everything else.

The more I thought of how Evan Knight had systematically gone about erasing as much as he could of another human's identity, the angrier I became. That last note had been Morgan's only direct admission of being gay. He had, albeit as one of his last acts on earth, finally opened his closet door. And Knight had robbed him even of that.

I wondered if Evan Knight ever gave one split second's thought to what he had done to another man's dignity? I doubted it. He simply had done his best to remove any possible link between Morgan and the books Evan had published under his own name, and Morgan's being gay was one of those links. To be honest, I really wouldn't have thought Knight was that smart to go to all that trouble. If there was only one copy of the manuscripts, and he had them, why should he care if someone found out Morgan was gay? Granted, there were a few oblique links between the letters and the books—and the little old lady in the fog story, of course—though the chance of anyone picking up on them was extremely remote. It wasn't as though people would be standing in line to read the letters of some to-all-appearances average Joe. His father's papers would get a lot more attention simply because of who Jerromy Butler was. As Collin Butler had said, his grandfather was an important and famous man. His father was not.

But I realized, too, that Morgan Butler's papers just might have attracted more interest if it were known that he was gay, and the chance was therefore greater that someone might stumble on Knight's secret as Taylor Cates apparently had. So maybe Knight was sharper than I gave him credit for being. But part of me still doubted it.

* * *

I had a message from Glen O'Banyon's secretary waiting on my machine when I returned to the office, asking me to call, which I did immediately. I was told he was in a meeting with a client, but would call me back as soon as he was finished.

I hung up the phone, sat back in my chair, and let my mind take over.

This was probably one of the most convoluted and ultimately frustrating cases I'd had in a long, long time.

And as so often happens with me, a new thought bubbled to the surface of my mind, like a gas bubble in a tar pit.

Taylor Cates was dead, and I had been going on the assumption, all this time, that he had been murdered, most probably by Evan Knight, to cover up Taylor's somehow-discovery that Knight had stolen Morgan's work. But the fact that Cates had been working on the Butler papers...and, specifically from what I could tell, on Morgan Butler's papers...for only about a week and a half before he was killed finally sank in. What could he have found in that time, especially since the missing letters had obviously been taken long before he even started? Taylor couldn't have taken them…Dave Witherspoon had been working on them first, and I'd checked both his and Taylor's cataloging notes against the remaining letters, and everything matched. Even if he had, as Dave Witherspoon said, been nosing around Morgan's papers while Dave was working on them, it's unlikely he would have risked trying to take anything.

So it was entirely possible that Taylor's death had nothing to do with Morgan Butler's papers.

Great! Now *you think of it!* my mind said with more than a touch of disgust.

I didn't have a single shred of direct evidence to prove that Knight was the murderer. I did have pretty solid proof that he had stolen Morgan's work, but what could I do with it? The only person who had a legal right to go after Knight for plagiarism, as far as I could tell, was Collin Butler, and I strongly suspected that he would want nothing whatever to do with claiming any rights to his father's books, even though a considerable amount of money was involved. On the contrary, I was pretty sure his homophobia would keep him from wanting it even known that his father wrote them.

For Taylor to have deduced from his reading of the letters remaining in the file that Morgan was gay is hardly surprising. I think anybody good at reading between the lines would easily make the connection. Even if none of the letters was missing, it would be impossible to say with certainty. But Morgan's last note was the "smoking gun" which removed any doubt.

So if Knight had taken the last note with the rest of the missing letters, why would he have had to kill Taylor? Taylor might have figured out enough to have been caused Knight considerable embarrassment, and might even have been able to make himself a considerable nuisance. But I just couldn't see it as a solid motive for murder. I know, murderers often have their own peculiar logic, but still…

The ringing of the phone jolted me back to the real world.

"Hardesty Investigations," I said, picking up the receiver.

"Dick, Glen. How are things going with the investigation?"

I sighed. "Funny you should ask," I said, and gave him a Reader's Digest version of where things stood at the moment. I tried to keep it limited to the facts and leave out my ruminations, but the end result was the same: I was pretty much going nowhere fast.

"Ah," O'Banyon said when I'd finished. "I was afraid of that. We had a board meeting last night, and Zach Clanton was demanding we pull the plug. That man acts as though every nickle the Burrows spends is coming directly out of his own pocket. He keeps pointing to the fact that if the medical examiner and the police consider Taylor's death an accident, we should accept it and get on with our lives. I told the board I'd call you today to check. So what do you think?"

"I don't know, Glen," I said. "I can see his point, I guess, but I really do believe Taylor's death was no accident. If the board wants to pull the plug, I'll understand. But knowing me, I think I'll keep going. I don't like just giving up."

"I understand," O'Banyon said. "And I'm pretty sure I can hold Zach off a while longer."

"I appreciate that, Glen," I said. "I do have a couple other things I want to follow up on."

"That's fine," he said. "If you need anything, don't hesitate to call."

"I won't," I said. "And thanks."

We said our goodbyes and hung up, and I went back to my thoughts.

* * *

One of the things I wanted to check on was Dave Witherspoon's new car and his trips to Cancun, and I'd start with the car first. I was sure he couldn't be making all that much money at the Burrows, and I remember his saying his father had worked in the coal mines, so that pretty much ruled out a wealthy family. It might have been possible if he and his partner Ryan shared their incomes. I didn't have any idea of what kind of work Ryan did, but I know two incomes made a big difference for Jonathan and me…especially since Joshua joined the family. But still….

I took out the phone book and looked up Dave's address. On the assumption that he might not return to work after his doctor's appointment, I left work early and took a drive to the address listed. It was in an area of older apartment buildings much like our own, with mostly on-street parking. I drove up and down the street for a couple of blocks in either direction, then did a figure-eight of the surrounding streets, looking for a white Datsun 280xz—it wouldn't be easy to miss—but didn't see one. On a hunch, I then drove through the alley behind Dave's building. Off the alley directly behind it was a small six-space parking lot, and sure enough, one of the spaces held the Datsun. I slowed down enough to check and, I hoped, memorize the license plate number, then drove home.

* * *

I've always been pretty good about leaving my work at work, and I get irked with myself when for some reason I can't do it. The fact that during our group hug that evening I was thinking about who took Morgan's suicide note did not bode well for the evening, and sure enough, I spent the majority of the night thinking about the case to the degree that even Joshua noticed it. I was sitting there staring blankly at the TV, my mind a million miles away, when Joshua climbed up on the couch beside me and stood up so he could bend over and whisper in my ear: "Can I have another cookie?"

When without thinking I offhandedly said "Sure," he jumped off the couch and ran into the kitchen. The next thing I heard was a piteous "But Uncle Dick *said* I could!" followed by Jonathan' stern: "Well, Uncle Dick was wrong. You know it's almost bedtime."

Damn! I'd lost track of time again. But I had to give Joshua credit for recognizing an opening when he saw it.

And Jonathan, bless his heart, recognized that I was preoccupied and, after putting Joshua to bed and reading to him until he fell asleep and going to bed ourselves, Jonathan devised another form of distraction which totally took my mind off everything but what was happening at the moment. Afterwards, completely happy and relaxed, I felt myself drifting off to sleep.

Okay, so let's shift focus from Evan Knight to Dave Witherspoon, my mind began.

Damn!

* * *

As soon as I was sure the DMV was open in the morning, I called my contact Bil (yeah, only one "l"—that's the way he spells it) Dunham, gave him the Datsun's license plate number and asked him to check it out for me. He called back within half an hour to tell me the car was indeed registered to Dave Witherspoon, that there were no liens against it, which meant he'd paid cash, and had been purchased new four months ago. Four months ago? That was way before the Burrows ever opened, while the collection was still at the Burrows estate. *Yes,* another observed, *but so was Dave Witherspoon.* Nothing like being slapped in the back of the head with a shovel! It all fell into place! Witherspoon had started working for the foundation while Knight was still in Europe. Knight had no idea at the time that there would even be a separate library. I'm sure he didn't anticipate anyone going through the Butler papers in his absence. He may well have left some key clue among Morgan's papers that Witherspoon picked up on.

Knight obviously had taken Morgan's manuscripts some time before—he'd started publishing them while Chester Burrows was still alive—but it might not have occurred to him at that time to take the letters as well, and by the time he got back from Europe, Witherspoon was already cataloging and recording them. It would have been next to impossible for Evan to take them at that point. However, it would have been simple enough for *Witherspoon* to take the letters he wanted and just record the ones he left. He could very well have made a connection to the books being published under Evan's name and taken the letters himself to try to cash in on some of Knight's undeserved fame and fortune.

But regardless of who took the letters, Witherspoon undoubtedly found out what Knight was up to, and decided to blackmail him—where else might he have come by the money for two trips to Cancun and a new car?

Okay, so taking almost every letter in which Morgan referred to the fact that he was writing would be one thing: why take the letters that might hint at Morgan's being gay? Witherspoon had denied he had any idea of Morgan's homosexuality, but it was hard not to see it even in the letters remaining in the collection. Putting together Morgan's references to his writing and the obvious undertones of homosexuality in his letters to Scot, making the connection would be a lot easier for almost anyone to pick up on.

Uh, yeah, a mind voice said, *but if Knight was going to kill somebody, wouldn't it be Witherspoon? Taylor Cates is the one who's dead.*

* * *

Okay: having, in my own mind if nowhere else, established a fairly firm case for Dave Witherspoon's being a blackmailer, what about the possibility of his being a killer to boot? I rather hated to give up on the idea that Knight was the killer, and of course I wouldn't, completely. Again I was boldly striding into Terra Incognita armed only with speculations and theories, but I had to follow it through. Dave and Taylor had a long history of mutual antagonism. Taylor had managed to get Dave fired, and Dave believed it was so Taylor could take over cataloging the Butler papers. However if Witherespoon had found out about Knight's theft, he couldn't be sure Taylor wouldn't find it, too. He may have killed Taylor to forestall that possibility. And as a bonus for eliminating Taylor, he was pretty much guaranteed to get his job back and continue whatever it was he was doing on the side.

Taylor was by all accounts a pretty savvy guy. When he took over the Butler cataloging from Dave, he might very well have figured out that some letters were obviously missing from the file of a guy so anally retentive that he kept copies of everything he wrote. And from there it wouldn't be too great a leap to make a connection to the books Evan Knight was claiming to be his own.

Desperate situations calling for desperate solutions, I decided that if I ever hoped to untangle this mess of maybe's and what if's, the most direct way was to confront Evan Knight with what I knew. I certainly didn't expect a confession, and I knew I was putting myself at strong risk, if he *had* killed Taylor Cates, of being his next potential target. But the more I thought about it, the less reason I saw for him to have killed Taylor—unless, of course, Taylor *had* made the connection and Knight figured it was easier to kill him than to have two people know his secret.

Being more than a little foolhardy but not totally stupid, I also decided to cover my ass by having a talk first with one of my contacts at Police headquarters. I knew I could trust either Marty Gresham or Mark Richman, Craig's father, to keep what I told them confidential until I was able to provide them with the proof they'd need that a crime had been committed: in this case, two crimes—plagiarism and murder. I knew of course that plagiarism was hardly in the same league as murder, and I wasn't even sure if you could go to jail for it. But I knew you could go to civil court over it, and I knew that Knight would not only be discredited but very likely forced to repay the money the books had earned—to whom, I also wasn't sure.

I'd not talked to either Marty or Mark in some time, and I knew that both were always very busy with their jobs. However, as a lieutenant in the Administrative Division, Mark Richman had even more responsibilities and things to worry about than Marty, who had recently made Detective in the Homicide Division. I knew putting Marty on to a possible murder would definitely pique his interest, but I felt I could trust him to give me the leeway I needed rather than trying to jump in immediately.

I looked at my watch and saw it was 10:30. Picking up the phone, I dialed the City Annex, which housed the police department headquarters, and asked to speak to Detective Marty Gresham. I had no idea if he'd be in or on a case somewhere, but luck was with me and after a moment's pause I heard Marty's voice: "Detective Gresham."

"Marty!" I said: "It's Dick Hardesty."

"Dick!" he said, sounding as if he were sincerely happy to hear from me. "It's been a long time! What's up?"

"I've got something going on I wanted you to know about, just in case," I said. "Any chance you might be free for lunch?"

"Sure," he said. "We just finished up a case and I've got a stack of paperwork to get done, but I can spare a few minutes."

"Your wife still packing your lunch?" I asked.

I could almost hear him grin. "Not since the baby came—which is about the last time I heard from you, as I recall."

I realized with some surprise that he was right: I'd called to congratulate him when I heard he'd had a little girl, but that was…well, several months ago.

"Sorry to say you're right," I said. "How's the baby doing?"

"I'll show you her picture when I see you. Etheridge's okay? Noon?"

"Etheridge's is fine. See you there."

* * *

I arrived at Etheridge's at about ten 'til noon, hoping to beat the crowd and get a table. I was just finishing my first cup of coffee when Marty Gresham walked in. I almost didn't recognize him out of his uniform, but now that he was a detective he got to wear street clothes. And he surely did look good in them. He came over, hand extended, and after we'd shaken, sat down across from me.

"So, what's going on?" he asked, picking up the menu the waiter had left for him. I knew he was on a tight time schedule, so I didn't mind his getting right to the point.

I sketched it all out for him: Taylor Cates' apparently accidental death and the background of everything going on at the Burrows which led me to suspect that it was not an accident. He, not surprisingly, had never heard of Evan Knight...or of Jerromy Butler, for that matter.

My narrative was interrupted briefly while the waiter came with Marty's coffee, took our orders, and again, while I was still talking, when he brought our food.

"So," I said, finally wrapping it all up, "I've got three things going on here at the same time...plagiarism, blackmail, and murder. I have pretty positive evidence to support the plagiarism, but the 'evidence' for blackmail is mostly circum-stantial, and solid evidence for the murder is totally nonexis-tent at this point. Since the one thing I know without question is that Evan Knight is the key element, I've decided to approach him with what I've figured out, in hopes that might somehow break some sort of solid evidence loose from the logjam that exists now."

Marty, who'd been largely silent, eating and drinking his coffee as I talked, put down his cup and wiped his mouth with his napkin.

"You're taking a pretty big risk, here," he said. "You could end up getting yourself killed."

I shrugged. "Which is exactly why I'm talking to you," I said. "I intend to let Knight know that I've told you—I won't mention your name, obviously—so that just in case he may think of trying something, he'll know he can't get away with it."

Marty just looked at me for a minute. "Still a pretty big risk," he said. "Why don't you just turn everything you've got over to us, officially."

I finished another bite of my BLT before responding. "And what could you do with it? Plagiarism's a civil crime, true, and I'm sure you could get him on that with what I know, but I'm more interested in finding out exactly why and how Taylor Cates died. The police have already accepted the accidental death idea. To have them have to go back to square one and try to make a winnable case would take a heck of a lot more time and taxpayers' money than I'm sure they'd care to expend."

Marty gave a slight shrug, which I took to be of acknowledgment.

"No," I continued, "I really think I'm in a better position,
based on everything I've been able to piece together, to follow
it through to the end."

Marty still did not look totally convinced.

"If I'm right," I said, "and Knight did *not,* despite what I
first assumed, kill Taylor, I don't think he'd resort to trying
to kill me just to keep his secret. He's going to be pretty
damned upset at the idea of being hauled into court for
plagiarism, but it's a lot easier to deal with than a murder
charge.

"My money is on Dave Witherspoon, and maybe Knight
will be able to give me something I can use to prove it."

The waiter came to take Marty's plate, and refill our coffee.
When he'd gone, Marty sat back in his chair. "Well," he said,
"you know that if I have reason to believe that a murder has
been committed, I'm obligated to act on it."

"Understood," I said, taking a forkful of potato salad from
my side dish, "but technically that should involve a little more
solid evidence than either one of us has at this point. I can
assure you that the minute I get *any* solid evidence, you'll be
the first one I call."

He took a sip of coffee. "Well, while it's against my better
judgement, I guess I can give you that. But for God's sake,
don't do anything stupid! You're getting pretty close to it as
it is in trying to confront this guy."

I sighed. "I know, and believe me I don't have a death wish.
I'll be careful."

We sat in silence for a moment until I said: "Now, how
about letting me see that picture of your daughter?"

* * *

There were one or two things I wanted to check before I
tried contacting Evan Knight. One of them was to talk to Dave
Witherspoon again. I really needed to feel more confident than
I did about exactly who, Knight or Witherspoon, had taken
Morgan's letters. If Dave had taken them, that would cinch
my blackmail theory. If Knight had taken them, though,
Witherspoon would have had to come up with some other basis
for the blackmail, and the fact that I didn't have any idea what

that basis might be bugged me.

After leaving Marty with the usual promise to keep him fully informed, I drove to the Burrows and pulled into the parking lot to the side of the building. The Datsun was there.

Again, I went directly to the cataloging room and rang the bell, and the red-head once more came to let me in.

"Can't keep away, huh?" he asked with a grin as he held the door open for me.

"It's getting to be my home away from home," I replied. As he closed the door behind me, I said: "Is Dave Witherspoon around?"

"Sure," he said. "Hold on just a second and I'll get him for you."

He handed me a clipboard with an apparently new, formal check-in sheet and pencil, then moved off toward the stacks at the far end of the room. I signed, dated, and entered the time in their appropriate spaces, then exchanged a nod and smile with Janice, who was working at her usual table.

A moment later Dave appeared and came over to me.

"Dick," he said by way of greeting. "Ken said you wanted to see me?"

"Yeah," I said. "I've just got a couple of quick questions. You started working on the Butler papers while they were still at the Burrows estate, right?"

"That's right. Evan Knight had started the cataloging some time before, but hadn't finished."

"Were Morgan Butler's papers separate from those of his father?"

I watched his face for any reaction, and there was none.

"Actually, no. They were all pretty much mixed together. Evan had been separating them as he went along, but I just continued doing the same thing as I went through the materials Evan hadn't gotten to."

"And you cataloged them as you came to them?" I asked.

He shook his head. "No, I just separated them out into another box Evan had started for him, and put them in chronological order for specific cataloging after I'd finished his father's."

"But you didn't read them?" I asked.

"Not really," he said.

Why didn't I believe him? I would have expected him at least to look a bit puzzled as to why I'd asked, but he didn't.

"You'd completely cataloged Jerromy Butler before

you...left?"

He nodded. "Yes. I had just started on Morgan's and hadn't gotten more than a third of the way through before Taylor got me fired."

"I really admire you for having taken your getting fired so well," I said. "I think I'd have been ready to kill the guy." I'd deliberately used the word "kill" hoping it might get some sort of reaction from him, but it didn't. Not so much as the quiver of an eyelash.

"As I told you," he said casually...maybe a tad too casually..."I understood. Taylor was being Taylor. A bastard, but still Taylor. And it all worked out in the long run."

Yes, it had. And just maybe not...double entendre intended...by accident. I remembered what his partner Ryan had said about Dave when we'd had lunch: "He sees something he wants, he goes for it." Well, he'd wanted his job back.

I didn't see anything else I might be able to get out of him at that point, so I thanked him for his time, and he went back to whatever it was he was doing while I picked up the clipboard and pencil and signed myself out.

Besides, I thought as I walked up the steps to the main entrance, it might be good to keep him on his toes by stopping by frequently to ask him a question or two.

* * *

The more I thought of it, the more likely it became that Dave Witherspoon had definitely taken the letters. Again, Evan Knight didn't strike me as a candidate for Mensa. If he even thought about removing Morgan's letters, he probably figured he had plenty of time to do it himself. He didn't foresee the moving of the collection, and specifically that anyone other than him might start cataloging the Butlers' papers.

I was just unlocking the door to my car when I remembered something that sent me back into the library and up to Irving McHam's office.

"Come," McHam's deep voice said in response to my knock at his office door. He seemed a bit surprised to see me when he looked up from some papers on his desk as I entered.

"Mr. Hardesty. I wasn't expecting you."

"I'm sorry to bother you," I said, "but I have a quick question you might answer for me."

He gestured me to a seat, but I declined. "Thanks, but I

won't be but a moment," I said.

"So what is it you want to know?" he asked, leaning back in his chair.

"There was a fire at the Burrows estate shortly before the collection was moved," I said. "Do you remember exactly when that happened?"

He thought a moment, then said: "Sometime in January. The 24th, I believe. Why?"

"I was just curious," I said. "I can imagine it gave everyone involved a real scare."

"That it did, indeed."

"I'd imagine it was particularly so for Evan Knight, since he'd worked there for so long." I paused just for a second, but not long enough for him to reply before I said: "Oh, that's right...he was in Europe at the time."

McHam shook his head. "No," he said, "Evan had returned the week before the fire. He was still recovering from the news that the collection was to be moved. I suppose he really should have been notified just as a courtesy, but really no one knew where he might be at any specific time and the moving of the collection wasn't really his concern in any event."

"Ah," I said. "Well, thank you for your time. I'll let you get back to work now."

"You're quite welcome," he said, immediately dropping his eyes back to whatever it was he'd been reading when I came in.

* * *

So, conjecture time again. Knight comes back from Europe, learns not only that the collection is being moved but, quite probably, that someone...Dave Witherspoon...is cataloging the Butler papers. He has no way of knowing what Dave might discover, so he sets a fire in hopes that any evidence linking "his" books to Morgan's papers would be destroyed. It's entirely possible, of course, that the fire was completely accidental and Knight had nothing to do with it, but it made sense that he might. But in either case, the fire didn't touch Morgan's papers and Dave Witherspoon had gotten enough from them to begin his blackmail.

And again I had to consider what I was going to do about Knight. If I was able to determine that he had killed Taylor, the answer was obvious: turn him in and let the judicial system do whatever it wanted with him. But if he hadn't, that still left me with the fact that he had stolen another man's work, and that, too, was a crime. Every penny he had made from Morgan's work belonged to…who? Collin Butler? I'd thought that one out earlier, and decided he probably wouldn't want to be linked in any way with his father's books…including the money they earned. God knows he didn't look like he needed it.

And when I'd thought about it earlier, I'd assumed that Collin Butler was the only one who had a legal right to the profits from Morgan's books. But I realized now that I was wrong: Morgan had specifically donated them to the Burrows collection and therefore the Burrows Foundation would have claim to whatever the books had earned.

The most important thing for me was that Morgan be given the recognition he deserved, of which Evan Knight had deprived him. But I realized, again ironically, that it's quite possible that if it *weren't* for Knight's stealing them, they may not ever have been published.

Life is truly strange.

* * *

I have no idea where the rest of the day went, but suddenly it was time to head home for the weekend. I didn't really want to put off the inevitable, but Knight could wait until Monday.

* * *

Nice weekend. Went by much too fast, of course, and nothing much was accomplished. It's amazing how much time grocery shopping and laundry-doing and dry-cleaner-going and fish feeding and plant watering and housecleaning—an absolute necessity with a four-year-old around—take out of a Saturday. And Saturday night we took Joshua to an early showing of a kid's movie Jonathan thought, rightly, he'd enjoy.

Sunday was paper for me and church and Sunday School for Jonathan and Joshua and, instead of going out to brunch, we made a picnic lunch and drove up to the Jessup Reservoir, about 20 miles away. There were more people in the picnic area than I'd anticipated, but Joshua got to play with a couple of kids his age and feed the ducks and get his shoes soaked by wading into the water before we could stop him, so it all worked out.

As I said, a nice weekend.

* * *

No point in putting it off. As soon as I got to the office Monday morning, I called Evan Knight. Luckily, he was home.

"Evan Knight," the voice said as the receiver was picked up.

"This is Dick Hardesty," I said. 'We have to talk."

"I thought we just had," he replied.

"Yeah, well, this was before a bunch of things came up," I said.

"Well I'm really pretty busy." It was clear from the tone of his voice he didn't want another conversation. "I'm going over the proofs for my next book, and I'm on something of a deadline. So…"

"It's your books we have to talk about," I said.

There was a decided pause, then: "What about my books?"

"Your books and blackmail," I said.

This time the pause was so long I was afraid he might have hung up…except I'd heard no 'click' and there was no dial tone.

Finally: "I don't understand."

"I think you do," I said, "and you can talk to either me or the police. The choice is yours."

"Okay. When and where?"

"The Carnival, 3:00."

He hung up without another word.

* * *

Oh-kay, Hardesty, a mind voice said with mild exasperation. *Now what?*

Well, first and foremost, I just wanted to see what might come of it. I hoped that whatever Knight's reaction might be, it would point the direction I should go next. And while I have been known to be wrong in my assessment of people, I think my ability to recognize when I'm being conned or lied to is a little better than average. I knew I was basing my recent shift away from thinking of Knight as a killer on the fact that if he were going to have killed anyone, it would have been Dave Witherspoon when the blackmail first began (and I hadn't a clue exactly when that was). No, I was now leaning toward Dave Witherspoon as Taylor Cates' killer, and I hoped Knight might give me something to support that contention.

* * *

Jonathan's call shortly after lunch to remind me to stop by the photographer's to pick up our pictures was a welcome reminder that life did exist outside of murder investigations. Sometimes I got myself so wrapped up in a case that I lost track of that fact.

I arrived at the Carnival around ten 'til three and was, except for the bartender and one other customer, the only guy in the place. I ordered a Manhattan and, leaving a bill on the bar, took it to a table under the small front window...which was too high off the floor to be able to see out of while seated. The juke box segued from Elton John's newest, "Sad Songs" to another top-ten, "Let's Hear it for the Boy." Though I've never really paid that much attention to what was on the top of the music charts, I happened to like them both.

At exactly 3:00, the door opened and Evan Knight walked in. He looked around the room, spotted me, and without so much as a nod of acknowledgment, went directly to the bar. A moment later he strode over to the table, all but slammed his beer down, and took a seat.

"Okay," he said. "So what the hell is this all about?" But before I had a chance to open my mouth, he continued: "I'm sorry if my banging your boyfriend pissed you off, but that's no cause to start making all sorts of ridiculous accusations. There are libel laws, you know, and I could haul your ass into court."

Ah, yet another 'a good offense is the best defense' ploy. Too bad I wasn't buying it.

"You could," I said, "but we both know you won't. Plagiarism's a crime, too, as I think you know, and I know you've been publishing Morgan Butler's novels under your own name."

"Prove it!" he said, picking up his beer to take several deep swigs.

"As a matter of fact, I can," I said. "And I know all about Dave Witherspoon's blackmailing you because of it."

He looked at me scathingly. "*You* should be a writer," he scoffed. "That's some imagination you've got."

"Glad you like it," I said. "Did you know Dave Witherspoon killed Taylor Cates?"

He'd picked up his beer again and had it halfway to his mouth, but stopped in mid-motion and then put it back on the table.

"Are you out of your fucking mind?"

I shook my head. "Afraid not," I said. "I had you pegged for it until I found out it was Dave and not Taylor who was behind the blackmail. And if you think for one split second that when Dave gets busted for blackmail he won't do everything in his power to pin Taylor's death on you, you're kidding yourself."

Knight leaned forward in his chair, menacingly. "You know what I think?" he said. "I think you're making this whole thing up just because the thought of someone else screwing your boyfriend drives you nuts, and you'll say or do anything to get back at me. I think you don't have one single bit of proof of any of this crap, and until you do, you can just go fuck yourself."

With that he stood up and walked out of the bar.

Well, that went well, one of my mind-voices observed.

* * *

I decided not to return to work, and instead drove to the photographer's studio to pick up our pieces of immortality. They weren't exactly cheap, but the per-day cost spread over a hundred or so years was rather reasonable. And she'd done a really great job. She gave me the card of a friend of hers who owned a framing shop and said he did excellent work. I thanked her, paid her, and carefully carried the equally-carefully-wrapped prints to the car and set them carefully on the back seat. With my track record for breaking things, "carefully" was definitely the operative word.

I hadn't really given that much thought to my meeting with Evan Knight. I'd lobbed my hand grenade and had no control over what bits and pieces might start falling around me as a result. I'd just have to wait and see.

I got home far enough ahead of Jonathan and Joshua to set the photos out on the couch, propped up against the cushions so they could see them the minute they walked in. I was in the kitchen fixing my Manhattan when I heard the door open.

"Wow!" Jonathan said, obviously spotting the photos immediately. "These are *great!*"

Joshua seemed equally impressed, particularly by those that had him in them. He grabbed one of himself in his sport coat and bow tie and ran into the bedroom "to show Mommy and Daddy."

I realized, as he said that and raced out of the room, that he had been with us now for the better part of a year: his fifth birthday was coming up in August. Good Lord, where does the time go?

I showed Jonathan the card the photographer had given me, and after studying the pictures for a few minutes, he went directly to the phone to call the framer. I knew they were probably closed for the night, and I was right. "Maybe we can go over there tomorrow?" he asked. "I can't wait to get them framed and up on the wall. And I have to write all the relatives and send them copies, and...."

His enthusiasm reminded me again of just how much alike he and Joshua were.

* * *

The phone rang just as I was finishing the crossword puzzle and thinking about having another cup of coffee.

"Hardesty Investigations," I said, picking up the phone, as always, on the second ring.

I recognized Glen O'Banyon's voice immediately. "We have another one," he said, and I didn't have to ask 'another what?' I knew.

Shit!

CHAPTER 12

"Who?" I asked, though I had a queasy feeling in the pit of my stomach that said I knew.

"Dave Witherspoon," he said. "A passing patrol car found him around one o'clock this morning on the front steps of the Burrows. I don't know any other details right now. I just thought you'd want to know."

"Thanks, Glen," I said. "I'll see what I can find out and get back to you. Are you in court today or at the office?"

"I'll be in the office most of the day," he said. "And I'll let you know if I find out anything more."

"Okay," I said. "I'll get right on it."

We exchanged good-byes and hung up.

What had been a queasy feeling in my stomach washed through my entire body and I couldn't help but listen to a very strong mind voice which said: *Congratulations, Hardesty—you just got Dave Witherspoon killed!*

Damn it, Hardesty, the voice continued. *Why in the hell don't you think before you open your mouth? Not only did you have to tell Knight you knew he was being blackmailed, but you had to say you knew it was Dave Witherspoon. And then you had to go and all but paint a bullseye on the guy's back by suggesting that Witherspoon wouldn't hesitate to turn him in if he thought it would help himself. Truly stupid!*

But talk about being truly stupid, how could Knight have been so dumb as to go out and kill the guy within twelve hours of my telling him I knew what was going on? That just didn't make any sense. I tried to make myself feel better by telling myself I really hadn't thought of Knight as a murderer. And why? Just because I didn't think he killed Taylor Cates? Like that made a bit of difference now.

Sheesh!

* * *

I knew that there was a good chance that Tim, as assistant medical examiner, would be working on Witherspoon's body, or at least that he would be able to tell me what the autopsy found, but I also knew they probably couldn't have found much yet, even if they'd begun their examination. Still, I called Tim's work number and left a message asking him to call.

I next called the City Annex and asked to talk to Marty Gresham. I was told he was out on a case, but left my number for when he returned.

I needn't have bothered, because I'd no sooner hung up the phone when it rang.

"Hardesty Investigations," I said, picking it up.

"Dick, it's Marty," the voice said. "We need to talk."

"I know," I said. "Dave Witherspoon, right?"

"You heard, then?"

"About ten minutes ago."

"Can you come out here to the Burrows, then? Right away?'

"Sure," I said. "I'm on my way."

* * *

The front of the Burrows was cordoned off, and a hastily made sign saying 'Please use side entrance' had been placed, like the announcement of a garage sale, on the outside of the yellow tape near the sidewalk. There were no police cars around, and no one standing inside the cordoned-off area.

I parked in the side lot, and used the side door to get into the building. It was very quiet, even for a library, and for a moment I wondered if anyone were there. There were a few people in the main room of the first floor, though, apparently going through their normal routines, so I continued down to the cataloging room. The door, of course, was closed but looking through the window I saw Janice and two or three of the other workers at their tables, going through the motions of working. However, even through the closed door, I could sense a different atmosphere in the room.

I didn't see Marty or McHam, or anyone else whom I hadn't seen there before, so headed up to Irving McHam's office. As I approached, I could hear voices from inside. I knocked.

"Yes?" McHam's deep voice responded, and I turned the knob and opened the door. McHam was behind his desk, with two men seated in front of him with their backs to me. They both turned around and I saw it was Marty and some guy who looked vaguely familiar, but who I don't think I'd met before.

The unknown man, who looked like he'd just stepped off the cover of True Detective Magazine, immediately got out of his chair and said to McHam: "Well, I think we're through here for the moment." Marty also rose to his feet. "Thank you for your cooperation," the guy continued. "We'll be in contact again if we need anything else. Now, if you'll excuse us, we have to talk with Mr. Hardesty."

Both he and Marty turned toward me, ready to leave, as McHam also got out of his chair. "If you would like to talk here," McHam said, "I really have many things to do in other parts of the library. You're free to use my office. No one will disturb you."

"Thanks," the guy said. "If you're sure it won't be any trouble."

McHam gave a dismissive wave of his hand. "Not at all," he said, moving toward the door. "Take as long as you need."

He passed me with a nod of his head, and left, closing the door behind him.

"Dick," Marty said moving toward me for our usual handshake, while indicating the other detective,"this is Detective Carpenter."

Carpenter? I knew a Detective Carpenter on the force, but this certainly wasn't him.

The man stepped forward to shake hands. Apparently my confusion showed, because he grinned as he took my hand. "You know my brother, I understand," he said. "…and his partner, Detective Couch."

Aha! I thought. Yes, I did indeed know detectives Carpenter and Couch. I'd had dealings with them on several past cases. Carpenter was a decent guy I rather liked. Couch was a homophobic asshole with a capitol 'A'.

"You've heard about our encounters, I gather," I said.

"Oh, yes," he said, still grinning. "You are not one of Detective Couch's favorite people."

"And you can't imagine how upset I am over that," I said, returning the grin.

Marty crossed the room for another chair, which he brought over for me, then turned the other two chairs around so we could sit facing one another.

After we'd all been seated, I jumped right in. "So what happened?"

Detective Carpenter leaned forward, resting his elbows on his knees.

"A patrol found the body this morning around one a.m., though the actual time of death hasn't been determined. It's a pretty quiet area, with not a lot of traffic at night. He apparently fell backwards down the front stairs. He was lying on his back with his head toward the foot of the stairs. There was a broken bottle of whiskey near the body, and the officers who found him said he reeked of alcohol. It appeared he was drunk and had fallen backwards, hitting his head. However, that didn't explain why he'd be here at that time of night, and considering the other recent death here and the circumstances surrounding it, we're definitely treating this one as a possible homicide."

"And we'll be taking another, closer look at the Cates case as well," Marty added. "I've told Detective Carpenter about our conversation—I was sure you wouldn't mind."

"Not at all," I said.

"Would you mind going over it one more time for my benefit?" Carpenter asked, and I did, adding what I'd learned and pieced together since Marty and I had our conversation.

"So you think Witherspoon killed Cates and was blackmailing Knight?" Carpenter asked, sitting back in his chair. "And Knight then killed Witherspoon?" He shook his head. "That was a pretty stupid thing for him to do right after you'd talked to him."

"I agree," I said. "But he might have thought that by getting rid of Dave Witherspoon, he might then somehow be able to get rid of any proof that Witherspoon was blackmailing him—and, by extension, any proof that he had stolen Morgan Butler's work. Knight doesn't know that Scot McVickers kept all his letters and there's enough proof in them to convict him of plagiarism. Maybe he figured if there's no proof of blackmail, there would be no reason for anyone to think he killed Witherspoon. Have you talked to Ryan...I don't think I know his last name...Dave's partner?"

"No," Marty said, "we went over there first thing this morning to talk with him, and he wasn't home. Looking in through the front window—they live in one of those courtyard-apartment buildings—we saw the place had been ransacked, which makes sense if Knight was looking for whatever it was Witherspoon had on him. We called the super, who let us in, but he said Witherspoon's roommate was out of town and isn't due back until this afternoon."

But then why was Witherspoon killed at the Burrows? Why not in his own apartment?

"Can you get us copies of those letters you were telling us about?" Carpenter asked. It was obvious that Carpenter was the senior member of the team, and Marty was learning the ropes from him.

"I'm sure I can," I said.

We talked for a few more minutes, then Carpenter thanked me for coming over, and we all got up to leave, Marty carefully putting all three chairs back in their proper places. I promised that I would contact Wayne Powers about the letters and let them know if I found out or thought of anything that might be of further interest to them.

I paused about halfway out the door.

"Oh, and one more thing," I said. "If you do arrest Knight, and if you get a search warrant for his house, would you be sure they specifically include book manuscripts?"

Carpenter looked a little puzzled, but nodded. "Will do," he said.

We all shook hands again, and as they went to the cataloging room to see if they could find out anything from Dave's coworkers, I headed back to the office to try to talk myself out of the persistent and very unpleasant feeling that I'd been responsible for Dave Witherspoon's death.

* * *

Well, the whole matter of the plagiarism and the blackmail and the deaths of Taylor Cates and Dave Witherspoon was largely out of my hands. It was up to the police now. When I returned to the office I saw I had no messages, which meant that Tim hadn't tried to get in touch with me. Well, he was probably busy...maybe with Dave Witherspoon.

Damn! There was that wave of guilt again!

To take my mind off it, I called Glen O'Banyon's office and, on being told that he was with a client, I left my number and asked to have him call me just as soon as he could.

I fixed a pot of coffee and sat back down at my desk, staring into it as though it held some deep secret. Fortunately, the ringing of the phone pulled me back to the real world.

"Hardesty Investigations," I said, setting the coffee cup down on the desk.

"Dick, hi." I recognized Tim's voice immediately. "Sorry I didn't get back to you sooner. We just finished with Dave Witherspoon...I gather that's why you called me."

"Yeah," I said. "What can you tell me about it?"

"Not too much," he said. "Blunt trauma to the back of the skull, very similar to that earlier death at the Burrows."

"Caused by the fall?" I asked, knowing full well that this

one was no accident.

"Hard to say, but probably not. With Cates, the size and shape of the wound indicated almost a puncture, and could have been from his hitting a corner of the metal stairs as he fell. With this one—an almost identical wound, he fell down concrete steps with no sharp edges that could cause a wound of that shape."

"Any indication of a murder weapon?" I asked.

"Not at the scene," he said. "A piece of pipe, maybe? We'll be examining the wound more closely to get a better idea of what it might have been."

"The police say there was a broken bottle of booze by the body, and that he reeked of alcohol."

"Yeah, that's another interesting thing," Tim said. "He may have had a drink or two earlier in the evening, but his blood alcohol levels were well within limits. The smell of alcohol was pretty strong, though…almost like he'd spilled it all over himself."

"Or someone else had done it for him to make it look as though he were drunk," I said. "Did you determine a time of death?"

"Somewhere between ten p.m. and midnight, roughly," Tim said.

"Well thanks a lot for the information, Tim. I owe you."

"Ah," Tim said, "sounds just like the old days."

I knew he was referring to the time before he met Phil or I met Jonathan when, as I'd mentioned, Tim and I used to spend some very pleasant…uh…single-guy time together…and I laughed.

"Yeah," I said. "Sorry I can't repay you like I used to, but we wouldn't want to break up two happy homes, now, would we?"

"Nope," Tim said. "But a little nostalgia's no crime."

"I'll drink to that," I said.

"And on that happy note, I've really got to run," Tim said. "Talk to you soon. Give my best to Jonathan and Joshua."

"And you to Phil. So long."

* * *

Talking to Tim—even albeit about dead bodies—lifted me out of my guilt trip. But I also realized I was experiencing a little something akin to post partum depression. I mean, I'd been working on this case for what seemed like a long time, and suddenly, in one poor guy's assisted fall down a flight of stairs, it was over. Well, *it* wasn't over; there'd still have to be a charge and a trial and a conviction, but *my* direct involvement was finished. I'd be an onlooker from here on out.

Not having heard from Glen O'Banyon yet, I took a quick minute to call Wayne Powers to see about borrowing the letters again. He wasn't home, so I left a message, and had no sooner hung up the receiver when Glen called.

"What's going on?" he asked, and I told him everything I knew, including my conversation with Marty Gresham and his partner and my talk with Tim.

"There is one minor side issue," I said, "and while it doesn't really involve me at all, directly, I am concerned about it on Morgan Butler's behalf."

"And what is that?" O'Banyon asked.

"*If* the police find more manuscripts in Knight's house, and I have a hunch they will—I know he was getting another book ready for his publisher—it raises the question of what to do with them, and who has the rights."

There was a slight pause, then O'Banyon said: "Well, the Burrows has the rights, unless Morgan assigned them to his son. I know he left a will, and that his bequest to the Burrows collection is specifically in it, but I don't know if he made any separate or specific mention of unpublished manuscripts. I can check, though."

"I don't know if anything can be done with those manuscripts already published under Evan's name, as far as giving Morgan credit for them," I said, "but if there are unpublished manuscripts, I'd really like to see them published under Morgan's name. Plus, they could bring in quite a bit of money to the Burrows Foundation."

"A good point," O'Banyon said. "I'll definitely check into it. We've got enough trouble with Collin Butler as it is...we don't want another squabble over rights to Morgan's books."

"I'm sure Collin would fight for them," I said, "but not for the money they could bring. I think he'd want them just to make sure they were never published. It may sound a little odd, but I feel I owe it to Morgan to be sure that doesn't happen."

"Well let me get back to you on that," he said. "I'll have one of my associates look into the will immediately."

There was another pause, then he said: "Well, I'd better

set up a meeting with the Board to let everyone know what's going on. Thanks for everything, Dick."

"You're welcome," I said. "It's been an interesting case."

* * *

I'd put the photos to be framed in the back seat of my car before leaving for work, and had arranged to meet Jonathan and Joshua at the framer's, which turned out to be in the basement level of a very nice little art shop in one of the more trendy parts of town.

Seeing the fragile nature of many of the glassware and sculptures on display as we entered, Jonathan wisely picked a fascinated Joshua up and carried him through the danger zone.

"Put me down!" Joshua insisted. "I wanna *see!*"

"When we get downstairs," Jonathan said, nodding me toward a neatly painted sign near the stairway.

I had no idea there were so many different types and styles of picture frame available, but this place seemed to have them all. It took nearly half an hour to make the right selection…which is to say one Jonathan and I agreed on…for each of the three photos we were planning to hang. The process was interrupted twice by first Jonathan's and then my hurrying over to scoop Joshua off the stairs as he tried to take advantage of our distraction to go up and play with the "toys" on the main floor.

Told that the newly framed pictures would be ready within the week, we left and celebrated Joshua's getting out of the place without breaking anything by going to Cap'n Rooney's Fish Shack for dinner. It occurred to me that we ate there so often we should buy stock in the place.

* * *

When we got home, I called Wayne Powers' number, and found him home. I asked if I could borrow the letters again, explaining that the police wanted copies of those which could prove some of Morgan's other papers had been stolen from the Burrows collection.

"I'll be home all morning," Powers said, "if you'd like to come by and get them. Though to be honest, I feel a little awkward about …well, you know…these are personal letters to Scot, and..."

"I understand, of course," I said, and I did. "I can come over around 9:30, if that's okay. And if you have the time for me to go quickly through them while I'm there, I'll be able to take only the letters I think would be pertinent to their investigation."

"I'd appreciate that," he said. "So I'll see you in the morning, then."

"Yes, and thanks again."

* * *

It wasn't until Joshua was in bed and asleep that I had a chance to fill Jonathan in on everything that had happened during the day.

"You mean Evan didn't write all those books?" he asked, incredulous. "I knew he wasn't the nice guy I thought he was at first, but that he'd steal another writer's books? And then *kill* somebody?" He shook his head. "Wow."

He was quiet for a minute, then looked at me, his face serious. "I guess it's true what they say."

"What's that?" I asked.

"You can't tell a book by its cover," he said, and grinned.

I groaned and reached over to grab him by the back of the neck. "Time for bed, Jonathan," I said.

"Make me!" he said, defiantly.

"My thought exactly," I replied.

* * *

Ever since I first discovered sex, I have noticed that it is an excellent way to relieve tensions, and I awoke the next morning feeling much more positive about the world in general. A case was, after all, just a case, and they aren't always pleasant. I was truly sorry Dave Witherspoon was dead, but I couldn't let myself take the blame for it.

Joshua, in the few minutes before his before-bedtime bath, had apparently picked up a new word from a medical show we'd been watching on TV: 'hyperventilating'. He must have used it six times during breakfast. He wasn't, he assured me when I told him not to play with his cereal, playing with it, he was hyperventilating it. The fact that he had no idea what a word meant didn't slow him down. If he liked it, he used it.

"As soon as you're old enough to read," Jonathan told him, "we'll get you a dictionary so you can look up words to see what they mean."

"I can read now!" the boy responded, and in fact he could make out quite a few of the more common words in his story books. "I'm hyperventilating," he said firmly, as though that settled the debate once and for all.

* * *

I arrived at Wayne Powers' house right on time (I was getting much better at not arriving fifteen minutes early every time I went somewhere), and was greeted at the door by an eager Andy, butt and tail both waggling. Wayne invited me into the kitchen for a cup of coffee, and had the box of letters open on the kitchen table.

Having read all the letters at least twice—and, in the case of those which hadn't been removed from the Burrows collection, four times—I was able to move through them rather quickly as we sat and drank our coffee. I set aside those few which had direct reference in incidents in the books, and those in which he talked about writing constantly. There were maybe fifteen letters when I finished. And when I reached that final letter—which of course I did not take, since it had no bearing on the plagiarism—I wondered again what had happened to the copy, torn from the spiral notebook.

Wayne and I had another cup of coffee and talked for a few minutes after the letters I wasn't taking were returned safely to the box. The more time I spent around Wayne, the better I liked him. He was, as Morgan had been, a high school English teacher, and retired about the time that Scot died. He'd traveled extensively, read voraciously, and had many interests. I told him about Jonathan and Joshua and something of my life, and he had the tact and diplomacy to at least appear to be interested. Andy, with his head on my lap, was obviously enraptured hearing me talk…as long as I kept stroking his head.

I invited Wayne to have dinner with us as a small token of my appreciation for his help, and I knew Jonathan would enjoy meeting him. He accepted with thanks, and I told him we'd call to set up a date.

While he went to get me a manila folder to put the letters

in, I asked if I could use his phone to call the City Annex to
see if Marty Gresham might be in. I thought I might be able
to go directly there from Wayne's house rather than going to
the office first. But no luck on that one; neither Marty nor
Detective Carpenter…Dan Carpenter, I learned…was in, but
I left my office number and asked them to call.

* * *

There were two calls waiting when I got to the office: Glen
O'Banyon and Marty Gresham. I tried Glen first, in case he
might have something for me I could pass on to Marty. I was
both surprised and relieved when I was put right through.

"Hi, Dick," he said. "Just wanted to let you know that I sent
one of my junior associates down to probate to check Morgan
Butler's will. It took a while for them to find it, since they put
records in storage after ten years, but he found it. There is no
specific reference to any books, though the bequest to the
Burrows Collection does state 'all personal papers,' which
would cover them."

"Ah, good," I said. "Now we have to find out if there are
any more unpublished works out there. Will you be initiating
a suit against Evan Knight for the books he already published?"

"I think we'll hold off a bit on that until we see how this
murder thing goes," he said. "But I've called a meeting of the
board for tonight at nine at the Burrows. Can you make it?
I think the board would like to hear everything directly from
you."

"Sure," I said. "But isn't nine a little late?"

"The library's open until nine," he said. "And this will give
us more privacy, and give everyone time to have dinner first.
Use the side entrance and come to the conference room next
to McHam's office."

"Okay," I said. "I'll see you at nine."

As soon as we hung up, I called the City Annex and asked
for Marty's extension. The phone was picked up immediately.

"Detective Gresham," the voice said.

"Marty, Dick. I got the letters. Do you want me to bring
them over?"

"Actually," he said, "we were just on our way out. Things
are really moving in the Witherspoon case. Are you going to
be at your office? We'll stop by there as soon as we can. We
can pick up the letters and fill you in on what's happening."

"Great!" I said. "I'll be here. You know where my office is, I assume?" Marty had never been here, but I had worked with the department long enough that I was pretty sure they knew where I could be found.

"Yeah," Marty said, "I know. We'll see you when we get there, okay? Sorry I can't be more specific on the time."

"No problem," I said. "Later, then." And we hung up.

* * *

As soon as I got to the office, I made copies of all of the letters in the manila envelope and put them in another folder. The police didn't need the originals, I was sure, and this way I could get them back to Wayne without delay. I was tempted to go over Morgan's letters one more time, but as I was making a fresh pot of coffee my mind started wandering again to Dave Witherspoon's death, and why he had been killed at the Burrows rather than at his own apartment, which had been ransacked. Knight apparently knew Ryan was out of town—how I didn't know—and might have called Dave and lured him to the Burrows so he could be sure no one would be home when he ransacked the place.

But that didn't make even an iota of sense if he was going to kill the guy anyway. He couldn't be in two places at once, obviously. He either had to be ransacking the apartment or at the Burrows killing Dave. It was possible, of course, that he'd killed Dave first and then gone to the apartment. But then, again, why didn't he just kill Dave at the apartment?

Well, maybe Marty could fill in some of the details. I wondered if they had arrested Knight, or if they'd gotten a search warrant for his house. I sure did hope they'd put the manuscripts on the warrant! Were there any more books? If so, how many?

And again I blamed myself for having confronted Knight and told him I knew about Dave's blackmailing him. That may well have set him off. He killed Dave and ransacked his apartment looking for whatever Dave had on him. I wondered if he had found it.

Of course it was any direct link to the books which would be Knight's primary concern, and especially the "lady in the fog" letter. I couldn't really see the letters' very few and clouded hints of Morgan's being gay being of that much concern to Knight, and I wondered again about the suicide note. Other than being close to solid proof that Morgan was gay, it didn't even hint of his writing, and by itself wouldn't have all that much value as a blackmail tool.

Well, Witherspoon had undoubtedly just taken anything he thought he might be able to use.

I pulled myself away from ruminating long enough to call downstairs to the diner for a BLT, a side of cole slaw, and a large Coke. I waited about ten minutes, then, putting a note on the door for Marty in case he came while I was downstairs, I ran down to pick up my order.

I'd just finished the last of the cole slaw when I heard a knock at the door and looked up to see two figures behind the opaque glass. Hastily tossing the evidence of lunch into the wastebasket, I called: "It's open," and Marty and Dan Carpenter came in.

I'd moved another chair closer to the desk in anticipation of their arrival and, after standing for a handshake and offering them a cup of coffee, which they declined, motioned them to a seat. Sitting down myself, I pushed the manila envelope across the desk to Marty, who was seated closest.

"These are copies of the originals," I said. "I assume they'll do?"

"That'll be fine," Marty replied.

I sat back in my chair. "So...what's going on?"

As he had done in McHam's office, Carpenter leaned forward in his chair, elbows on his knees.

"We served a search warrant on Evan Knight this morning," Carpenter said. "We don't have enough to arrest him, yet, but we're going over Witherspoon's apartment for fingerprints. We're also doing a fingerprint check on what's left of the whiskey bottle found by Witherspoon's body. Knight denies everything, of course. He claims he had an all-nighter with a hustler, but of course didn't get the guy's name."

"Did the warrant turn up any manuscripts?" I asked.

Carpenter nodded to Marty, who said: "They found a typewritten manuscript on his desk, and a box full of handwritten spiral notebooks that appear to be some sort of manuscripts, though I don't know how many books they might represent. We confiscated them as possible evidence, though."

"Great!" I said. That meant Morgan could have at least a couple of his books published under his own name—including, I hoped, the book Knight was proofing for his publisher. "Any evidence of blackmail? Anything from Witherspoon's apartment?"

Marty shook his head. "He'd had a fire in his fireplace recently, though," he said. "We collected the residue, but I don't think there will be much they can find out from it."

"So do you think you'll be able to arrest him?" I asked.

Carpenter shrugged. "It depends on what our investigation comes up with. I'd say, off the record, that the odds were better than even. But we'll just have to see."

Well, that was something. I knew the plagiarism charge would stand up with or without the blackmail, and since I didn't know for an absolute certainty that Knight had murdered Dave Witherspoon, at the very least he would be exposed as a plagiarist, totally discredited in the writing world, and, depending on what the Burrows Foundation decided to do about it, maybe sued for every nickle he had.

Carpenter put his hands on the edge of the arms of his chair and pushed himself up to a standing position. "Well, we'd better get busy. Thanks for the letters. Will you need them back?"

I didn't, of course, but I felt a bit uncomfortable for Wayne, Scot, and Morgan to have Morgan's very personal letters in a police file somewhere. "If you don't mind," I said.

"No problem," Marty said. "Thanks again for your help, Dick. We'll keep you posted."

He stepped quickly forward to shake hands, then turned to join Carpenter, who was already at the door. Carpenter turned partly toward me, nodded a goodbye, and they left.

* * *

On my way home, it occurred to me just how dramatically my life had changed since I met Jonathan. I think I could count on one hand the number of times I'd gone out at night without him...well, maybe two. But it wasn't many compared to my single days when sometimes I wouldn't even make it home at all for two days at a stretch. I'd stop by a bar for happy hour, pick somebody up, spend the night at his place...all part of the game. Well, we all make our choices, and I made mine, and I was happy with it.

The evening at home went as usual, up to and just beyond Joshua's bedtime ritual, when instead of going back to the living room and talking or watch TV, I got ready to leave for the Burrows. Jonathan, who had been studying his horticulture books earlier, got out some stationery and prepared to write notes to his relatives, enclosing a photo of Joshua with each.

"It shouldn't take too long," I said as I gave him a good-bye hug, "but if it drags out, don't feel you have to wait up for me."

"Okay," he replied. "But I'll probably still be up. I'll want to hear how it went."

* * *

I got to the Burrows at about ten 'til nine, and took a few minutes to check out the wide front steps. I couldn't tell exactly where Witherspoon's body had been found, but I noted the steps were flanked by two eight-to-ten-foot arborvitae which, if Witherspoon were lying close to the edge of the steps, might have made it harder to see him, especially late at night.

Again, the questions formed. What the hell was he doing there at that time of night? Did he maybe have a key to the building? I rather doubted it, but I'd have to check. At the top of the steps on either side of the main doors were large clay planters; the two closest to the door, but about three feet from the building, held small trees; two others on each side, up against the building, held flowers. On closer look, I saw the flower planters weren't quite touching the building, by about enough space to reach a hand behind them.

Convenient place for a blackmail drop off, I thought. Maybe that's what Witherspoon was doing there? Picking up a payment?

The front doors opened as a few people were leaving the building, and as I saw the woman usually behind the main desk approach the door with a key, I hurriedly entered.

"I'm sorry, sir," the woman said, raising a hand as if to stop me, "but we're closed."

"I know," I said. "I'm here for the board meeting."

"Ah, yes," she said, letting me pass and proceeding to lock the door. "You know where the conference room is, I assume."

"Yes, thank you," I said, and started up the steps to the second floor.

* * *

Glen O'Banyon was already there, as were Marv Westeen, Charles Peterson, and I assumed the fourth man, whom I hadn't met, was Tom McNabb. No sign of Zach Clanton. Glen re-introduced the board members, and I shook hands with each in turn.

Zach Clanton blustered in at around five after, making his general displeasure at having had to give up part of his evening known without saying a word. When everyone had been seated and settled in, Glen asked me to explain to the rest exactly what had been going on, and I did my best with what was a pretty complex story, involving two deaths, plagiarism, blackmail, and murder. I told them everything up to and including my visit with detectives Gresham and Carpenter, and the fact that more of Morgan's manuscripts had been found.

"I may be stepping out of my territory here," I said, "but I would sincerely hope that in addressing the many wrongs in this case, you would include those done to Morgan Butler as a human being. Here was a man forced to live his life in the closet, and to hide his true self from everything and everyone except Scot McVickers. I believe as strongly as I possibly can that Morgan hoped that one day, even though he himself wouldn't be alive to see it, that his books would be published and, by doing so, he could at last let the world know who and what he was. Evan Knight robbed him of that with the books he published under his own name, but there is still a chance to give Morgan what I really believe he always wanted, and publish the remaining books under his own name."

"Hah!" Zach Clanton exclaimed. "You think for one minute Collin Butler would stand for that? Not on your life! And Jerromy Butler would turn over in his grave if it got out that his son was gay!"

"But the books belong to the Burrows," I said, looking to Glen O'Banyon. "You can do whatever you want with them."

"The books, yes," Glen said. "But the name...we probably could win on that, if it went to court, but it could be a long and expensive fight."

Damn!

I turned to Zach Clanton. "You know Collin Butler," I said. "Is there any way he could be convinced not to fight letting his father have what I believe he wanted so badly?"

Clanton shook his head. "You don't know Collin Butler!" he said. "He's a bulldog, just like his grandfather. He won't let anything stand in the way of getting whatever he wants. He was in a car accident when he was twenty, and the doctors told him he'd never walk again. But he did, just by sheer will. He walked with a cane for years...still carries a walking stick, as a matter of fact, although now it's more an affectation than a need. He says it's a reminder to him that he can beat the world. He plays golf, for chrissakes."

And my mind suddenly was playing Frank Sinatra singing *On the Road to Mandalay*, full volume: *"And the dawn comes up like thunder out of China, 'cross the bay"!*

CHAPTER 13

I had to talk to Evan Knight, and it couldn't wait. I managed to sit there until Glen told me I could go while they moved on to some other business, and then I all but ran down to the main floor and the telephone behind the main desk. It was quarter 'til ten, but I was sure Knight would be up...if he was even home.

Most of the lights on the main floor were off, but I could see well enough to find the phone and dial.

"Hello?" I noticed that he dropped his standard "Evan Knight" greeting.

"Evan, this is Dick Hardesty..."

"What the fuck do *you* want?" he demanded, cutting me off. "Haven't you done enough already?"

A dial tone told me he'd hung up on me.

I dialed again.

"Leave me the fuck alone," he said angrily, and I knew he was about ready to hang up again.

"Wait!" I said. "I know you didn't kill Dave Witherspoon, but I need you to help me prove it!"

There was a very long pause and only the lack of a dial tone told me he was still on the line. Finally: "How?"

"Can I come over?" I asked. "Right now?"

Another pause, then: "If this is a trick...."

"No," I assured him. "No trick. I swear. I can be there in fifteen minutes."

Yet another pause. "All right, but..."

"No trick," I repeated. "I'll see you shortly."

I paused only long enough to call Jonathan and tell him where I was going, and that I'd be home as soon as I could.

"Be careful!" Jonathan urged.

"I will," I assured him. "See you later."

* * *

A very surly and haggard-looking Evan Knight met me at the door and led me into the living room without a word. He pointed to a chair and I sat down. He dropped heavily onto the couch, one leg folded under his butt. He still hadn't said a word, obviously waiting for me to speak first.

"You don't stand a chance on the plagiarism," I began, "or,

I'll wager, denying the blackmail. And even if they didn't say so, you know they've pegged you for Dave Witherspoon's murder. The police are going over Witherspoon's apartment with a fine-tooth comb for fingerprints or other evidence. So the only way you can beat a murder charge is by being totally honest with me. You really haven't got anything to lose...or much of a choice for that matter."

He was still staring at me sullenly. "So what do you want to know?"

"Tell me about the blackmail."

"I knew it was Witherspoon the minute I got the first demand letter—he sent me a copy of one of Morgan's letters mentioning an incident in *Chesspiece*—and I confronted him, but he insisted on playing coy. He never did admit it, but it couldn't have been anyone else."

"You set the fire at the Burrows estate?" I asked, though I was 100 percent sure he had.

He shrugged. "I panicked," he said. "I'd gotten back from Europe and suddenly I get this copy of one of Morgan's letters. I didn't know what else might still be in there that Witherspoon might find, so the same night I got the demand, I went over to the estate...I had a key...and set a fire in the room where the Butler papers had been kept, and then I called the fire department. I didn't want to destroy the whole collection—Chester Burrows had been too good to me and I couldn't do that to him. I didn't know Butler's papers had been moved to another room while I was in Europe. And when I had a chance, later, to go through them, I noticed that a hell of a lot of them seemed to be missing."

"You hadn't read them all when or before you took the manuscripts?"

"No," he said, shaking his head. "It didn't occur to me that I'd have to. I'd read them over quickly, but wasn't really looking for specific tie-ins to the manuscripts."

"So you paid the blackmail," I said. "How?"

"Cloak and dagger shit. I think Dave really got off on his little games," he said. "I put the money in an envelope and left it at the library."

"Behind one of the planters at the top of the front stairs," I said.

He looked at me oddly. "How did you know that?"

"I just knew," I said. 'A very lucky guess' would have been closer to the truth. "Was this a one-time deal?"

He gave me a slight sneer. "What do you think? It was the only time we played that stupid little hide-the-envelope game, though. The second time I got a demand letter, right after the second book was released, I had a little talk with him. I knew he wouldn't stop, so I made him an offer...I'd 'hire' him as a 'research assistant' at a weekly 'salary', which I figured would be cheaper in the long run."

"And he went along?"

"He did. Especially after I told him that if he didn't, I'd kill him."

"Would you have?" I asked.

Another sneer. "Kill him? Don't be ridiculous!"

"And you can prove that you 'hired' him?"

"It's all in my bank records. Plain as day."

"So no more money drops behind the planter?"

He shook his head. "Only that one."

We were both quiet a moment while my mind went running off in a couple different directions at once. Finally I said: "I'm curious; did you take the suicide note, or did Dave?"

He looked at me. "Suicide note? What suicide note?"

"You didn't see it on the last page of the last spiral notebook?"

He shook his head. "No. I just saw he hadn't finished it, so I put it back."

"And Dave didn't mention it in his demand letters?"

"No."

Odd, I thought. Of everything stolen from Morgan's papers, I'd have thought that one would be the one Witherspoon would be sure to have used as proof Morgan was gay.

"But he did say he had proof that Morgan was gay, didn't he?"

"No," he said. "What difference would that make to me?"

"Just that Morgan's being gay could be seen as another link to the manuscripts," I replied.

He snorted. "Lots of people are gay who don't write books," he said.

He had a point.

"So who killed Dave?" he asked.

"You can read about it in the paper," I said. "Just be glad you're off the hook."

"Off the hook...yeah," he said contemptuously. "My life's ruined, my reputation destroyed, I'm going to lose every cent I have...yeah, I'm 'off the hook' all right."

"Better than the rest of your life in prison," I said.

He shrugged.

As I got up to leave he said: "So you're going to talk to the police again?"

I nodded. "And they'll be talking to you again, too, I'm sure. I might suggest you voluntarily do everything you can to make things right with the Burrows Foundation over the manuscript theft, both with the money you've made from the books and as far as giving Morgan Butler credit for his own work. You might be able to avoid a bunch of civil charges that way. The important thing is that you initiate the procedure and don't wait until the Burrows Foundation comes after you."

And, without an exchange of good-byes, I walked to the door and left.

I couldn't wait until morning, but I had no choice.

* * *

Jonathan was asleep on the couch in front of the TV when I got home. I turned off the TV and went over to kiss him on the forehead. He awoke with a start, then grinned sleepily. "How did it go?" he asked.

And, pulling him up off the couch and leading him to the bedroom, I told him.

* * *

"Detective Gresham," the voice said.

I took another deep swig of coffee, still trying to shake the cobwebs from not having had much sleep, before saying: "Marty, we've got to talk; the sooner the better."

"I was just going to call you," he said. "We've got some news. Just a second," he said, and I heard the suddenly muffled sound of him saying something to someone...detective Carpenter, I'd guess...and then clarity as he said: "We can come right over."

"Great," I said. "See you then."

I wondered what their 'news' might be, but hoped it would support the neat tower of cards I'd constructed, rather than knock it down.

I knew who killed Dave Witherspoon and I knew why and I knew how. And I knew that Dave Witherspoon had *not* killed Taylor Cates. Proving it...well, that would be up to the police.

I'd just give them what I saw as the facts, and let them take it from there.

I just hoped I was right.

* * *

Marty and Dan Carpenter arrived within twenty minutes. I offered them a cup of coffee from the just-made second pot of the morning, and we all sat down.

"We got the reports on the fingerprints," Carpenter said. "Evan Knight's fingerprints were all over Witherspoon's apartment—we knew they were his from the things taken from Knight's house during the execution of the search warrant. So that nails him for breaking and entering, at least. The murder is a little more iffy. They picked up a partial thumb print on a piece of the whiskey bottle by Witherspoon's body, but they weren't either Witherspoon's or Knight's, and they don't match any on record."

"I think I know whose they are," I said. And with that I started dismantling my little tower of cards, laying each one out in front of them.

"Taylor Cates supposedly fell down a flight of metal stairs," I began. "The cause of death was a small wound to the back of the head, apparently from hitting a sharp corner of the stairs as he fell. Dave Witherspoon had a similar wound, but there was nothing on the stairs to have caused it. And no possible weapon was found in either case.

"Dave Witherspoon was a blackmailer, but Evan Knight wasn't his only target. It was the second target who killed Taylor Cates...by mistake. He didn't know who was blackmailing him, but he knew whoever it was was working on Morgan Butler's papers, and he somehow found out it was Taylor. He had no way of knowing that Taylor had only been working on them since Dave was fired. I was the one who told him about that, I'm sorry to say.

"But chances are that Witherspoon, who didn't have any idea that Taylor had been murdered, made another blackmail demand, and the target realized his mistake. I think Dave had made the same drop-off spot—one of the planters at the top of the Burrows' front stairs—arrangements with the second target as he had with Knight, and was killed when he went to pick up the latest payment. Knight wouldn't have had any reason to be there, since he was paying his blackmail in the form of a 'salary' to Dave. He was ransacking Dave's apartment only because he panicked after I told him I thought Dave had killed Taylor but might try to pin it on him. If he could find the letters Dave was using for blackmail, he could deny he was being blackmailed at all. "

Both Marty and Carpenter had been listening closely to everything I'd said, but Marty gave me a bemused little smile and said: "Okay, Dick, you've got us. But can we cut the 'target' stuff and get a name...and how he did it? I know you're enjoying this, but we do have a job to do."

I grinned, probably a bit sheepishly. "Sorry, guys," I said. "Every now and then I fall victim to the Inspector-in-the-drawing-room syndrome.

"The evening Taylor was killed...the night of the Burrows' opening ceremony... Jonathan and I were walking up to the place when we were passed by a guy with a gold-knobbed walking stick. It wasn't until last night that I realized that guy had to have been Collin Butler. And once I realized that, everything fell into place. Witherspoon was blackmailing Evan Knight because of Morgan's manuscripts, but he was blackmailing Collin Butler because Dave had figured out Morgan was gay, and had Morgan's suicide note to prove it. Collin Butler couldn't bear to have that knowledge made public, especially considering who his grandfather was.

Dave, again, had no idea that Taylor had been murdered, let alone that the killer was the guy Dave was blackmailing. If he had, he would have been smart enough to take a hint and drop the blackmail. But he didn't, and when Butler got another blackmail demand just at the time he expected to be given a seat on the Bob Jones University Board of Trustees, he realized—maybe partly as a result of my having told him Taylor wasn't the only one who'd worked on the Butler papers—he'd killed the wrong guy. He couldn't risk losing something he wanted so badly by having a bunch of rock-bound fundamentalists know his father was gay. He'd already killed once: he didn't hesitate to do it again.

"I'm not sure how Collin got into the cataloging room the night of the opening, but apparently he threatened Taylor, who didn't have a clue who Butler was, even though they'd known each other when they were kids, and when Taylor tried to get away from him, Butler chased him through the stacks and hit him with the walking stick as Taylor tried to make it to the back exit.

"I'm willing to bet you anything that if you get that walking stick, it will match the wounds on both Taylor and Dave." Carpenter shook his head. "Now *that's* a story!" he said. "Yeah, it is, isn't it?" I said. "Now all you have to do is go out and prove it."

* * *

And prove it they did. The partial thumb print on the whiskey bottle was a perfect match with Collin's; his walking stick matched both wounds, and though he had carefully wiped the heavy knob clean, a small speck of Dave's blood was found in the space where the knob joined the staff.

Evan Knight was charged and convicted for breaking and entering but, because he made full restitution…which included selling his house…to the Burrows Foundation, they chose to take no further action against him. The Foundation demanded he also make a formal acknowledgment of Morgan as the rightful author of the four books published under Evan's name, and the books' publisher, after some hesitation but unwilling to lose a cash cow that Morgan's talents represented, agreed to publish the book Knight had been proofing under Morgan's name. There were four other books in the box confiscated during the search of Knight's home, and they also were destined for publication under Morgan's name.

Collin Butler, fighting…unsuccessfully…two charges of first degree murder, had no time to contest his father's unspoken wishes.

* * *

The story of Collin Butler's murder conviction on both counts appeared in the Sunday edition of the paper, which Joshua and I were reading upon our return from brunch. All three of us were seated on the couch, with Joshua leaning up against me pointing at the pictures and asking his usual ten thousand questions.

Jonathan, who had been reading through the Books section, leaned over toward me, holding the paper open.

"Look, Dick!" he said. "They've got an article on Morgan and his new book…and there's a picture! He was a nice looking guy!"

It was a photo I'd not seen before…a head shot. He was

indeed handsome, but what got to me was the fact that he was smiling.

At last.

The End

All Dorien Grey books also available as print books and also as e-Books (Downloads) on the GLB Publishers' Internet Site in your choice of printable formats.

The Butcher's Son
1-879194-86-4   US $ 8.00   e-book
      Print book   US $ 14.95
www.glbpubs.com/tbs.html

The 9ᵗʰ Man
1-879194-78-3   US $ 8.00   e-book
      Print book   US $ 14.95
www.glbpubs.com/9th.html

The Bar Watcher
1-879194-79-1   US $ 8.00   e-book
      Print book   US $ 14.95
www.glbpubs.com/tbw.html

The Hired Man
1-879194-76-7   US $ 8.00   e-book
      Print book   US $ 15.95
www.glbpubs.com/thm.html

The Good Cop
1-879194-75-9   US $ 8.00   e-book
      Print book   US $ 15.95
www.glbpubs.com/tgc.html

The Bottle Ghosts
1-879194-73-2   US $ 8.00   e-book
          Print book   US $ 15.95
www.glbpubs.com/tbg.html

The Dirt Peddler
1-879194-72-4   US $ 8.00   e-book
          Print book   US $ 15.95
www.glbpubs.com/tdp.html

The Role Players
1-879194-49-X   US$ 8.00   e-book
          Print book   US$ 15.95
www.glbpubs.com/trp.html

The Popsicle Tree
1-879194-55-4   US$ 8.00   e-book
          Print book   US$ 15.95
www.glbpubs.com/tpt.html

GLB Publishers, POBox 78212, San Francisco 94107

DID YOU KNOW?

The Dick Hardesty series has its own web site for your quick perusal:

http://www.dickhardestymysteries.com

Dorien Grey has his own website

http://www.doriengrey.net

where you can keep up with what's going on in his world, and what's coming up in the future. You can also read the first chapter of any of his books here, see photos of featured bookstores carrying his books, as well as gain insights into other aspects of his life.

You are also welcome to contact Dorien directly by email at doriengrey@gmail.com with any comments, suggestions, or constructive criticism.

And of course the main web site for all the print books and e-books by GLB Publishers is:

http://www.glbpubs.com